DAUGHTER OF

JERUSALEM

JOAN WOLF

WORTHY
PUBLISHING

Published by Worthy Publishing, a division of Worthy Media, Inc., 134 Franklin Road, Suite 200, Brentwood, Tennessee 37027.

HELPING PEOPLE EXPERIENCE THE HEART OF GOD

eBook available at worthypublishing.com

Audio distributed through Brilliance Audio; visit brillianceaudio.com

Library of Congress Control Number: 2012954114

For foreign and subsidiary rights, contact Riggins International Rights Services, Inc.; rigginsrights.com

Published in association with Natasha Kern Literary Agency

ISBN: 978-1-936034-67-3 (trade paper)

Cover Design: Faceout Studio, Jeff Miller
Cover Images: © Shutterstock

Printed in the United States of America
13 14 15 16 17 LBM 8 7 6 5 4 3 2 1

For my mother and father in memoriam.

⤿

NOTE ON LANGUAGE

At the time of Christ the spoken language among Jews was Aramaic. Hebrew was known only by the highly educated, who studied it so they could read the scriptures. A simplified form of Greek was the universal language of the widespread Roman Empire, and most Jews probably spoke this marketplace Greek as well. The Gospels of Matthew, Mark, Luke, and John were written in Greek. Only the Romans spoke Latin. The characters in this book are supposedly speaking Aramaic. What you are reading is a modern English "translation" of that language.

"The way Ms. Wolf handles this often misunderstood and controversial woman is nothing short of a literary triumph. Bravo!"

—Margaret Brownley,
New York Times best-selling author,
Dawn Comes Early and *Waiting for Morning*

"In *Daughter of Jerusalem,* Joan Wolf has given us a treasure: a new, vibrant perspective on the life of mysterious Mary Magdalene. As the story unfolds it is impossible not to feel afresh the excitement we knew at our early explorations into our faith."

—Stella Cameron, *New York Times* best-selling author,
Court of Angels series

"Wolf weaves an original and intriguing tale of treachery and lost love with the discovery of forgiveness, hope, and redemption. An inspiring story not to be missed."

—Cathy Gohilke, award-winning author, *Band of Sisters*

"At last, a Mary Magdalene we can believe in and root for. Joan Wolf eschews the stereotypes to portray Christ's beloved female disciple not as a prostitute or 'fallen' woman but as a complex, autonomous, intelligent person of beauty and passion as well as piety. Enthralling."

—Sherry Jones, best-selling author,
The Jewel of Medina and *Four Sisters, All Queens*

"Compelling, thought-provoking fiction. Joan Wolf is a brilliant story-teller, recreating the world that Jesus walked."

—Patricia Rice, *New York Times* best-selling author,
The Trouble with Magic

"The fictional story of Mary Magdalene drew me in from the first page. Rich with details and wonderful characters, this inspirational tale tugged at my heart and kept me up way past my bedtime. Truly one of the best books I've read in a long while."

—Beth Wiseman, best-selling author,
Daughters of Promise series

"Daughter of Jerusalem is a powerful story . . . . Joan Wolf creates [Mary Magdalene's] world with vivid grace."

—Mary Jo Putney, best-selling author, The Lost Lords series

"I loved reading the Gospel stories from the perspective of a woman. . . . A must-read for those who enjoy historical fiction!"

—Melanie Dobson, award-winning author,
The Silent Order and *Where the Trail Ends*

"A moving portrait of one of the most curiously overlooked women in history. Wolf deftly shows us . . . that our greatest worth is to be found in the soul."

—Iris Anthony, author, *The Ruins of Lace*

"Meet Mary of Magdala, a woman of great courage and love, a woman for all seasons."

—Catherine Coulter, author, *Backfire*

Part 1

Daniel

Chapter One

IT WAS DEEP AUGUST when my father and I made the journey from my old home in Bethany to what was to be my new home in Magdala. We traveled with a party of friends from Jerusalem going to visit family in Galilee, and we joined up with other groups in Jericho because it wasn't safe to travel the route along the Jordan if you weren't with a large caravan.

Papa was taking me to live with my mother's sister, my aunt Leah, because I did not get on with my stepmother. He had married Judith shortly after my mother died, when I was three. She was never nice to me. As I grew older, I learned to stand up for myself. We disliked each other intensely and made no attempt to hide our feelings.

A neighbor once told me that Judith was jealous of me. Instinctively, I knew that to be true. On the surface, Judith had the authority in the house, but I always felt that I had more power because I was better than she was. I wasn't petty minded, and people liked me. My little half brother, Lazarus, and half sister, Martha, loved me more than they loved their own mother. But Judith had brought several highly profitable olive groves to Papa when they married, so he always took her side.

When I was ten, and the confrontations between us were growing worse, my father decided to send me to live with Aunt Leah. He told me it was for Aunt Leah's sake; her husband had died, and she had no children of her own. I would be a comfort to her, he said. My mother would have wanted me to go.

I knew the real reason behind my banishment was that he was tired of having to listen to Judith's complaints. He saw an opportunity for peace in his house, and he was going to take it.

It's not that I didn't love my Aunt Leah. She lived with her husband and his brothers in a house on the Sea of Galilee, and she always stayed with us in Bethany when she came to Jerusalem for the holy days. She was my mother's only sister, and there had always been a special bond between us. If my aunt had lived in Bethany or anywhere close by, I would have been thrilled to make my home with her. But I could not feel happy about being sent to Galilee.

Judeans believed Galilee was a barbarian place. All my life I had heard that Galileans weren't strict Jews, the way we were in Judea. They were lax in their practices, unclean in their table manners, and poorly educated. None of the great Temple scholars came from Galilee. Nobody of any importance had ever come from Galilee. I couldn't understand how my father, who had often said these things himself, would want me to live in such an uncivilized province.

When I told him this, my father got the hard expression on his face that meant he wasn't going to change his mind. So Judith packed my belongings, and my father and I left Bethany, the only home I had ever known, to make the long, hot walk north to Magdala in Galilee. Lazarus and Martha cried and clung to me when I left, making me feel even worse, and I was thoroughly miserable as we joined the group of people who were to be our companions on the road.

The trip north wasn't as horrible as I feared. The farther we walked, the lovelier the landscape became. In August, Bethany was hot and brown and dry; Galilee, in contrast, seemed cool and lush. Dark evergreen forest covered the hillsides, and the sheep looked fat and healthy in their lush pastures. The wheat had been harvested, but everywhere figs hung ripe on trees, and we could see men at work harvesting dates.

After two days of walking we arrived at the southernmost tip of the Sea of Galilee. The sun was setting as we came into the village, and the lake waters reflected back the streaky gold colors of the sky. The hills on the western side of the sea rose like shadow guardians out of the sunset. It was the most beautiful sight I had ever seen.

One of the men in our party saw my face and chuckled. "It's nice, isn't it?"

"I never saw so much water!"

The man laughed. "One day perhaps you will visit the Great Sea, where you can sail for days and never see land. Then you will understand just how tiny this so-called Sea of Galilee is."

One of the men traveling with us was from Capernaum, another city on the lake, and he was quick to defend his native province. "You have nothing nearly as beautiful in Judea. The Dead Sea is ugly, and nothing can live in it. *Our* lake teems with fish. You can't get fish like ours anywhere in Judea."

The Judean exploded into a defense of his province, but I stopped listening to the squabble. Instead I stood quietly, looking at the beauty that lay stretched out before me, praying in my heart that God would let me find happiness in this new place.

IT WAS TOO LATE to go on to Magdala, so my father and I spent the night at one of the inns that served travelers and merchants along the well-traveled route. We set forth early the next morning, taking the road that ran along the west side of the lake. The first town we came to was Tiberias, a new city that was still being built by Herod Antipas, the ruler of Galilee.

I was hungry, but we didn't stop. My father told me Tiberias was a Roman city and that no good Jew would sully the soles of his sandals by stopping near it.

"It's almost as bad as Sepphoris," my father said with disgust, as he marched me along, determined to put the polluted city behind us as quickly as possible.

"What's Sepphoris?" I asked, skipping along beside him.

My father spat, something he rarely did. Then he told me that Sepphoris, the capital of Galilee, was a den of sin. It had been built by Herod the Great using Greek architects and was the seat of the Roman occupation in Galilee. Herod Antipas, my father said, his voice dripping with scorn, was as in love with the Greeks and Romans as his father had been.

It was early afternoon when we arrived in Magdala. As the first houses started to appear, I noticed that most of them were built of a light-colored stone, not the mud bricks we used in Bethany. It was very pretty.

"There is the house," my father said, and I stared in amazement. Built of stone, it was situated directly on the lakeshore. And it was huge! It had two stories, supported by a series of stone arches. Gardens stretched out on either side, and the roof was tile, not the packed clay I was used to.

The people who live here must be very rich, I thought. My father was considered a well-to-do man in Bethany, but our house was tiny compared to this.

I felt my chest growing tight with anxiety as my father opened the gate that gave onto a path to the front door. Close up, the house looked even more enormous, sprawling over a huge plot of land, with outbuildings and an orchard of date palms and fig trees.

"Papa," I whispered, as I trailed behind him, "are you certain this is the right place? This house is so big!"

He didn't appear overwhelmed. "Benjamin has obviously done well with his business."

He kept going, and I followed reluctantly, forcing one foot to move after the other. I was frightened and had a dreadful feeling I might cry. I never cried, and I was proud of that distinction. No matter what Judith said, no matter how many times my father locked me up in my room, I never cried. I *would not* start now.

But the outlines of the huge house had become suspiciously blurry. I ground my teeth together to gain control.

The gate banged behind us, and someone called out my father's name. We stopped and waited while a well-dressed boy came down the path toward us. He addressed my father politely: "You must be Jacob bar Solomon. Welcome to our house, sir. I am Daniel, Benjamin's youngest son."

My father smiled and reached out to embrace the boy. "I thank you, Daniel bar Benjamin," he replied, turning the full strength of his charm on the boy. My father was a very handsome man, with thick black hair only beginning to turn gray, dark brown eyes, and imperious black eyebrows. People often joked that there was no way he could deny my paternity, I looked so much like him. I was never quite sure I liked the comparison. Certainly I had his hair and eyebrows, but my nose did not jut out like his, and my cheekbones were high and thin, not broad and solid.

Lately I had taken to stealing peeks at myself in Judith's polished bronze hand mirror, and I had been pleased with what I saw. Judith caught me once and called me ugly names, and I lost my temper and told her she looked like a cow. That was when my father made the decision to send me to live with Aunt Leah.

My father introduced me to Daniel, and we stood, silent in the sunlight, looking at each other. He was the handsomest boy I had ever seen, with clean, dark brown hair and reddish brown eyes. We knew immediately that we would like each other.

"Welcome to our house, Mary," he said and smiled. Daniel had a wonderful smile; it lit up his thin, boyish face and made me feel that I truly was welcome here.

"Come into the house with me," he said, glancing back at my father and then again at me. "I'll find Leah and my mother to greet you."

MY AUNT WAS WAITING just inside the front door. and I ran into her outstretched arms. They closed around me tightly. "Mary," she said, her lips pressed against the top of my head, "I'm so glad you have come to me."

I was glad too. Daniel's smile and Leah's welcome had washed away the tears that had threatened on the path, and my old confidence came rushing back. My father said, "You have contributed greatly to the peace of my household, Leah, by having Mary live with you. I thank you with all my heart."

"We are happy to have her," another voice said, and I lifted my face from my aunt's shoulder to greet Daniel's mother, Esther, the matriarch of the family.

Her eyes were the same color as Daniel's, and she looked at me for a long moment before she said, "I hope you are used to working, Mary. In this family, everyone has responsibilities."

I bowed my head respectfully and assured her I would happily do whatever she might ask. I felt Aunt Leah take my hand and squeeze it, and I squeezed hers back.

Suddenly I was glad to be here in Magdala, in this house set on the beautiful Sea of Galilee, where Daniel lived.

Chapter Two

It DIDN'T TAKE LONG for me to learn that fitting into a large, new family wasn't going to be so easy. The head of the household and the family business was Benjamin, Daniel's father; next in authority after Benjamin was his younger brother, Joses. Counting from Benjamin down to the youngest baby, the household numbered thirty-two people in all. For a girl from a small family of five, it was overwhelming.

Aunt Leah had been married to Benjamin's other brother, Isaac. When Isaac died, Leah, having no other place to go, remained with her relatives by marriage. That's why she had been so happy when my father asked her to let me come live with her. I was someone of her own blood.

She was so sweet and gentle that I often thought my mother must have been like her. I had no memories of my mother, but that didn't stop me from missing her. If she had lived, she would have taken care of me and loved me. If she had lived, I would never have had to deal with Judith.

Esther, Lord Benjamin's wife (we were all supposed to call him *Lord* to show our respect for his position), put me to work right away. Even though some girls came from the village to help, there was still a lot to be done each day. Just getting enough water for the daily household needs was a huge task, as were milking the goats and making cheese and curds from the gathered milk. The daily bread had to be baked and the food for supper gathered and cooked. Squeezed in between these chores were the ongoing tasks of spinning cloth, making the cloth into garments, and caring for the large vegetable garden.

I tried hard to do everything the way Esther wanted, but I had learned little about housekeeping or cooking from Judith. Nothing I did had pleased her, and she banished me from her kitchen.

Aunt Leah gently tried to show me what to do, but I was miserably homesick for Lazarus and Martha. I would often slip away into the courtyard to play with the young children. It was much more satisfying than trying to carry out tasks that everyone scorned me for doing poorly.

Eventually Esther settled on the jobs most suited to me. I would rise early and prepare the day's bread, do the weeding in the vegetable garden, and help look after the children. I didn't mind doing any of these things and tried to go about my work as quietly and competently as I could.

My biggest misery of the first few months in Magdala came from the girls my age, the daughters of Benjamin and Joses. They all slept together in one of the big upstairs rooms, and none of them was nice to me. Fortunately, I got to sleep in a small room with my Aunt Leah so I didn't have to put up with their snide comments at night, but they kept it up in the daytime. Or they just turned their backs and ignored me. I knew I shouldn't respond, but it was hard to keep a quiet tongue.

I explained this to Daniel one day, when he came home from the synagogue. He saw me in the vegetable garden viciously pulling weeds and came to speak to me. He was the only male in the family who did not work in the family business of salting, packing, and shipping fish. Instead he went into town every day to study with the rabbi. Lord Benjamin's plan for his brilliant youngest son was to send him to Jerusalem when he was sixteen to complete his studies at the Temple and become a scribe.

On this particular afternoon I watched him making his way along the narrow garden paths, and I smiled. He was twelve, two years older than I, tall and slim and elegant looking in his immaculate white linen tunic and cloak of fine blue wool. Its ritual blue tassels swung rhythmically as he strode along.

It was not the first time we had talked together in the garden, and he grinned as he came up to me. "You are certainly attacking those weeds, Mary." He looked around. "Where is Rachel? I thought she was supposed to help you today."

"She said she had a headache and went to lie down." I ripped out another weed and tossed it into my basket.

Rachel was Joses' daughter and my chief tormenter. I thought the rest of the girls might be friendly if not for Rachel's influence. They seemed to be afraid of her.

"Come and sit down," Daniel said, gesturing toward the wooden bench that was nestled in the shade of the house.

I sat next to him, licking the perspiration from my upper lip. I poured a cup of water from the jug I had brought with me and offered it to him. He took a sip and then gave it back to me. I drank thirstily.

"Is Rachel still making life difficult for you?"

I put the cup down on the seat next to me with a loud click. "She hates me. I have tried to be nice to her, Daniel, but she goes out of her way to be mean. And she makes all the other girls act mean too. I don't know what's wrong with her."

"She's jealous of you," Daniel said.

I frowned. "What does she have to be jealous about? *She's* the granddaughter; I'm only a poor cousin."

"You're prettier," he replied and stretched his legs comfortably in front of him.

"Much good that does me."

He turned his head to look at me. "Before you came, Rachel was the prettiest of the unmarried girls. You've taken her place, and she resents you for it. Give her time, and she'll come around. She's spoiled, that's all."

"I don't care about Rachel," I said with a sniff. I turned my face away so he couldn't see my expression and regarded the sparkling lake that lay beyond the walls of the house. "I just want the other girls to like me. I have to spend so much time with them, and they're either mean or they act like I don't exist." I swallowed. "It's horrible."

Daniel took my hand. "I'm your friend, Mary. Try to remember that when they upset you; you do have a friend in this house. And my sisters and cousins will come around eventually. They're good girls at heart, truly."

I turned back to him. He was so handsome, with his warm red-brown eyes, chiseled nose, and neat ears.

Without thinking, I blurted, "You were lucky you didn't get your father's ears."

He looked startled, and then he burst into laughter. I put my hand over my mouth and stared at him in dismay. "I didn't mean to say that."

"I'm embarrassed to admit it, but I've had the same thought myself." He was breathless with mirth.

Lord Benjamin had huge ears. Sometimes, as we all sat in the courtyard in the evening, I would find myself staring at them. Aunt Leah had once leaned over to remind me that I wasn't being very polite.

"They're enormous," I said now with awe.

"They are, aren't they? My mother once told me large ears were a sign of God's special blessing."

"I never knew that."

Daniel grinned. "She made it up. I'm sure of it."

We both laughed.

After that day, Daniel made a point of seeking me out when he got home from school. Spending time with him made all the difference in the world to me. I was no longer alone in the hurly-burly of this big, confusing family. And he was right about the girls too. As time went by they did soften their attitudes, and I actually began to feel at home in Magdala.

Chapter Three

I STOOD ON A bench and surveyed the courtyard where I had brought the nine children in my custody to play. Like everything in the house, the courtyard was large, with three fig trees strategically placed to give the greatest amount of shade.

I wasn't looking for shade at the moment, however. I was enjoying the feel of the warm spring sunshine on my head and shoulders. I inhaled the soft air, relishing the scent of the almond blossoms the breeze carried from the garden. I could hear the faint hubbub of men on the shorefront haggling over the price of fish. Lord Benjamin was the biggest employer in the area; most of the fishermen in town sold their catches to him. Lord Benjamin once told me that their fish was sold as far away as Rome. I was very impressed.

This would be my second spring in Galilee, and I was a very different person from the girl who had first arrived in Magdala. I was a real part of the family now, assured of my place and my status. Even my girl cousins had become my friends—with the exception of Rachel, who was just as nasty as ever.

Sometimes I felt sorry for Rachel. Ruth had told me that nobody liked her because she was such a bully. Ruth and I had become very close, so now Rachel didn't like Ruth either, even though Ruth was her sister. *It must be horrible to be a jealous person*, I thought, with the superiority of one who has never had that particularly spiteful feeling.

I no longer missed Bethany. The previous spring, when we went into Jerusalem for Passover, I had spent a month in Bethany with my family, and I was glad when it was time to return to Galilee. I had wished I could bring Martha and Lazarus with me, but leaving them wasn't as hard as it had been the first time.

I thought of my little brother and sister as I stood on the bench surveying my charges, who were playing a throwing game with a ball I had made by winding cord. They became more and more noisy as the game went on, and I was just telling Amos to lower his voice when Daniel came strolling out of the house eating a slice of bread.

I frowned at him. "You sneaked that from the kitchen."

He grinned. "Leah is such an easy mark."

"Daniel!" The cry went up from all nine of the children. "Play with us! Play with us!"

Dinah came running up to me and grabbed my hand. "You too, Mary! You too!"

Daniel finished his bread, and the two of us joined in the game. Twenty minutes later I called for a respite, and the children sat cross-legged on the ground and drank water from earthenware cups I had filled and passed around.

They were lovely children, full of life and exuberance but obedient as well. After they had finished their water, I distributed small clay animal figures and told them to play quietly. Then I went back to Daniel.

This time together had become part of the pattern of our days. Daniel would come home from the synagogue, change into the same plain tunic and brown robe that the rest of the men wore, and then join the children and me. His father never expected him to join his brothers and cousins on the shore, doing the hard physical labor of packing salted fish into great wooden barrels for shipping.

Daniel was his father's pride and joy, and as long as the rabbi continued to sing his praises, he was excused from physical labor and left to do almost anything he wished to do.

What he wished to do was to spend time with the children and me—mostly with me. For my part, I looked forward to this moment all day long. "What do you and Daniel *talk* about?" Ruth had once asked.

I answered, "The scriptures." I don't think she believed me, but it was true. Daniel told me about what he was studying with the rabbi, and we would discuss some of the questions the rabbi had posed. We were fortunate to have such a scholarly rabbi at our synagogue in Magdala. Daniel said that none of the other towns around the lake had anyone nearly as learned.

I loved to listen to Daniel talk. He was much more interesting than any of the men who stood up to speak in the synagogue. When Daniel talked about the Lord and His covenant with the Jews, it made me understand how fortunate I was to be one of God's chosen people. Daniel said he liked to discuss things with me because I had a quick mind and I made him think. I treasured those words as the greatest compliment I had ever received. That was what was so splendid about Daniel. He would have liked me just as much if I hadn't been pretty.

Lately he had been intrigued by the story of Judas Maccabeus, the hero who raised a Jewish army and drove the Syrian empire out of our lands. I heard about every battle that Judas ever fought and every campaign he ever planned. If anyone else had dwelled on these military details, I would have found it tedious, but I loved the fire that came into Daniel's eyes and the flush that rose in his cheeks as he related the heroic deeds of Judas and his brothers.

"David led an army and won back our lands," I pointed out to him this afternoon, as the children played. "Why isn't David your hero? He was our greatest king, after all. Surely he was a greater man than Judas."

"Of course I revere David. But the important thing about Judas, Mary, is that he did all of this only a hundred and fifty years ago! Now here we are in the same situation, only this time it's the Romans, not the Syrians, who are occupying our lands. We must find another Judas Maccabeus to rise up and lead us. We need the Messiah to come!"

This was not a new refrain, nor was Daniel the only man in Magdala to speak of the Messiah. Our people were growing increasingly weary of the Roman occupation, which our own kings had invited and seemed happy to collude with. Herod the Great and his son, Antipas, had built great palaces modeled after the buildings of Greece and Rome. Magdala itself was too small a town to have Romans stationed here, but Capernaum, only a few miles away, had a large Roman army presence. Everyone in Magdala hated the Romans and longed to be rid of them.

I decided to change the subject. "Tell me the story of Esther."

The fiery look faded from his face to be replaced by amusement. "Again?"

"I could say the same thing when you start talking about the Maccabees," I retorted.

I loved the book of Esther. There was so little in our literature about women, and I thought Esther was just as great a hero as David or Judas Maccabeus. After all, hadn't she saved the Jewish people from total destruction? Not even David or Judas had done that. Maybe Esther was even greater than they were!

I secretly loved to pretend that I was Esther, that I was the one entering the harem of the great king of Persia . . . that I was the one he chose to be his wife because of my great beauty . . . that I was the one who foiled the dastardly designs of the villain Haman. The king must have loved Esther very much, because he pardoned her for interrupting his religious service and hanged her enemy, Haman, high enough for all of Susa to see.

Daniel crossed his arms behind his head, leaned against the fig tree, and started the story.

I thought as I listened, *When we're married, we will name our first daughter Esther.*

Chapter Four

REMEMBER WHAT A SCARED little chicken you were when you first came to live with us?"

I stared at Daniel and replied with dignity, "I have never in my life been a scared little chicken."

"Well, an unhappy little chicken then," he amended.

Ruth and I were supposed to be spreading clothes to dry in the autumn sun, but Daniel had appeared and told her he would help instead. She had given me a look, rolled her eyes, and gone off to begin her next chore. She wouldn't give us away. She never did.

Daniel and I festooned the bushes with clothes and then went to our spot in the corner of the garden out of sight of the house. We sat side by side with our backs propped against the thatched stone enclosure that held the gardening tools.

I rested my head on his shoulder and inhaled the familiar scent of his body. I sighed with happiness.

"The rabbi said today that he has made arrangements for me to study with the best teacher in Jerusalem," Daniel said.

My happiness dimmed. Daniel would turn sixteen in another

month, and when we went to Jerusalem for Passover in the spring, he was to stay behind to begin his studies at the Temple.

I removed my head from his shoulder. "I don't want to talk about that."

"I know you don't. But avoiding the subject isn't going to make it go away."

I raised my legs to rest my forehead on my knees. "I know." My voice came out sounding muffled. "But we still have a few months together. We shouldn't spoil them by worrying about the future."

"Maybe we should."

I turned my head to look at him. His profile looked stern, as if he was trying to hold back some emotion.

"What's wrong, Daniel? You want to go to Jerusalem. The rabbi in Magdala has nothing more to teach you, and you're hungry to learn. Nothing has changed."

He didn't look at me. "On my way home I stopped to buy some dates at Abraham's market stand, and his son asked me how my beautiful cousin was doing and whether he would see you on the Sabbath."

He still wasn't looking at me.

"And . . . ?" I prompted.

He met my eyes at last. "I wish you weren't so beautiful, Mary! All the boys in town stare at you."

I knew this was true, but it had been true ever since I had grown breasts last year. Why should it bother Daniel now?

I turned to him, tucking my legs under me. "Daniel, will you please tell me what is *really* wrong?"

A muscle jumped in his jaw. "Last night my father told me that Joses has agreed to a marriage for Anna. It's Tobias ben Joseph. They will be betrothed next month."

"Why should that concern you?" I said.

He answered in a fierce voice. "Don't you see, Mary? You'll be fourteen soon yourself, and the men will be begging to marry you. And I'll be in Jerusalem studying, a boy with no money and no hope of getting any until I qualify as a scribe."

I almost laughed. I would have if he weren't so upset. I pressed a little closer to him and took his hand.

"Daniel, I'm flattered that you think so highly of me, but be sensible. No father wants a girl who has only a pretty face to recommend her for his son. I have no great family connections, no notable housewifely skills, no money." I held his hand to my cheek. "The only man who will ever want to marry me is you."

He still looked worried. "But what if someone does ask for you? What will we do then?"

I smiled at him. "I'll refuse him. No one can make me marry if I don't want to."

He sighed. Then, slowly, he grinned. "I don't believe anyone has ever made you do anything you didn't want to."

"I have perseverance. You have nothing to worry about. I'll simply stay here until you're ready, and then we will marry."

He looked around to make sure there were no observers, and then he pulled me against him and kissed me.

THE DECEMBER RAINS WERE dark and chilly as usual, but the week after Hanukkah we suddenly had an unusual burst of mild and sunny weather. Everyone reveled in it, and one evening it was even warm enough for us to go out into the courtyard, which was sheltered by the surrounding walls of the house. I sat on a low bench with a group of children gathered around me. We were playing a word game, and occasionally I glanced away from the uplifted little faces to where Daniel was sitting beside his eldest brother, Samuel.

Samuel was the only member of the family besides Rachel who disliked me. He wasn't unpleasant; he just acted as if I didn't exist. When we met unexpectedly, he would avert his eyes as if I were unclean. I couldn't imagine what I had done to offend him and did my best to stay out of his way.

It was unusual for Daniel and Samuel to be talking so comfortably. The age gap between them was many years, and Samuel always seemed more like Daniel's uncle than his brother.

Samuel was unfortunate to have been the only son to inherit his father's ears. True, they were not so tremendous as Lord Benjamin's, but they were big enough to be remarkable. He also had inherited his father's bulky body and wide, flat nose.

Poor Samuel, I thought, as I compared him to the elegant young brother sitting beside him.

Suddenly there was activity at the far end of the courtyard, and I turned to see Abigail, Samuel's wife, getting laboriously to her feet. Esther and Miriam, Joses' wife, rushed to join her. Abigail was nine months gone with child, and I thought her time might have come. Esther turned and beckoned to Aunt Leah, and the three women supported Abigail as they all entered the house.

"Where are they going, Mary?" a small voice asked.

I smiled into the curious face of Dinah, one of Joses' granddaughters. "Abigail is going to have a baby. Isn't that nice? You will have a new little cousin to play with."

Dinah looked around the courtyard and shook her head decisively. "I already have enough cousins."

I smothered a laugh. "Well, this little cousin won't be big enough to join our group for a long time."

Dinah smiled. She loved having my full attention. "Good."

Lord Benjamin leaned over to slap Samuel on the back. "This time you will have a son, eh?"

Poor Abigail had thus far only given Samuel three daughters. Everyone was praying for a son.

Samuel gave a strained smile. "I certainly hope so," he replied.

⁂

I WENT TO BED that night expecting to hear of a new child in the morning. I knew that childbirth was dangerous—my own mother had died having a baby. But Abigail had given birth three times with no trouble. After saying a prayer for her, I fell into my usual sound sleep.

Aunt Leah had not yet returned to her sleeping mat when I awoke. I pulled my wool cloak over my tunic, draped my veil over my hair, slipped my feet into sandals, and went out into the courtyard to the large baking oven.

I was always the first one up because my morning job was to grind the grain for the day's bread. I used a hand mill to do this, and after that I mixed the meal with water, salt, and a bit of leavening. Then I kneaded it into dough to be baked later in the day.

I was kneading vigorously when Aunt Leah came out of the house. She looked tired.

"Mary," she said in her softest voice.

I smiled into her weary face. "Is it a boy?"

My aunt shook her head. "No, another girl."

"Too bad," I said sympathetically.

She just stood there looking at me, and my hands grew still on the dough. "Is something wrong?"

"Abigail died," she said.

I had been three years old when my mother died. I had no memory of her, but all my life I had longed for her. I still did. So those two words, *Abigail died*, hit me like a punch in the stomach. "What happened?"

My aunt took my hand. "We couldn't stop the bleeding, my dear. Miriam is very skilled, but even she . . ."

"The baby?"

My little brother had died along with my mother. I remembered that too. Such a tiny little life, so quickly extinguished.

"She is alive."

I swallowed. "That is good." I swallowed again. "But she will never know her mother."

"No," my aunt agreed. "She will never know her mother."

I started to cry. Leah put her arms around me and held me close. We both knew that I wasn't crying for Abigail.

Chapter Five

Aſter the warm spell in December, winter set in for good. With the cold and rain cooping us up in the house, Daniel and I were forced to meet more briefly and with less intimacy than we had become used to, which frustrated both of us. Then, as January came to a close, I noticed something odd happening. Samuel was noticing me.

It was very strange. Where once he had never looked at me, now I caught him staring at me. He even smiled at me once or twice. I found the new Samuel unnerving, and I redoubled my efforts to avoid him.

When it wasn't raining, I would take the children outdoors for at least part of the day, and one particularly nice afternoon two weeks before Purim, we were in the courtyard playing a game of hide-and-seek. The children loved to hide, which made me the seeker. Their giggling always gave them away, but I made a great show of looking in peculiar places for them or not quite seeing them, which they loved.

We had been at it for a while when I noticed Samuel watching us from one of the doorways. Ivah, Joses' grandchild, had mischievously pulled my veil off, and as no one else was around, I hadn't bothered to replace it. The girls loved to play with my hair, which was long and straight. It was easy for them to braid, and I squealed and scolded when they pulled too hard. They loved that too.

As soon as I saw Samuel, I tried to hide my hair. "I'm sorry, Samuel, to be so disheveled," I apologized as I gathered it into a messy knot. "One of the children pulled my veil off when we were playing."

He advanced into the courtyard, paying no attention to his little daughter, who had run up to him. "Your hair is very beautiful, Mary. It shines blue in the sun, like the wing of a raven."

I gave him an uncertain smile and then turned to one of the children. "Ivah, fetch me my veil, please." Obediently, she ran to get it.

"There's no need to be fearful," Samuel said, regarding me with a look that made my stomach feel sick. He kept coming closer. "I am a member of your family, after all."

He stopped beside me and reached out to take a strand of hair that had escaped the knot between my fingers. He rubbed it between his fingers, as if evaluating a piece of material. "It's like silk," he said.

His eyes glistened, and my heart began to pound. I hated his touch and wanted to push him away. But he was Lord Benjamin's heir, a man of great importance in the family. I felt trapped and began to pray to God for deliverance.

"What do you think you're doing?"

The words ripped across the courtyard, causing both Samuel and me to jump.

It was Daniel.

Samuel dropped my hair and swung around to face his younger brother. "I thought you were supposed to be studying." He sounded furious.

Daniel was striding across the courtyard toward us. He retorted, "I was studying, but when I looked into the courtyard, I saw you stalking Mary the way a wolf stalks a lamb." He was pale, and his narrowed eyes shone like fire. He looked startlingly dangerous.

I grabbed my veil from Ivah and clapped it on my head. The two brothers glared at each other with open fury.

Little Zebah slipped her hand into mine. "Why are they angry, Mary?" She sounded as frightened as I was. I shook my head, speechless. "I want to go away from here," the girl whimpered.

I didn't know if it would be better to go or to stay and try to keep them from killing each other.

Daniel's eyes swung away from Samuel and met mine. "Zebah's right. Take the children somewhere else."

I nodded, rounded up my charges, and herded them out of the courtyard and toward the house. As we walked away, I said brightly, "I'll tell you a story. Which one do you want to hear?"

"The one about the man who was swallowed by a whale!" Amos yelled.

There was a commotion of agreement.

"All right," I said. "We'll go into the front room, and I'll tell it to you."

≈

WE WERE STILL IN the front room, and I had moved on to the story of Noah and the flood, when Daniel found me. "I have to talk to you," he said in a clipped voice.

I gestured to the children, indicating that I could not leave them.

"Get Leah or Ruth," he commanded, and I ran out of the room.

I found Aunt Leah alone in the kitchen, and I asked her to watch the children for a short time so I could speak to Daniel.

"Why can't Daniel speak in front of the children?" She was looking at me worriedly.

I told her about how strange Samuel had been and how he and Daniel had looked ready to come to blows.

She shut her eyes. "Mary, do you know how much trouble all this could cause?"

I swallowed hard. I was beginning to realize that I did. "But Samuel has never liked me, Aunt Leah!" I cried.

"I suppose you had better speak to Daniel." Her voice was almost inaudible, and she went ahead of me into the front room. The look she shot at Daniel was somber, but then she turned to the children and engaged them in a song.

Daniel and I slipped away to the empty courtyard.

"This way," he said, leading me to the door of one of the storerooms. He pushed it open and we stepped inside.

The room was filled with the barrels used for packing fish, and the smell of wood and dust was strong in the air. Daniel left the door open a crack so we could see each other.

The expression on his face as he looked down at me was unlike any I had seen before. His nose looked sharper, almost like a hawk's beak, and his eyes wore a strangely intense expression.

"What has happened?" My voice trembled despite my efforts to sound calm.

"Samuel wants to marry you," he said. "That's what he told me after you left. The rutting old goat, he wants to *marry* you!"

I stared at him in horror. "But he's never liked me, Daniel! Remember how I once asked you what I might have done to offend him?"

Daniel laughed harshly. "He was afraid to look at you. He lusted after you, and he was married to another woman. You were a temptation to him. That's why he never looked at you."

I shuddered at the thought of Samuel lusting after me. "What are we going to do, Daniel? I can't marry Samuel!"

He reached out and pulled me close. I rested my cheek against his linen tunic and felt the beating of his heart. I put my arms around his waist and held him tightly.

He said my name and I looked up at him. He bent his head and kissed me.

We had kissed before, but this was different. This kiss was full of urgency, full of need. This was a kiss I could feel all the way down in my stomach. My head fell back, and he cupped a hand behind it to support me. His strong young body was pressed against mine, and I was dizzy with what he was making me feel.

"Mary." His voice was husky and shaking. "This isn't right." He put both his hands on my upper arms and put me away from him. His grip was so hard it hurt me. "I should not have kissed you like that."

"It felt right to me." I lifted my chin, daring him to disagree.

A flash of amusement flitted across his tense face. "I love it when you raise your chin like that." He drew a deep, steadying breath. "I love all of you, my beloved."

"I love you too, Daniel. I have always loved you."

His face took on the dangerous aspect it had worn in the courtyard. He looked out the cracked door and said, "I would like to murder Samuel."

"You can't hurt Samuel! That would make everything worse."

It never occurred to me that, if it came to blows, Samuel was much heavier than Daniel and would undoubtedly be the victor. The way Daniel looked . . . it never occurred to me at all.

He straightened to his full height. "I'll speak to my father about us. I'll tell him how we feel, that we wish to be married someday. I won't allow you to be married to Samuel."

From the courtyard Leah's voice sounded, calling my name.

Daniel said, "Go out first. I'll wait for a bit. We don't want anyone to see us come out of here together."

I bit my lip, gave him another fearful look, and slipped out the door.

⁓

Neither Samuel nor Daniel appeared at supper that night, but as Ruth and I were walking toward the kitchen to help with the dishes, she hissed in my ear and pushed me into the closet where the Passover supper pots and plates were kept. All the precious dishes were lovingly wrapped in linen and carefully stacked.

Esther kept a ritually clean kitchen at all times, but for Passover she had special, treasured dinnerware. Unlike the stories I had heard in Judea about Galileans, she was very strict about following the dietary laws.

Ruth and I stood close together in the small closet, whispering so as not to be heard by anyone passing by. "My mother told me that this afternoon Samuel asked Lord Benjamin if he could marry you!"

My heart began to race. "What did Lord Benjamin answer?"

"He said no."

My relief was so intense that my knees almost gave way. "Give thanks to the Lord, for he is good," I said fervently.

Ruth was looking bewildered. "How ever did Samuel come to do such a thing, Mary? You always complained he didn't like you."

I told her about what had occurred that afternoon in the courtyard. "I was terrified. Samuel was so close to me, and his eyes were glittering in a horrible way. He looked as if he wanted to eat me up." I shuddered. "Then he touched my hair."

"No . . ." Ruth breathed in shocked sympathy. "That's disgusting. How did you get away?"

"Daniel came into the courtyard."

Ruth's mouth opened in a big O. She seemed torn between fascination and terror. "What happened then?"

I swallowed. "They had a big argument. Oh, Ruth, I thought they were going to punch each other! Then Daniel told me to take the children inside, and I did."

Even to Ruth, I didn't think I should mention my later meeting with Daniel in the storeroom.

Ruth patted my arm. "Well, you can consider yourself safe from Samuel. Lord Benjamin has already made plans for him. He's been negotiating for Samuel to marry Naomi, the daughter of Saul bar Levi."

Saul bar Levi had one of the biggest fishing fleets in Magdala; his daughter would be a good match for Lord Benjamin's heir.

"Was Lord Benjamin angry with Samuel?"

"If he was, he'll get over it. It wasn't your fault that Samuel made a fool of himself."

I prayed she was right.

"There is one more thing, though . . ."

The expression on her face alarmed me. "What?"

"My mother also told me that Lord Benjamin expects to collect a big bride price for you. She said that two well-placed men from the town have already inquired about getting you for their sons."

I had never seriously thought that I might be the object of marriage offers. I knew that the young men in town admired my looks, but their fathers would be looking for more than just a pretty face.

The Jewish custom was that the prospective husband's family had to pay a bride price to his prospective in-laws as compensation for the loss of her services to their household. However, the wife was also expected to bring something to the husband's family. Social status and sterling housewifely skills were the minimum a family would require before parting with a substantial bride price.

I said, "Your mother must be wrong. Why would any father want to pay to bring me into his family?"

Ruth said, "Those boys want you for the same reason that Samuel wanted you. And there will probably be others."

"No," I said. "No and no and no. This can't be true."

Ruth took my two hands and looked into my eyes. "Mary, listen to me. I'm not your friend because you're beautiful; I'm your friend because I like you. You're generous and kind and funny and fun to be with. But men aren't always interested in those things. They think of something else when they look at a woman."

I thought of Samuel's glittering eyes, and suddenly I was angry. "A Jewish man is supposed to think about a woman's wifely qualities. When the scriptures talk about a wife, they say that 'charm is deceptive and beauty fleeting.'" I lifted my chin. "A Jewish man is supposed to wed a woman whose housewifely accomplishments are richer than the 'finest of pearls.' That's what the scriptures say!"

"That may be true, but remember, they also tell us that Jacob preferred Rachel over Leah because Rachel was so beautiful. And David had Bathsheba's husband murdered because he wanted her beauty so much. I don't believe the scriptures mention Rachel or Bathsheba's housewifely skills."

I wanted to stamp my foot, but I was afraid we might be heard from outside the closet. "Daniel doesn't love me for my looks; he cares about *me*," I said.

"Yes, he does." Ruth leaned forward to kiss my cheek. "But you and Daniel . . . well, you two are special. The rest of us will never have what you have."

I heard a note of regret in her voice. "Will you be content to marry the man your father picks for you?" I asked.

"How would I go about choosing a man myself? I don't know any men. None of the girls in this house knows any men. We must rely on our fathers for that sort of thing."

Suddenly my heart was wrung for my friend and for all the poor girls who didn't have a Daniel in their lives.

Ruth said, "We'd better go before Esther begins to look for us."

I agreed, and we listened for noise in the hall outside. When we heard no one, we slipped out the closet door and walked softly through the hall and into the kitchen.

Later that night, as I was lying on my sleeping mat, some of Ruth's words came back to me. In matters of marriage, she had said, girls must rely upon their fathers.

But Lord Benjamin is not my father. My father lives in Bethany.

I wondered if I might have found a way of escaping any marriage offers Lord Benjamin might receive for me.

Chapter Six

Jewish women are not taught to pray as the men are. Our learning is practically limited to prayers to be said over the preparation of food. But my studies with Daniel had made me feel that the Lord was ever-present, and I prayed often. I loved the psalms in particular. It comforted me to think I could look to the Lord the way a sheep looks to its shepherd, to know that the Lord would never let me be orphaned, that I would always find shelter in the shadow of His wings.

My father had abandoned me, and Lord Benjamin had never made me feel like a full member of his family. So I turned to the Lord for what I lacked in paternal care. The Lord cared about me. If I prayed hard enough, He would take pity on Daniel and me and allow us to marry.

During those difficult days Daniel and I were rigidly monitored. Samuel had told his father about Daniel's protective way toward me, and every time Esther saw me, she glared as if I were a snake in her bosom. Rachel kept trying to find out what I had done to make Esther so angry. Daniel and I were able to see each other only at supper, where we were placed at opposite ends of the table.

On the second day of the week, the women of the household went into town to do the shopping. The open-air marketplace in Magdala was much larger than one might expect for a town of a thousand people. It was Magdala's location on the lake road that made us an easy stopping place for the merchants traveling north to Caesarea Philippi and Damascus, south to Jerusalem, west to Sepphoris and to Caesarea, on the coast of the Great Sea, and sometimes even all the way into Egypt. We never knew what we might see when we went to market.

This particular market day was bright and sunny, and all the women of our family joined the buzzing, gossiping crowd as they flitted from stall to stall. Ruth and I slipped away from Aunt Leah as she was bargaining for some newly harvested flax. We were standing in front of a stall near the synagogue wall, admiring pretty earrings a merchant from Sepphoris was selling, when Daniel appeared at my elbow.

I gave him a surprised look. He was supposed to be studying in the synagogue.

He put his mouth close to my ear. "I told the rabbi I needed some fresh air. We must talk, Mary."

We looked at each other, and then, at the same moment, we turned our eyes to Ruth.

She sighed. "All right. What do you want me to do?"

Daniel said, "Keep out of the sight of my mother and yours. That way they'll believe that Mary is still with you. We won't be long, Ruth. I promise."

Ruth looked at me, and I mouthed the word *please*. She glanced over her shoulder to see if Esther or Miriam was around and then said, "All right. I'll sit in the shade of the synagogue porch. Come and get me when you're ready."

She moved off into the crowd, and I pulled my veil far down over my forehead to hide my face. Daniel said to the jewelry merchant, "Can we use the tent behind your stall for a few minutes?"

The big man looked at the two of us and shook his head. "It would be sinful of me to allow such a thing. You two are clearly unwed. It would be wrong of me to assist in your sinful behavior."

Daniel reached out, and I saw that he had a shekel in his hand. It disappeared quickly into the merchant's robes, and he gestured for us to enter into the small canvas enclosure.

I followed Daniel through the opening in the canvas. The odor inside was stifling—male sweat mingled with rotten fish. The miserable place held a sleeping mat, an empty wineskin, a half-eaten loaf of bread, and an uncovered bowl of olives that had attracted a swarm of flies. My nose wrinkled, and I instinctively took a step back.

Daniel said, "I'm sorry I had to bring you in here, Mary, but I couldn't think of any other way for us to be alone. My mother is watching me as a lioness watches a threatened cub. I think what happened with Samuel has made her afraid that you and I are more to each other than the brother and sister she always thought we were."

I tried to ignore the smell and put an urgent hand on his sleeve. "Ruth told me that your father expects to get a big bride price for me! She said that two men have already asked for me for their sons!"

I felt his arm go rigid under my fingers. His expression was grim. "That's what I've been afraid of."

I shook his arm. "Listen. I might have a solution for us. If I go back to Bethany and live with my father again, Lord Benjamin won't be able to arrange my marriage. That will be for my own father to do. I'll explain to my father about us, and I'm sure he will let me wait for you to finish your studies. It's prestigious to be a Temple scribe. My father would be proud to have someone like that in his family. I know he would."

A thin line appeared between Daniel's black brows. "What about Judith?"

"Don't worry about Judith. She's so stuck-up that she would love to impress all of Bethany by having a Temple scribe in her family."

He inhaled deeply. "That would be a solution indeed."

I added triumphantly, "And I could even visit you in Jerusalem! People from Bethany go into Jerusalem all the time."

We smiled at each other in the dimness of the merchant's foul-smelling den.

Daniel said, "You'll have to ask your father for his permission to go home. I can write whatever you want to say and have it sent by the messenger who takes letters to the synagogues in Judea."

I agreed. "I think we should also ask my father to send someone to bring me home. Maybe he would even come himself!"

I could see it all in my mind—my triumphant departure, Lord Benjamin's fury—and then I thought of Aunt Leah. I would ask my father to let her come too. I shuddered to think of leaving her behind to face Lord Benjamin alone.

The opening to the tent parted, and the merchant peered in. "How much longer are you two going to be?"

Daniel produced another shekel. "Not long. Be patient. We'll only be a moment."

Once again the shekel disappeared into the man's surprisingly clean garments, and he closed the canvas behind him.

Daniel said, "We have to hurry. What do you want me to say?"

"Tell him I want to come home because Lord Benjamin is trying to make me marry someone I hate. And tell him that Aunt Leah must come with me." I bit my lip. "Do you think I should tell him about us in a letter? Or should I wait until I get there?"

We looked at each other, trying to decide. "Perhaps you shouldn't be too specific," Daniel said at last.

"I think you're right."

"Perhaps I'll add that the reason my father wants you to marry this man is because the bride price is so big. If your father thinks he can collect a big bride price for you, he might be more inclined to let you come home."

"Very clever, Daniel." I glanced nervously at the tent opening. "I think we had better go."

He bent his head and gave me a quick, hard kiss. "Be patient, my love."

I managed a trembling smile, and we both slipped back into the world.

❧

LATER THAT WEEK LORD Benjamin formally announced to the family that Samuel would be marrying Naomi, and all the men of the family were delighted with such an advantageous match. Samuel didn't look delighted, but then, he had always been an expressionless man.

Fifteen days after my letter had been sent, my father's response was delivered to the synagogue in Magdala. It was a breezy end-of-winter day, and I had taken the little girls out into the garden to admire the almond trees, which were in bloom. I was explaining to them about how the tree would produce its nuts, when I saw Daniel coming toward me. It wasn't until I saw the scroll in his belt that I realized he must have heard from my father.

Daniel came up to us and offered a bag of sweets to the children, who shrieked with delight. While they crunched on their treats, Daniel drew me aside.

"You have the letter?" I asked.

"Yes."

"Have you read it?"

"Yes."

The grim look on his face was making me nervous. "What does it say?"

He pulled the parchment out of his belt and unrolled it. "Listen," he said:

To my daughter Mary: I have received your communication, and what you ask is impossible. You are a part of Benjamin's household, not of mine, and you must abide by his wishes. He has housed and fed you all these years, and he would never choose a man for you who was not fit to be your husband. It is my wish that you abide by his decision. Peace comes through obedience, my daughter. Your father, Jacob

I stared at the paper in Daniel's long, slender fingers and couldn't believe what I had heard. My father didn't care about me. He didn't care about me at all. I wasn't a part of his household. As far as he was concerned, I was a stranger.

I looked up into Daniel's bleak face. "How could he do this to me?"

He stuffed the paper back into his belt and put his hands on my shoulders. "Mary. Love. Don't look like that. I will fix this. I'll make it all right with my father. I'll make him allow us to marry."

I swallowed. "How can you make him do that? He doesn't like me, Daniel. I don't think he's ever liked me."

He looked so much older than his sixteen years. "I will do it." He traced the curve of my cheek with a gentle forefinger. "It will be all right. I promise it will be all right."

"Is something wrong?" It was Dinah's little piping voice, and she pulled at my skirt to get my attention. She had finished her treat.

I managed some kind of a smile. "No, Dinah. Nothing is wrong. Have all the children finished their sweets?"

"I haven't," Zebah said, her mouth still full of dried fig. "Dinah gobbled hers."

"I did not," Dinah said, turning to glare at her cousin.

Daniel squeezed my arm and said, "I'll talk to my father tonight," and turned away.

"Daniel's nice," Dinah said. "I like it when he brings us treats."

I watched him walk away, with the pale sun shining on his black hair, and I was afraid.

I COULDN'T EAT A thing at supper, and Aunt Leah asked me twice if I was feeling ill. When the meal was finally finished, I saw Daniel and his father disappear toward the back of the house. I knew they must have gone to the room Lord Benjamin kept for his private use, and I was so nervous that if I had eaten, I would have thrown all of the food right back up on the tile floor. Half an hour later, while I was in the kitchen helping with the dishes, Ivah peeked in and said, "Mary, Lord Benjamin wants to see you in his room."

The kitchen went silent. No one moved. Everyone looked at me. Rachel hissed in my ear, "What have you done this time?"

I kept my face blank, stiffened my spine, and walked out. I could feel the eyes boring into my back as I left the room.

Lord Benjamin's private room was small, but it had its own lamp, and there was a rug on the floor and a cushion on the bench. He was sitting on the bench, and Daniel was standing next to him. They both looked at me as I came in and closed the door behind me.

The lamp was lit, but it was difficult to decipher Lord Benjamin's expression. I stood in front of him, my eyes cast down. Daniel moved to stand beside me, but I didn't dare look at him.

Lord Benjamin said, "Mary, I have given Daniel permission to become betrothed to you."

My knees wobbled, my ears hummed, and for a horrifying moment I was afraid I might faint. I blinked to clear my vision and focused on Daniel's father. "Thank you, sir," I said uncertainly.

He looked back at me, his face unreadable.

I turned to Daniel. He smiled and nodded, and joy exploded inside me like the rising sun. I smiled back. I could feel my joy radiating out to encompass Daniel as we stood there together.

Lord Benjamin rose. "I will give you five minutes alone, and then I'll come back." He looked at his son. "Remember our agreement."

Daniel's voice was firm. "Yes, Father. We will obey your wishes."

Lord Benjamin walked past me and left the room, leaving the door open behind him. I stepped into Daniel's arms.

He held me tightly, and I slid my arms around his waist and hugged him back. For a moment we just stood there, locked together, as close as we could get. When Daniel pushed my veil back and rested his lips against my hair, I managed to croak, "How did you do it?"

His mouth moved against my hair as he answered. "I told him that if he wouldn't let me marry you, I'd go out to the desert and join the Essenes."

I pulled away to look up at his face. "The Essenes? You wouldn't do that!"

"I might have," he replied grimly. "I just might have."

42

I knew little about the Essenes except that they were a strange group of religious extremists who lived in the wilds of the Judean desert. I simply couldn't imagine Daniel as one of them.

Daniel said, "Listen, Mary, this is what my father agreed to. We can't marry until I have become a scribe and can support you, but we can become formally betrothed at Shavuot."

I was dizzy with happiness. Lord Benjamin had said *yes*. I had heard him with my own ears.

"There is one other stipulation," Daniel went on. "We must keep our betrothal a secret until after Passover. Samuel and Naomi are having their betrothal ceremony right before we leave for Jerusalem, and my father doesn't want us to do anything that might draw attention away from Naomi."

This seemed reasonable. It was certainly true that my betrothal to Daniel would cause more of a sensation in the family and the town than Naomi's to Samuel.

I felt like jumping up and down and screaming for joy, the way Dinah did when she was happy. "The Lord has answered our prayers," I said.

Daniel grinned. "We're going to be betrothed."

I grinned back. "We're going to be betrothed!"

We were holding hands and laughing like idiots when Lord Benjamin came back into the room.

Chapter Seven

I KEPT MY PROMISE to Daniel and told no one but Aunt Leah about our betrothal. She knew how I felt about Daniel, but we never openly spoke about it—except for her guarded comments that I should be careful where I bestowed my heart. Her astonishment when I told her of Lord Benjamin's approval told me just how much she had doubted we would ever get it. But she was almost as happy for me as I was for myself.

"Daniel is such a fine young man, Mary," she said, holding my face between her hands as we stood in our tiny bedchamber. Her brown eyes were serious. "You must try to be worthy of him."

I knew I would never be worthy of Daniel. No woman could be. But he loved me, and if he searched the world over, he would not find a single person who could love him more than I did. I knew I had been blessed by God to have Daniel's love in return. "I'll try my best," I promised.

She held me to her and said with awe, "I never thought this could happen. Good for Benjamin."

SAMUEL AND NAOMI had their betrothal ceremony two days before the family left for Jerusalem to celebrate Passover. Every year the families from our town would make up a caravan and travel together. It was safer to journey in numbers, and it was also more fun.

The warming weather had dried up most of the winter mud, and the roads weren't yet dusty. The sun was just right, warm on our heads and shoulders but not too hot. The hillsides of Galilee were covered with wildflowers, and the stretching fields of barley and wheat glittered like splashes of sunshine under the blue arch of the sky.

Almost everyone walked, but most families had donkeys to carry their tents, food, and the fine linen clothing that they would wear to the Temple. There were many other caravans on the road, and we filled the air with our singing. The little ones sang the pilgrimage songs I had taught them, and the joyous sound of hundreds of voices rose toward the heavens as we marched along the well-worn path that followed the Jordan from Galilee into Judea.

At night, around the cooking fires, the men would talk about the success or disappointment of the flax harvest and how good or bad the fishing had been, and—as always when a group of Jewish men got together—they talked about how much they hated the Romans. Second to the Romans, they hated Herod Antipas, the Galilean king, because he collaborated with the enemy. And they hated the most prominent symbol of the occupation, the Roman procurator who ruled Judea, because Rome had banished the Jewish king, Herod Archelaus, for incompetence.

I liked to eavesdrop on these conversations because Daniel was passionate about politics. He was passionate, too, as were most of the other men, about his hopes for the coming of the Messiah.

Daniel had often recited to me the exact passages in scripture that predicted the Messiah's coming. The Messiah would be a war leader like David and Judas Maccabeus, only greater. It was the Messiah whom the Lord had anointed to restore the lands of Israel to the Jewish people. The Messiah was destined to reign over all the world.

At night, I contemplated the idea of the Messiah as I lay in the tent that I shared with Aunt Leah and some of the children. It was exciting to think that a great king would arise from our midst, but I had difficulty picturing how it could happen. Our people were farmers and fishermen. Our leaders were priests, scribes, and Pharisees—religious men, not soldiers. When the Roman centurions rode their big horses into Magdala, we all backed out of their way. They wore helmets and breastplates and carried spears. They had conquered the world. How could the men of my little nation hope to defeat them?

Thankfully, it was up to God to answer that question, not me.

IT TOOK US FOUR days to reach our usual campsite on the gentle slopes of the Mount of Olives. Every year we set up our tents in this same place, away from the crowds that were crammed like bees in a hive within the city walls.

We arrived just as the sun was setting over Jerusalem, and I managed a short escape from the bustle of getting settled so I could look across the Kidron Valley to the holy city itself.

This particular picture was imprinted on my mind, and I treasured it. I could close my eyes and call it up whenever I wished, and I did so frequently when I prayed. When I looked across the valley at Jerusalem, I didn't see the Upper City, where the rich lived amid an array of magnificent palaces, or the great mass of the Citadel, or the huge barracks of the Antonia, where the hated Roman troops were housed.

My eyes were filled with the shining white splendor of the Temple, the center of the Jewish world, rising high above the ancient city walls.

Tonight, with the red sunset sky casting a glow on its marble purity, it was a breathtaking sight. My heart swelled with pride and awe as I regarded it.

I liked seeing the Temple from a distance better than I did being inside the building itself. We always visited at Passover, when the presence of the Lord seemed lost in the mass of people and animals that were crushed within its walls. But here, on the Mount of Olives, the Lord was very present to me, and I recited to myself the great words of the covenant He had made to Abraham: *I will be your God, and you will be my people.*

I was so moved that tears stung my eyes. As I stood there, with the radiant glory of our Temple before me, I asked the Lord humbly how I had ever deserved to be so happy.

THE FOLLOWING MORNING OUR group set out early for the Temple. The road from the Mount of Olives was already crowded with pilgrims waiting their turn to pass through the Valley Gate, the one closest to the Mount. It was dry underfoot from so many feet, and dust rose into the air as we walked. Ivah started to cough, so I tied a cotton scarf over her nose and mouth.

It should have been a short walk, but at Passover it always took hours. The closer we got to the gate, the more packed together the crowd became. Merchants were lined up along the way, hoping to sell a lamb or some pigeons and doves for Temple sacrifice. The loud voices, promising cheaper prices if we bought from them, scraped on my nerves, as did the whining of the multitude of beggars. People pushed and shoved to get to the merchants, and I picked Ivah up so she wouldn't be stepped on.

We finally reached the Valley Gate, which was guarded by a detachment of bored-looking Roman soldiers. I walked through, still carrying Ivah, and one of the soldiers peered at me and made a rude remark as we went by.

"Disgusting pigs," Ruth muttered from behind me, and I heartily agreed.

The crowd outside the walls was nothing compared to the crowd inside. Merchants were lined up all along the narrow streets, shouting out their wares in Greek and Aramaic, and the air was filled with the bleating of frightened animals.

I always tried not to think about the rivers of blood that would be shed on the Temple altars. Lord Benjamin always bought our lamb inside the Temple, even though it was more expensive. To be accepted as a sacrifice, the lamb had to be declared unblemished, and the priests often declared the lambs that came from outside unfit, forcing the poor pilgrim to buy a second lamb, this time from the Temple. Lord Benjamin said it was a way for the priests to make money, and the only way to avoid the swindle was to take no chances and buy your lamb from them.

The smells were almost as overwhelming as the noise and the crowds. Food from all the countries of the Empire was being sold at market stands, and those odors, combined with the stench of sweat and the pungent oils that people had anointed themselves with, were enough to make my stomach churn.

When we finally reached the Temple, we had to separate so each of us could take a *mikvah*, the ritual bath that was necessary before one could be admitted to the Temple proper. About half the family had gathered in the Court of the Gentiles by the time I joined them, my *mikvah* finished. The court was almost as crowded and noisy as the streets had been. The money changers were set up, ready to exchange foreign currency into ritually clean shekels, and the merchants were spread all over the vast area, selling a variety of sacrificial birds and animals as well as ritually pure lambs. Some enterprising souls were even trying to sell souvenirs to visitors from foreign lands.

Once all the family had gathered, we went up the stairs into the next court, the Court of the Women. This was where the real Temple started. It was open only to Jews, unlike the Court of the Gentiles, and merchants were not allowed in here. This court was meant for relaxing, for socializing, for meeting old friends. It was also the place where worshippers made their donations to the upkeep of the Temple. Lord Benjamin had given each member of his household a shekel for the Temple treasury, and I felt very important as I dropped my offering into one of the huge chests shaped like a ram's horn.

As the family dispersed to seek out friends they hadn't seen since last Passover, I attached myself to Daniel, and loyal Ruth attached herself to me. The Court of the Women was the place where all the famous scholars taught their students, the place where Daniel himself would shortly be a student. We followed him as he walked about, listening to the scholars as they questioned their students.

I tried not to dwell on our coming separation. How was I going to get through each day without seeing him? Without speaking to him? I couldn't bear to think about it, so I tried to concentrate on what was being said by the scholars.

Beside me Ruth squealed, and I watched as she and another girl embraced and began to chatter. I turned back to the discourse Daniel was listening to so intently. The scribe was speaking about the Messiah, and for the first time I began to wonder if such a being might come in my lifetime.

❦

THE WOMEN AND CHILDREN remained in the Women's Court, while the men went through the magnificent bronze Nicanor Gate to ascend to the next court, the Court of Israel. From this vantage point, they could witness the priests making sacrifices and burnt offerings upon the altars in the Court of the Priests.

Women weren't allowed beyond the Women's Court, which suited me well. I found the thought of all that blood running down the Temple funnels into the valley below distressing. On these occasions I always remembered one of the psalms that Daniel had taught me, the one where the Lord says that He needs no bulls or goats from us as sacrifice, that all He wants from His people is our worship and thanksgiving.

Apparently the priests of the Temple hadn't taken that psalm seriously.

Finally the men returned, and it was time to leave the Temple area. Lord Benjamin, Esther, Joses, Miriam, Samuel, and Naomi were going to remain in the city to dine that evening with Aaron bar David, the wealthy merchant who shipped the family's fish to all the lands of the Roman world, while the rest of us were returning to the Mount of Olives.

As Ruth and I chatted idly, waiting for Ezekiel, Lord Benjamin's second son, Lord Benjamin announced that the invitation to dine with Aaron bar David had been extended to Daniel and me.

Daniel had no part in the business, but he was going to be a famous scribe someday. I could understand why he had been invited.

But me? Our betrothal was still a secret. Why would Lord Benjamin have asked this merchant to invite me?

Daniel said, "I am honored, Father, but a little surprised."

Lord Benjamin smiled genially. "I met Aaron bar David in the Temple today, and I happened to mention that you would be remaining here in Jerusalem to study. He saw that I would miss you sorely, and he included you in his invitation so that I could have more time with you before we must part."

I was pleased. What a nice man Aaron bar David must be.

Of course, this still didn't explain my invitation. It had been strange enough to include Esther, Miriam, and Naomi. Women normally didn't dine with men not of their family, but Aaron bar David lived in Sepphoris, and everyone said that they did many strange things in that Romanized city.

"But why should Mary go?"

It was Rachel, and she looked to be almost bursting with fury.

"I know that Mary will miss Daniel too," Lord Benjamin replied benevolently. "It won't harm her to come, as long as her aunts are present as well."

In all the years I'd lived in his house, I never realized what a kind man Lord Benjamin was. I gave him my most radiant smile.

He didn't smile in return. He just nodded once and turned away.

Chapter Eight

AARON BAR DAVID'S HOUSE was in Jerusalem's Upper City, where the wealthy had their homes. The beautiful buildings with their lovely gardens, and the broad, gracious, tree-lined streets, were in sharp contrast to the narrow twisting alleyways and tightly packed mud-brick houses of the lower city. Herod the Great's immense palace was in the Upper City, as were the houses of the priests and Pharisees who made up the Sanhedrin, the ruling council of our religious life.

Naomi and I gaped as we passed one imposing residence after another, until finally Esther snapped at us to stop behaving like bumpkins, and we lowered our eyes in proper decorum. Daniel murmured in my ear, "Some of this money could be used for better purposes, I think."

I pictured all the beggars on the streets of the lower city and murmured my agreement.

A servant opened the gate at the entrance to Aaron's house, and we crossed a stone courtyard with a spouting fountain to arrive at the massive front door. It sprang open before we reached the top step and a servant bowed to Lord Benjamin and bade us follow him upstairs.

The upper room was huge, with most of it taken up by a low

carved wooden table with gold inlay. Couches were placed around three of the sides, with the fourth side left traditionally empty. At the servant's direction, we took our assigned places, Lord Benjamin to the right of the host seat and Samuel to the left. After them came the next two men, Joses and Daniel. The four of us women, Esther, Miriam, Naomi, and I, were placed at the bottom.

Once we were seated, the servant said, "The master is concluding a conference. He will be with you in a moment," and he glided away, closing the door behind him.

I clasped my hands nervously in my lap. I had never been in such grand surroundings, and I hoped I would do nothing that might embarrass Lord Benjamin and Esther. Naomi, who was sitting across from me, shot me an awed look, and we shared an anxious smile.

Lord Benjamin and Samuel were speaking softly and Daniel was staring into space when the door opened again and Aaron bar David came in. His hair was sparse, and his face was deeply lined. He had a broad, curved nose and beneath it a pair of thick, very pink lips. His belly bulged under his immaculate white garments. *He may be rich,* I thought, *but he's ugly.*

I immediately felt guilty. I knew I put too much emphasis on physical attractiveness. *Poor man,* I scolded myself. *He can't help the way he looks. He's probably very nice.*

Lord Benjamin introduced those of us Aaron didn't know: Daniel, then Esther, Miriam, Naomi, and me. When Aaron's eyes fell upon me, I smiled and ducked my head respectfully. He smiled back, parting his thick pink lips to show a set of surprisingly decent teeth. "I'm pleased to meet you, Mary," he said.

I was a little startled by his use of my name. I murmured, "Thank you," and went back to looking at my plate.

The supper, served by Greek slaves, was a more lavish feast than I had ever eaten. There were large loaves of delicious bread flavored with olive oil, mint, cumin, cinnamon, and even locusts. There were platters of partridge and quail, fruits and dates and olives, and a variety of roasted vegetables. There was plenty of rich red wine and pitchers of water to mix it with.

I knew Esther had been worried that a Jew from Sepphoris might not serve the meal properly, but we followed all the rules of ceremonial cleanliness. We washed our hands before the meal was served and after every course. The water the servants offered was taken from the stone jar in the corner of the room, so we knew that nothing had been mixed with it. I could see the relief on Esther's face when she realized she wasn't going to have to eat with unclean hands.

The men talked business, and we women savored our food and were silent. I could see that Esther was trying to assess what kinds of spices had been used in the dishes. When the men's conversation finally began to peter out, Esther ventured a comment. "This is a very beautiful house, Aaron bar David."

He looked down at her from his place at the head of the table. "My main house is in Sepphoris, but this is useful for when I stay in Jerusalem."

He has two houses? I thought in amazement. Then Aaron spoke my name and inquired if I had ever visited Sepphoris.

I was so surprised that I almost couldn't answer. Things must be very different in Sepphoris if it was proper for a man of Aaron's stature to speak to a young girl like me. "N-no, Lord," I stammered, "I haven't."

"None of us women has been to Sepphoris," Esther said pleasantly. "Will you tell us a little about it?"

Aaron bar David was happy to oblige. He told us that when Herod Antipas had decided to make Sepphoris the capital of Galilee, he had rebuilt the city in the Greek style he so admired. All the public buildings, the king's palace, and the homes of the residents had been inspired by the Greeks. Aaron's pink lips stretched in a smile. "Some say that Sepphoris looks almost as Greek as Athens," he said.

Daniel's eyes met mine across the table. His face was expressionless, but I knew what he was thinking. We were Jews, not Greeks. We shouldn't be copying the ways of a pagan people.

When we had finished dinner and were ready to leave, Aaron bar David did something else that surprised me. He took my hand, held it, and wished me well.

My first impulse was to snatch my hand away from his, which was hot and damp, but I let him have it for a moment before I withdrew it as gracefully as I could. I stuttered some kind of a thank-you and was very glad to follow the others out.

~

THE FAMILY REMAINED AT our campsite on the Mount of Olives for two more weeks. Then, when everyone else left for home, Aunt Leah and I went to Bethany to stay for a month with my family as we always did after Passover.

Even though I was still furious with my father, I pretended that all was well so I could see Daniel. I managed to get into Jerusalem to visit him several times during my stay, which was both wonderful and frustrating. We had to meet in front of his teacher and fellow students, and it was awkward to speak to him as if he were just an ordinary cousin, when I wanted so much to throw my arms around him and kiss him.

I spent most of the time in Bethany with my little brother and sister. Lazarus and Martha were growing up, and we had lots of fun when we were together. The children had developed definite personalities. Lazarus was smart and amazingly kind for a young boy. And Martha was devoted to him. She was turning into a pretty girl, and her disposition was as sweet and kind as her brother's. It confounded me how such lovely children could have parents like my father and Judith. Sometimes I wondered if the two of them had been switched at birth for Judith's real babies.

I last saw Daniel the day before Aunt Leah and I were to travel back to Galilee. He took my hand before I left and said he looked forward to seeing me again in ten days when he came home for Shavuot. The touch of his hand made me tremble all over, and I squeezed his fingers and said I was looking forward to it as well. We parted with glowing hearts, full of hope and joy for our future together.

❧

LEAH AND I TRAVELED with a caravan of people from Bethany going to visit relatives in Tiberias. Two of Daniel's brothers met us in Tiberias and escorted us the rest of the way to Magdala.

Galilee looked beautiful. The hillsides were covered with hyacinths, gladioli, narcissus, and the red anemones I particularly liked. It seemed to me as if all of nature was rejoicing with me, and I skipped into the front room of the house with a big smile on my face.

Miriam was waiting for us. She greeted Aunt Leah and then told me that Lord Benjamin wished to see me in his office. Of course, I thought, he would want to ask me how Daniel was doing. I walked into his room ready to report on how brilliant his teacher thought Daniel was.

Lord Benjamin was sitting on his bench, in the same position as when he told me that he would allow Daniel to marry me. I felt Daniel's absence as sharply as a knife in my heart. I stopped before Lord Benjamin and said, "You wished to see me, my lord?"

He gave me a genial smile. "Yes, I wished to see you, Mary. I have wonderful news—you will be astonished at your good fortune. Aaron bar David, with whom you dined in Jerusalem, has asked for you in marriage."

The words bounced off my brain without sinking in.

Lord Benjamin continued in the same genial way, "He's one of the richest merchants in the country, and he has no heir. He's been married twice, and now he is looking to you to give him what he wants more than anything in the world: a son. You will live like a queen. You saw his home in Jerusalem, and it's nothing compared to his house in Sepphoris. I've been there many times, and I cannot even begin to recount to you its marvels."

As he began to talk about marble hallways, tortoise-shell tables, and plastered walls, I stared at him as if he was speaking a foreign language.

Finally I broke into his discourse. I took a step closer to where he sat in his lordly solitude, his broad cheeks creased with his fake smile, his big ears sticking out under his skullcap. I said in a loud voice, "What are you talking about? I'm going to marry Daniel."

All of Lord Benjamin's geniality vanished.

"This is a once in a lifetime offer. Aaron is giving a tremendous amount of money for you, and Daniel won't be ready to marry anyone for years. You will take Aaron bar David's offer and be grateful for it. The only things you have to offer are your youth and a pretty face. For that, you will live like a queen."

"But I love Daniel! And he loves me! I won't marry anyone else. I won't!"

He folded his hands on his big stomach. "Do you think you have a choice? Your father put you into my care. I'm your father now, and I say you will marry Aaron bar David, and that is the end of it."

If he had been angry, I would have been less frightened. It was his cool composure that scared me the most.

"Daniel won't let you do this," I said.

"Daniel will know nothing about it. You will be married and away from Magdala before Daniel hears a whisper of what has happened. Aaron bar David will be here in two days' time, and the wedding will be held the following day. It's all arranged."

All arranged. This . . . *outrage* had been planned from the time of the dinner party. *This* was why I had been invited to meet Aaron bar David. I stiffened my back and lifted my chin. "I won't do it, and you can't make me. I'll go to the rabbi. He'll stand up for me."

Lord Benjamin's face set like stone. "I've heard more than enough from you, Mary. You will wed this man. Refuse Aaron, and I'll disown you. Your own father will disown you. And if you run to Daniel and he marries you without my permission, he'll become an outcast from his family and his religion. He'll never be a scribe. He'll be a pariah, and the only work he'll ever know is that of a day laborer—if he's lucky enough to find someone to hire him."

His words struck me like physical blows.

"Do you want to do this to Daniel, Mary? Daniel whom you say you love?"

I struggled to find words. "But you told us we could marry!"

He shrugged. "This is the way things have always been. Why should you be different from any other girl?"

I felt my stomach heave.

"Go to see Esther. She has been making the arrangements for your wedding. And let us have no more of this rebellious talk."

I stared at Lord Benjamin and knew I was beaten. I couldn't rob Daniel of his future. I would have died for him. I wished I could die for him but it seemed all I could do was to marry someone else.

⸺

I RAN ALL THE way from Lord Benjamin's room to the tiny cell I shared with Aunt Leah. I was shaking all over as if I had a fever, and in truth I did feel sick. My stomach heaved, and I thought for a moment that I might vomit all over the floor. I collapsed on my sleeping mat and buried my face in my trembling hands.

I began to weep, deep wrenching sobs that wracked my body.

The door opened, and Aunt Leah came in. "Mary? Miriam told me to come to you. Are you ill?"

I looked up, and she cried out when she saw my face. She dropped to her knees and took me in her arms. "What has happened?" she asked.

Through my sobs I managed to tell her about my interview with Lord Benjamin.

"My poor lamb." Aunt Leah pressed my head to her breast and cradled me with her arms. "It was wicked of him to let you think you could marry Daniel when he had this in mind. I thought better of him."

So had I. So had Daniel.

I couldn't stop crying. "Lord Benjamin is an evil man, and I hate him! He lied to us! He lied to his own son!"

"Shh, shh," Aunt Leah crooned. She held me tighter, rocking me back and forth as if I were a baby. And like a baby, I burrowed into her, seeking the comfort no one could give.

"When is this marriage supposed to take place?" she asked after my sobs began to slow.

I said thickly, "Aaron is coming here in two days' time. We're to be married the following day."

I felt Leah's breath catch. "How clever. While we were in Bethany, Benjamin arranged a whole wedding for you."

"What am I going to do, Aunt Leah?" I wailed, pulling my face away from her tear-soaked shoulder.

She didn't answer.

"Tell me what I should do!" I stared up at her, desperate for her to save me from this hideous fate.

She looked desolate. "My darling girl, there is nothing you can do. Men make the decisions in this world, and we have no choice but to obey."

"But that's not fair! I have a soul too! Surely the Lord thinks I'm just as important as a man!"

"I don't think that He does," Aunt Leah replied regretfully. "Remember how the Lord asked Abraham to sacrifice his son, and Abraham was ready to obey? The Lord never asked Sarah how she might feel about that, did He?"

"N-no," I replied. "He didn't."

Leah sighed. "That's how things have always been and always will be."

They were almost the exact words Lord Benjamin had spoken.

"I'd rather be dead than married to Aaron bar David. He's old and ugly and disgusting." I shuddered at the thought of him touching me.

"Don't say that you'd rather be dead!" she rebuked sharply.

I'd never heard her sound so angry.

"Only a coward would say something like that, and you're not a coward, Mary. That I know for certain. You're not a coward."

She thought more highly of me than I did of myself. I said, "I can't live without Daniel, Aunt Leah. I can't. And I can't marry this awful man. I'll run away! I will!"

"Don't speak like a fool," she snapped. "You have no place to run. You will marry this man and go to Sepphoris with him, and you will make the best of it. That's what we women do: we make the best of it."

I sat there on my straw mat, with my robe and tunic pooled around me and Leah's hands hard on my shoulders, thinking frantically. I'd already tried to go home to my father, and he had rejected me. I could run away, but, if I couldn't run to Daniel . . . Aunt Leah was right. I had nowhere else to run. I couldn't destroy Daniel's future. I wouldn't.

I shut my eyes tightly. *Daniel*, I thought. *My dearest love.*

Slowly I opened my eyes. I wiped away my tears with my veil. My voice was so hard it didn't sound like my own when I said, "All right, then. I will marry Aaron bar David."

Chapter Nine

I HAVE LITTLE MEMORY of my wedding and the subsequent journey to my husband's home in Sepphoris. I protected myself from the horror of the experience by locking away the thinking, feeling part of me. My body was present, but my true self was shut away deep inside where no one could find it.

This was how I survived in my new life. I lived in a huge house, with Greek columns, beautiful mosaic floors, rich furniture, and I hated it. I hated every minute I spent there. I hated my old husband, who kept trying to make a child with me. I hated the gossamer silk tunics I wore in imitation of the Roman ladies. I hated the synagogue and the ladies who each tried to outdo the others with her jewels and her husband's social status.

I had enough sense not to tell my husband how I felt. I'd learned a hard lesson about men: never give them any more power over you than they already possessed. Aaron liked to dress me up and show me off to all his friends, and I went along with it like a child's doll that does the will of its owner. I raised unseen walls around me and let nothing or no one come in.

Aunt Leah had offered to come to Sepphoris with me, but I had refused. I knew she'd be miserable in a place that didn't follow the strict rules of Jewish law, and from what I had heard, Sepphoris was more Roman than Jewish. So I was alone. I spent all my free time in the garden, which really was quite lovely. And I thought about Daniel.

I was waiting for him to rescue me. On the horrible nights when Aaron came to my bed, I tried hard to see Daniel's face and not the old and ugly face of my husband. How I wished they were Daniel's arms around me and Daniel's lips touching my skin. I don't think I could have borne it if it hadn't been for this fantasy.

I had convinced myself that Daniel would never allow me to be married to someone else—that he would come to Sepphoris and take me away. I didn't worry about where he would take me. Daniel could read and write. We'd find somewhere in this great Empire where he could be a scribe. He didn't have to study at the Temple to write letters or keep books for other people. He could do that already.

⇌

IT WAS A FULL year before Daniel arrived. He came on Shavuot, the day we were supposed to have become betrothed. I was in the garden, speaking with our Greek gardener about planting rose bushes, when one of the housemaids came to find me.

"A man is here to see you, my lady. I told him that you were busy, but he was very insistent."

I replied impatiently, "If it's the goldsmith, tell him to go away. I don't want that bracelet he's been trying to sell me."

"It's not the goldsmith. He says he's your foster brother, my lady. He gave his name as Daniel."

I stopped breathing. She folded her hands and waited for my reply. "Where is he?" I managed to get out.

"In the foyer, my lady."

"Bring him to the small reception room. Offer him . . ." I stopped. Daniel couldn't eat anything that came from Aaron's unclean kitchen. "Offer him a cup of water, and tell him I'll be with him shortly."

The girl flew off to do my bidding, and I ran indoors to change into something more modest. In my bedchamber I pulled a simple cloak out of one of the large clothes chests and flung it over my thin dress. I pulled off my long gold earrings and covered my elaborately dressed hair with a silk scarf. At the last minute I stripped off my rings and bracelets too.

I was shaking as if I had the fever.

I paused at the doorway to compose myself before stepping into the passageway. I walked down the hall and through the main reception room and courtyard with deliberate slowness, my trembling hands clasped tightly in front of me, my breathing coming fast and short. After what seemed like an age, I arrived at the door of the small reception room.

He was standing in the middle of the marble floor, intently regarding the painted lilies on the plaster walls. I advanced a few steps and then stopped, drinking in the sight of him.

Although my sandals made no noise, his dark head swung around almost immediately. It was dim in the room, and I couldn't see his expression clearly. My heart was thundering.

He said, "I told your maid that I was your foster brother. It seemed easier that way."

I shivered at the familiar, beloved sound of his voice. I began to walk toward him, my knees so weak I wondered that I could stand up.

"You needn't have worried about the proprieties. Women in Sepphoris have more freedom than they're allowed in Magdala."

He made no move to meet me but stood still, his hands quiet at his sides. As he watched me approach, I checked a little, surprised at his stillness.

He was thinner than I remembered. Too thin, I thought.

I searched for something to say. "What did your father tell you about my marriage?"

He lips tightened. "When he came to see me in Jerusalem, you had already left for Sepphoris. He assured me that you'd been happy to win such a wealthy man for your husband. He told me to forget you, that I could marry much higher than a farmer's daughter from Bethany."

My mouth was so dry that it was difficult to form words. I longed for his embrace. "Did you believe him, Daniel? Did you think I was willing to marry Aaron?"

"Of course not. I thought he'd probably threatened you the way I'd threatened him." He narrowed his eyes, and his nostrils flared, and I knew the very thought of what his father had done was making him angry.

This reassured me.

"What did he threaten you with, Mary?"

At the sound of my name on his lips my heart leaped into my throat. I whispered, "He said that if you married me, he would disown you, that you'd become an outcast from all your people, that you'd never be able to become a scribe."

We stared at each other over the green and white marble that separated us. I said, "I couldn't do that to you, Daniel. I loved you too much to do that to you."

He nodded. His long lean body was taut as a strung bow. "I thought it might be something like that."

I cried, "Why didn't you come to see me? I've been looking for you and looking for you. I was beginning to fear that you believed him!"

He frowned. "How could you have expected me to come? You were married. There was nothing I could gain by seeing you other than tearing my heart apart even more." He shook his head, as if in despair. "Did you think I could bear seeing you as the wife of another man?"

Tears began to slide down my cheeks.

His voice sounded choked. "Don't, Mary. You never cry. Remember?"

"I cry all the time now. I cry every time I think of you."

He took a step toward me, and suddenly we were in each other's arms. I clung to him, breathing in his scent, pressing my cheek into his shoulder so hard the wool was leaving creases on my skin.

He held me so tightly that it hurt, and I reveled in it. *Daniel*, I thought. *Daniel, my dearest love.*

When I felt his grip loosen, I forced myself to let him go. I looked up, waiting for him to tell me he didn't care about the opinion of the world, that he'd take me away from Aaron and we would be together again.

He said hoarsely, "I've come to see you because I wanted you to know that I'm leaving Jerusalem and my studies. I'm going to join the Essenes."

I stared at him, not taking in what he had said.

"I'm going to Qumran. The Essenes have a great library there, and they're anxious to get me. I don't think I'll ever come back."

I heard the sharp intake of my breath. "The *Essenes?* You're leaving me to live like a beggar in the desert?"

His voice was patient, the way it had always sounded when he was explaining a passage of scripture to me. "The Essenes are not beggars. They're a group of holy men who pledge themselves to celibacy and a disciplined life of prayer. They choose to live in the desert because it's far from Jerusalem. They can live and pray in the desert unmolested by the corruption of the Temple and all it stands for."

I stared at him, speechless.

He began to pace up and down in front of the painted lilies. "Our people are in desperate need, Mary. A godless Empire occupies our country, and our own religious leaders have been corrupted by money. Animal sacrifice, and the money it brings in, is the business of the Temple these days, not prayer. I found that out during the year I spent in Jerusalem. We need to be saved from ourselves as well as from the Romans. We need the Messiah to come *now*, Mary, and that is what the Essenes pray for. They pray for the coming of the Messiah. That's why I wish to join them. The Messiah is our only hope of salvation."

If he joined the Essenes he would truly be lost to me forever. Even if my husband should die, Daniel would have sworn himself to celibacy.

"Don't do this," I pleaded. "Don't leave me, Daniel. Please don't leave me."

His red-brown eyes were somber. "I've prayed over this, Mary. I'm going to the Essenes to purify myself, so that I can pray for you as well as for the Messiah. God will surely listen to a prayer when it comes from a heart made pure by sacrifice."

I cared nothing for his purity of heart, but I knew, just by looking at him, that his mind was made up and that nothing I could say would change it.

A blessed numbness descended on my brain. I managed to choke out, "Then God bless you, Daniel."

He lifted his hand and touched my cheek. "God bless you, my most dearly beloved. I will pray for you as long as I live."

I stood perfectly still in the middle of the room, listening to the sound his sandals made on the floor as he left.

WHEN I FELT ABLE to move, I told the servants I was ill and slipped away to my room. One of the blessings of living in such a large house was that I had a bedroom to myself, and I crawled into the big, soft Roman bedstead and lay like a wounded animal seeking solitude to heal or to die.

I stayed in bed for a week. I vomited a few times, and I knew that Aaron hoped my sickness was because I was with child. I also knew that wasn't the case. I would never have a child with Aaron. My flesh and soul cringed away from him whenever he came near me. How could a child of his find a home within my body?

During that solitary week I thought long and hard about my life. Daniel wasn't going to save me after all. The hope I'd clung to during the last year had been smashed.

The more I thought, the more I realized what an unrealistic hope it had been. The dream of going out into the world hand in hand with Daniel was a child's dream. Daniel had known that. And he was paying for his father's evil too, hiding himself in the Judean wilderness with a sect of strange, celibate men.

Meanwhile I was left here in Sepphoris, married to an old man. But Aaron was very proud of me, and for most of the time I was perfectly free to do whatever I wished. I had no more bread to bake or laundry to wash or goats to feed. No more children to watch.

I tried not to think about how much I missed the children.

It was time for me to look ahead, not behind, time for me to make a meaningful life for myself in this foreign place. It was the only way I could show that Lord Benjamin hadn't defeated me.

On the seventh day I came out of my room and prepared to begin again.

Part 2

Marcus Novius Claudius

Chapter Ten

My new life began one afternoon six months later, when I met Julia Tiberia. I was wandering among the array of stalls in the Upper Market, trying to pass some time until I'd have to go home, when I stopped at the sandalmaker's stall. Another woman stopped as well, and as if at a signal we both pointed to the same pair of jeweled sandals. We looked at each other and burst out laughing. I insisted that she should have them, and she insisted that I should, and we fell into talk. As it turned out, neither of us bought the sandals; instead we continued to talk as we made our way down the hill from the Upper Market. Before we parted, Julia invited me to visit her.

The invitation shocked me. Jews didn't move in the rarefied atmosphere of Julia Tiberia's circle. I knew of her from the gossip spouted by my husband's friends' wives. She was the wealthy widow of Sepphoris' last Roman governor and had chosen to remain in the city after her husband's death. The gossipers said she wielded enormous social power among the Roman elite, a situation that very much annoyed the wife of the present governor.

Aaron was ecstatic when I told him about the invitation. He kept repeating her name as if he were reciting some holy text. He made me so nervous that by the time I left our house two afternoons later, I was wishing she'd never invited me.

I took a litter to Julia Tiberia's house in the Roman part of town. In Magdala we walked everywhere, but here women of the upper classes rode in litters. It was a rule I often flouted, but on this particular day I thought it was probably wise to do the correct thing.

The Romans, like King Herod, had copied Greek architecture, but the houses in this part of town were set farther back from the street than in ours. When I descended from the litter, I had to walk up a stone pathway, which was set in a courtyard filled with shrubs, flowers, and statues. The large bronze front door swung open just before I reached it, so I knew the house porter had been waiting for me. He greeted me in Latin.

I smiled apologetically and replied in Greek, "I'm sorry, I don't know your language. I'm Mary, the wife of Aaron bar David. Julia Tiberia is expecting me."

"Lady Julia is in the garden," he answered, switching easily to Greek. "I will take you to her."

The house was no larger than Aaron's, but it was much brighter. I realized, as we walked from the vestibule into the first room, that sunlight was pouring through an opening in the roof. A marble pool lay under the opening, which I later discovered was used to collect rainwater. Marble pillars supported the roof, the floors were made of marble tiles with contrasting colors, and the ceiling was covered with ivory and gold. As in Jewish homes, doors were placed along the side of the room, with latticework allowing the light from the court to enter.

The porter must have seen me gawking, for he said pleasantly, "This is the atrium, the room Lady Julia uses for entertainment. The next room, the peristylum, is for the family."

We passed through a narrow corridor and entered a room that looked like an indoor garden. The opening in the roof was much larger than in the atrium, and all sorts of beautiful plants and flowers bloomed among the palm and fig trees that grew in large pots around a central reflecting pool.

I glanced at the colorful mosaic floor and quickly looked away. The depiction of naked men chasing after beautiful young women would have been shocking even if they had been fully clothed. It is forbidden for Jews to have any representation of the human body.

"The garden is just beyond," the porter said, and we crossed the room and went outdoors.

Julia Tiberia was sitting at a white stone table with a papyrus scroll in her hands. She glanced up as we came in.

The porter said, "My lady, here is Mary, the wife of Aaron bar David."

Julia smiled at me and began to roll up the scroll. "How lovely to see you. Come and sit down, my dear."

I took the indicated bench and looked around at my lovely surroundings. The place was nothing like the simple garden I had at home. High marble columns enclosed it, and a part of it was covered for shade. In its center a marble fountain spouted sparkling clear water.

"Your house is very beautiful."

She looked pleased. "Thank you, my dear. I had it built after my husband died and I had to move out of the governor's palace."

"It's so bright! The houses I have lived in are much darker."

She bowed her head a little, accepting my compliment. "We Romans like living outdoors, and we strive to replicate that feeling even inside our homes."

With that topic of conversation exhausted, I suddenly felt very shy and inept. Julia Tiberia must have been in her forties, but she was still beautiful. Unlike most of the Romans I had met, her hair was light, and her eyes were blue. I had never known anyone with blue eyes before, and they fascinated me. She was a sophisticated woman of the world, and I wondered why on earth she had invited me.

Julia began our conversation deftly, asking me how old I was, where I had been born, and how I had come to live in Sepphoris. Her blue eyes were so intent, her expression so engaged, that I soon found myself pouring out my whole life's story. When I finally stopped and realized how long I had been talking, I was embarrassed.

"I am so sorry, my lady," I apologized feebly. "I didn't mean to bore you by talking about myself like that. You must think me very rude."

"Nonsense. I don't think you rude at all. You would have been rude if you had refused to answer my questions. I wanted to know all about you, Mary. You interest me."

"*I* interest you? But why?"

The blue eyes looked suddenly sad. "I once had a daughter who would be just your age if she had lived. I suppose you remind me of what I've lost."

"Oh, my lady," I said, "what a burden of grief you must carry."

"She lived to be ten. My only child. Yes, it is a great grief."

We sat in silence for a while. Then we spoke some more and had some refreshments, and she invited me to come back in the afternoon a few days hence, when she had no other appointments. I was happy to be asked and promised to come.

So began one of the most significant relationships of my life. Julia was unbelievably kind to me. She saw me as a substitute daughter, and I was certainly much in need of a mother. Through her I had access to a wide circle of highly cosmopolitan men and women whom I would ordinarily never have had a chance to meet.

Herod the Great's capital, Sepphoris was situated near two of the great commerce routes from Egypt to Damascus. Because of its strategic location, it had always attracted ambitious Romans who desired to prove themselves and thus move on to even higher office in Rome itself. These people all came to Julia's house, and, because I was her "adopted daughter," they befriended me.

I went shopping with the women, and we also went to the baths. Julia and I went to see plays at the theatre, and on the days when there were chariot races, we attended those too. I dined out at least three times a week.

And I did all this without the company of my husband. Aaron encouraged me. My Roman connections were generous in passing business his way, and he didn't want to do anything that might halt the flow of gold into his coffers.

This was heady stuff for a girl from a small Jewish market town. I was impressed by the fact that many of these Roman women were educated. They could read and write, and they passed papyrus scrolls of new poems among themselves with a careless ease that amazed and humbled me. From what I could gather, women even participated in some of the Romans' religious rites, as priestesses. And if a woman didn't like her husband, she could simply give him a writ of divorce, and he had no choice but to separate from her.

This was dramatically different from the status of women among my people, and I liked it. I was in awe of the accomplished women I met at Julia Tiberia's house, but most of all, I was in awe of Julia. Every Thursday she held a late afternoon reception, after the men had finished work and returned from the baths. Invited guests would gather in her atrium, where wine and plates of sliced eggs, snails, oysters, olives, and apples reposed upon a collection of beautiful small round tables made of expensive wood. Slaves walked around with silver wine cups as groups of people throughout the room engaged in vibrant conversation.

This was a pre-dinner gathering, deliberately simple, but it was also the most important regular social event in Sepphoris. If you weren't invited to one of Julia Tiberia's receptions, you were nobody, and everyone knew it.

Julia was able to wield this kind of power in part because her husband had been governor, but mainly because her father was an important senator. In addition, she was still a beautiful woman and smarter than most of the men who surrounded her.

I was incredibly fortunate to have met and interested such a woman. She took me in hand and did everything she could to turn me into a younger version of herself. She hired a tutor to teach me to read and write Greek, and she herself took on the task of teaching me Latin. After six months of relentless instruction, the people who came to her house didn't have to address me in Greek. I was almost as fluent in Latin as they were.

But it was learning to read that meant the most to me. All upper class Roman homes had libraries. Julia had inherited hers from her husband, and it was expansive. The library room, which opened off the atrium, was lined with cabinets holding the rolls upon which the books were written. Once I was literate, Julia allowed me access to all of them. It was she who opened my mind to the world beyond Galilee and Jerusalem.

It was also Julia who explained to me that when Aaron died, it was I who would inherit his money. Aaron had never said anything about this, so the revelation was a shock. Among my people, a woman never had her own money.

"Your position is well known throughout the city," Julia told me. We were sitting by the pool in her peristylum, drinking wine. By now I was so accustomed to the naked gods and goddesses, nymphs and satyrs that comprised her statues and floor mosaic that I hardly noticed them. She said, "Aaron bar David has no male heirs—no sons, no brothers, no cousins, no one. Under the law, Jewish as well as Roman, if there is no male heir, the money goes to the wife. You will be very rich one day, my dear Mary. Very rich indeed."

I stared at her. "Why hasn't Aaron said anything to me about this?"

Julia rolled her eyes. "Men," she said. "They never give up hope that their virility will magically return. He's probably still hoping for a son."

I shuddered at the thought. Aaron hadn't come to my bed for many months. He had tried very hard to remain capable, but it was no longer possible. For which I thanked the Lord devoutly every night.

Julia must have read my mind because she reached across and laid a comforting hand on mine. "Don't worry, darling. It won't come back. You're safe."

My mind was in chaos. "What would I do with all that money?"

She laughed. "Don't worry, my love. You'll find plenty to do with it." Her eyes glinted, blue as the sky. "Perhaps we might travel together. Would you like to see Alexandria?"

I nodded, speechless, as a vision of the outside world opened before my mind's eye. "Could we do that? Just two women?"

Julia gave me an amused look. "We would hire men, of course, to protect us from bandits, but a woman doesn't need a husband to do what she wants to do, Mary. That is, she doesn't if she has money. I have money for the same reason you will; my husband left it to me."

I asked a question I had often wondered about. "Did you never wish to remarry?"

Julia smiled serenely. "I have no need for a husband. If a woman has money, I think she is better off without one." She gave me an odd, glinting look that I didn't understand. "One can always enjoy the company of men without marrying them."

I thought she was talking about all of the men who frequented her receptions and lavished such attention on her, and I smiled back and agreed.

⁓

MY INTIMACY WITH THE powerful Romans was a topic of profound interest in the Jewish community. The synagogue Aaron and I attended catered to wealthy merchants, and they all wanted Roman patronage and hoped I could get it for them. Aaron was very generous with his donations, so we were in excellent standing with our money-loving rabbi.

If it were up to me, I wouldn't have attended the synagogue at all. I felt like a hypocrite, sitting on the women's side of the aisle, my elegant Roman hairdo covered by a veil, listening to the reading of scripture by men I couldn't bear.

For most of my life the two pillars of my existence had been Daniel and the Lord. Both had deserted me, so I had resolved to put them out of my mind. I had no temptation to adopt the religion of my new friends—all those gods seemed too absurd to be taken seriously. I still believed in the God of Israel; I just wanted nothing to do with Him. Like my father and Lord Benjamin, He had thrown me away.

Chapter Eleven

I WAS TWENTY-ONE when Marcus Novius Claudius arrived in Sepphoris to take over command of the Roman troops based in Galilee. His coming caused great excitement among the Roman population. He was a *legatus*, a senatorial officer, and he was also a member of the Claudian family, to which the emperor himself belonged. He was one of the most well-connected men ever to grace Galilee. Aaron told me the word was he had been appointed because the emperor feared a Jewish insurrection. Apparently, our new commander had shown himself an effective leader in other delicate political situations.

The idea of an insurrection seemed ludicrous if you lived in Sepphoris. But I hadn't forgotten the talk of a Messiah when I lived in Magdala, and I thought perhaps it was not impossible after all.

The women of Julia's circle were excited about the newcomer because he was young, handsome, and not yet married. My friend Cornelia Flavia, who was married to one of the officers stationed in the city, told me that the Sepphoris girls were fools to hope for anything from the legatus. "A man like that may not be married, but he is surely promised to the daughter of some wealthy senator in Rome.

The rich and powerful families always marry among themselves; they don't like to share with outsiders."

Julia, of course, intended to be the first one to entertain him, and as usual she got her way. Two days after the new commander rode into Sepphoris from Caesarea, he attended Julia's afternoon reception. He came in late, standing alone in the wide doorway between the vestibule and the atrium, looking at the group in front of him with all the unconscious arrogance of one in whose veins ran the blood of Caesar.

Gradually, without his seeming to do anything to attract it, the attention of the room focused on him. I stared along with everyone else.

He was a splendid-looking man, tall and broad shouldered, with hair as black as mine. He wore the white knee-length linen tunic that was standard garb for Roman men, but his was distinguished by a wide purple stripe to signify his senatorial rank.

The woman standing next to me said out loud, "Now *that* is a man."

Julia walked up to him, and he bent his head to receive her greeting. They spoke for a moment, and then she laid a light hand on his bare arm and began to take him around the room.

All of Julia's receptions were important, but for this occasion she had gathered together the highest of the city's Roman administrators. The bright silk colors of the women's stolas contrasted harmoniously with the white worn by the men. Julia had laughingly told me that Roman men would rather die than be caught wearing colors or silk. They wore white linen, whether it was a tunic or a toga, and that was that.

Sometimes, when I looked at those immaculate white garments, I imagined how hard it must be for the servants to launder them. I was wise enough, however, never to mention such a thought to my new friends. They would've been dumbfounded that I should even think of such a plebeian thing.

Magdala was very far away these days. I glanced down at my own dress, a stola that was a blue as clear as the flax on the Galilean hillside in spring. I loved the feel of silk against my skin, so much kinder than the rougher linen and wool I had worn at home.

As the guest of honor made the rounds, I continued my conversation with Cornelia. Her cousin in Rome had sent her a new poem, and she was telling me about it and promising to lend it to me. We were talking comfortably, when suddenly I felt Flavia close her hand around my wrist and whisper, "He's coming this way!"

I had no doubt whom she meant.

A moment later I heard Julia's voice. "And here are the two lovely young women you wished to meet, Legatus."

Flavia's hand fell away from my wrist, and we both turned to look at him.

His eyes were light green. Lion's eyes, I thought, as I looked up into them. Other than the eyes, it was a quintessentially Roman face, with a hawk nose, high hard cheekbones, and arrogant mouth.

As if from a distance, I heard Julia say, "Marcus Novius, I would like you to meet my dear young friend Mary."

He didn't look surprised by the Hebrew name, so I knew Julia must have told him about me. "Mary," he said slowly, as if savoring the sound on his tongue. "A beautiful name for a beautiful woman."

I stared at him. I couldn't help myself. He positively radiated masculine strength and power.

Everyone was looking at me, and I realized I hadn't spoken. I answered as coolly as I could in crisp Latin, "How do you do, Legatus?"

He smiled. It changed his whole face, making him look boyish and eager and delighted. It was a devastatingly attractive look. I had never met a man like this. Among my people there weren't any men like this. Because of the short haircut and shaved jaw, I could see how powerful his neck was; because of the short sleeves of his tunic I could see how muscular his arms were, how hard his forearms. Just looking at him as he stood there smiling at me made me lose my breath.

And that is how I met Marcus Novius Claudius.

~

DURING THE FOLLOWING WEEKS, he pursued me shamelessly. Wherever I was, there he was too. I knew people were talking about us. I knew I should warn him off.

Whenever I thought this way, however, I would roll my eyes. How did one warn off Marcus Novius Claudius? I doubted that an earthquake could do that, let alone a Jewish woman trying to make her way in an alien society.

There was also the fact that I enjoyed his company enormously. He was intelligent and witty and he knew so much about the world. He appealed to my brain and he made me laugh. *Why shouldn't I spend time with him?* I asked myself. I wasn't doing anything wrong.

But of course, there was a subterranean text to our meetings that I could not ignore, much as I tried to. Marcus' very presence stirred me in a way I had only felt once before, with Daniel. But with Daniel I had felt safe. I didn't feel safe with this man. I didn't feel safe at all.

I knew what Marcus wanted from me. I hadn't spent all these years in Julia's circle without learning something about the morals of the people who surrounded her. I knew that Julia had taken lovers from among the men posted to Sepphoris on either military or administrative duty. I knew that marital fidelity wasn't always honored among these aristocratic Romans. In this they were like their gods, fickle and faithless.

Despite my Roman veneer, I was still Jewish enough to know that adultery was a grave sin. I could truthfully say that, since Daniel left, I had never been tempted to betray my husband. I had had offers, but over the years I had perfected a way to refuse them, while at the same time managing not to offend the man I was rejecting.

But Marcus tempted me in a way I had never experienced before. When he put his hand on my arm, I shivered. When he bent his head to say something quietly into my ear, my heart pounded. I knew I was in grave danger, and I resisted. I had to give myself that amount of credit; I tried very hard to resist. But I was wavering, and I knew I needed help if I was to remain a faithful wife.

Julia Tiberia, the adviser for every other aspect of my life, was not the person to consult about this matter. In many ways she was a wise and ethical person, but she wouldn't understand my reluctance to give in to Marcus. In this, I knew she would be on Marcus' side, not mine.

My thoughts turned to my only living relatives, my brother, Lazarus, and my sister, Martha. We had corresponded regularly over the years I lived in Sepphoris, although I had refused to visit them while my father lived. Since they were observant Jews, I couldn't invite them to visit me. After my father died the previous year, I had spent a month with them in Bethany. It had been a wonderful if disturbing time—wonderful because it was so good to connect with the people who were truly my family, and disturbing because they made me realize how far I had traveled from the world of my childhood.

So it was then, when I realized the only sure way I could remain a faithful wife was to remove myself from the source of temptation, I decided I would pay another visit to my brother and sister. My hope was that by the time I returned to Sepphoris, either Marcus would have gone back to Rome, or he would have turned his attentions to someone else.

I came to this decision on a beautiful night in early March, when a group of us had been to the theatre and returned to Julia's for refreshments. Marcus hadn't attended the performance, but he joined us later as we sat around Julia's peristylum, chatting and enjoying the pleasant cool of the evening.

I was sitting on a couch by the pool, holding wine in one of Julia's beautiful cups and listening to the young man beside me talk earnestly about himself and his future hopes, when there was a little stir at the door, and Marcus came striding in. He had been at a military function and was still dressed in his uniform.

Marcus in uniform was, quite simply, stunning. I wasn't the only woman in the room who had trouble keeping her eyes off him. He ignored everyone—even Julia, who had gone to greet him—and walked through the gathering, straight to where I sat by the pool.

His eyes shifted briefly from my face. "Do you mind if I sit here?"

The question was directed to the young man who was sitting next to me. It was phrased as a question, not a command, but the young man jumped up as if the emperor himself had spoken.

"Not at all, Legatus," he said and moved away quickly, without even excusing himself to me.

"That was rather overbearing," I remarked as Marcus sat down on the couch, much closer to me than the young man had been.

He shrugged, then stretched his arm along the curved back of the couch and turned his body toward me. "What's the use of being the commander if you can't command?"

I smiled faintly. "I suppose that's so."

"How was the play?"

His lion's eyes were fixed on my face with total intensity. I could feel his gaze all the way down in my stomach.

"Entertaining enough, I suppose," I replied with forced lightness. "It was one of Plautus' sillier comedies."

The rest of the party had moved into the garden; later I would wonder if Julia had deliberately steered them all away from us. However it may have happened, when I glanced around for help, I realized that Marcus and I were alone. The murmur of voices seemed very far away. The moonlight was streaming through the open ceiling and reflecting off the pool. Suddenly I couldn't breathe.

He took my hand. I tried to pull it away, but he held it tight. He bent his dark head down to mine. "Mary, you must know how I feel about you. Stop pushing me away. We can do better than this, we two."

I forced myself to breathe. "I cannot become your lover, Marcus," I replied, wishing my voice sounded more forceful. "I am not a Roman, I am a Jew. My God isn't like your gods. My God demands that I be a faithful wife, as all the renowned women in our scriptures were faithful."

His eyes narrowed, and his gaze became even more intense. "Has that old man ever given you a single moment of pleasure, my love? I think not. I can love you the way you deserve to be loved, Mary."

He had called me his love. I felt as if my heart would burst out of my chest.

I pushed myself to my feet. "I can't stay here with you, Marcus!" I cried wildly. "Tell Julia I want a litter. I must go home! I must go home right now."

His green eyes glittered between his thick black lashes. "Don't fight me, Mary. You know you don't want to."

"I *have* to," I said desperately. "Go away, Marcus! Go away!"

Chapter Twelve

I scarcely slept that night, and in the morning I went to see my husband. He went most days to his warehouse in the city, but I was able to catch him before he left. When I asked to speak to him, he took me into the room off the courtyard where he kept his account books, his business papers, and his money chest.

While Jewish women in Sepphoris had adopted much of the Roman way of dress, Jewish men still kept to the robe and tunic that had been standard for our people for centuries. For a brief moment I compared in my mind the figure of my aging husband, with his big belly and skinny arms, to the figure of masculine perfection that was Marcus, and I winced.

Aaron sat on the stool behind the room's one table, which was empty except a carved wooden box. "What is it, Mary? I'm meeting today with a man from Lebanon who has wood he wants to ship to Rome. I don't want to be late for the appointment."

"I would like your permission to go to Bethany to visit my brother and sister, my husband."

He frowned suspiciously. "Why?"

I had spent half the night trying to come up with a good reason for the visit, but the best I could answer was "I miss them. They're my only close kin, and it will do me good to spend some time with them."

"You'll see them when we go to Jerusalem for Passover. You know I always allow you to stay with them then. I cannot afford to dispatch a contingent of men to escort you to Bethany just now. I'm too busy."

"Aaron, please. I want to go. *I need to go.* Don't deny me this, I beg you."

He narrowed his eyes and gave me a long look. "Does this have anything to do with Marcus Novius Claudius?"

My breath caught. "What do you mean?"

"I may be old, but I'm not a fool, Mary. Nor am I deaf. I've heard the gossip about the two of you. All of Sepphoris has heard it by now."

I swallowed. "Aaron, nothing has happened between us, I promise you. It's true that he has been pursuing me, and that's why I want to get away from Sepphoris for a while. And if the gossip is really rampant . . . well, surely you can see that it will be best for me to go to Bethany."

There was a calculating look in his eyes. "You have been refusing his advances, then?"

"Yes, my husband! I've been a faithful wife. I haven't betrayed your honor, I swear."

Aaron pushed his stool back and folded his arms on his chest. His bare toes, with their thick yellow nails, protruded from brown leather sandals as he stretched his legs in front of him.

"I said I wasn't a fool, Mary, but you are not a fool either. Has it never occurred to you how useful a liaison with Marcus Novius Claudius might be to the both of us?"

My mouth dropped open. "Wh-what do you mean?"

His voice was perfectly reasonable. "I'm telling you to give the Roman what he wants, Mary. It will benefit the both of us."

What could he mean? I didn't understand him at all. He was already getting most of the Roman business! I said carefully, "Aaron, what advantage could we possibly reap from my sleeping with Marcus Novius?"

He looked down at the empty table, then he looked up. His voice quivering, he said, "A child."

I understood immediately, and I was filled with pity. He was so desperate for a son that he would take one any way he could get one. I answered in the most sensible voice I could command. "Aaron, you don't want the child of a stranger and a pagan to inherit all you have. God has seen fit not to give you children, and you must accept that."

He slammed his hand on the desk. "I will not accept that! A Jew is the child of a Jewish mother, and you are a Jew. Your son will be a Jew, and that is good enough for me, Mary. I'll raise him, and he will be my son as well." He gestured around the office, at the chests filled with documents on papyrus rolls, at the big money box chained to the floor. "I built this business with my own sweat and blood. What's the purpose of my labor if I have no one to leave it to?"

I backed away. He was beginning to frighten me.

He shouted, "Did you really think I didn't know what was going on between you and the legatus? Everyone in this city knows what's going on. What I didn't know was that you were stupid enough to deny him. I have been praying all this last month that you would tell me you were with child."

His face was mottled with rage. My heart was pounding with fear. "If I should have a child, he wouldn't belong to you, Aaron. He would belong to Marcus."

"That isn't true! Your child will belong to your husband. That is the Jewish law. And don't think you can divorce me, Mary. The Romans may allow women to initiate a divorce, but we Jews are not so stupid as to give that power to a woman. You are my wife, and your child will be my child. Do you understand?"

I understood all right, and I fought back with as much reason as I could muster. "Aaron, you cannot push your wife into an adulterous relationship. That's against God's law."

He pushed his chair away and stood. "What do you care about God's law? You're more a Roman now than you are a Jew. And think of yourself, Mary. I have seen the legatus. He is exactly the kind of man any woman would like to have in her bed." For the briefest moment I thought I saw a glint of sorrow in his eyes, but then they hardened and he leaned toward me.

"I've seen how you are with the children at synagogue. You love children. Surely you would like one of your own."

His words struck a chord in my heart. I wanted very much to have a child—a child to love, to teach, to give my life a purpose. The desire was so strong that at times it was an ache. I thought I had reconciled myself to the fact that it would never happen as long as Aaron lived. But at his words, it was as if my very womb was calling out to me to be filled.

We stared at each other across the table. He read the emotions warring visibly across my face, and he nodded. "I don't think this is the time for you to go to Bethany. I think it will be much better if you remain here in Sepphoris and continue your visits to Julia Tiberia."

❧

I WENT OUTSIDE TO the garden and sat for a long time. Who would I be wronging if I followed Aaron's wishes? I thought of Marcus. Would I be wronging him?

I had no illusions that Marcus loved me. He desired me because I was a beautiful woman, and because I had put him off, I'd become even more attractive. I was sure Marcus Novius Claudius wasn't accustomed to being refused much of anything.

How far I had come from the innocent girl who had dreamed of marrying Daniel. How simple and pure my love for Daniel had been. I didn't love Marcus, at least not in the way I'd loved Daniel, but I wanted to sleep with him. It was time to be honest, and that was the truth. He stirred me deeply, and I wanted to find out what it might be like to have that sort of man make love to me.

Pain pierced my heart as I thought of what my life would have been like if I'd married Daniel. One thing I knew: I would most certainly never be contemplating sinning against my husband. Tears sprang to my eyes.

Stop this, I told myself. *You're a grown woman, and you know that if you wait for someone to hand you happiness on a golden plate, you'll wait forever. God isn't interested in your little life, Mary. It's up to you to grasp whatever happiness you can find and perhaps you can find some happiness with Marcus. Perhaps . . . oh, perhaps . . . there might even be a baby.*

I was still sitting in the garden when a servant arrived with a note for me from Julia Tiberia. She wrote that she'd received some bad news, and my company would be immensely comforting to her. Could I come tonight before sunset?

I wrote back immediately that of course I would be there.

⤜⤐

I ARRIVED AT JULIA's door at the appointed time, and the porter opened at my first knock. "My mistress is waiting for you in the garden, my lady," he said. "Shall I summon someone to show you out?"

I smiled. "No need for that, Plutus, I know my way."

He nodded and went back into the porter's box beside the door.

I walked the long length of the deserted atrium and then through the peristylum, which was empty as well. No slaves carrying water or newly washed linens were in sight, which was unusual. The large garden doors were open, however, and I stepped through them into the sweet, flower-scented air. The only sound was the trickling of water from the fountain. I looked for Julia, but she wasn't there.

I called her name, but it wasn't Julia who emerged from behind the statue of Venus holding a seashell. It was Marcus.

I was shocked. And angry. It was one thing for me to decide I might wish to be closer to Marcus, and another for Julia to put me into this kind of position.

I could feel the color flaming in my cheeks, and when he stood in front of me I said coldly, "I must tell you I had nothing to do with this meeting. I thought I was coming to see Julia."

His short black hair was still damp from the baths. His lion's eyes were drinking me in. He said, "I asked Julia to arrange this, Mary. She was kind enough to accommodate me."

My lips parted.

"Don't look so surprised. Surely you know how I feel about you. How obsessed I have become with you. I have been reduced to using a go-between, and I assure you that is not something I've ever done before. But"—his voice deepened—"you're driving me mad, Mary. Surely you must know that."

A pulse began to beat wildly in my throat. "I never meant to."

He gave a husky laugh. "I know, but it has happened anyway." He lifted his hands and put them on my shoulders. I could feel the strength of them through the thin gauze of my robe. "Tell me you don't feel the same about me, and I will go away."

My heart was hammering. He was so close that I could smell the sandalwood soap he used. My lips were dry and I moistened them with my tongue. He stared at my mouth.

"Tell me you don't want me," he said.

"I . . . don't think I can do that," I whispered.

He smiled. Then he bent forward, and his mouth came down on mine. A dark hood dropped over my mind, and a rush of sweet fire ran through my body. He kissed me until I could hardly stand, and I was clinging to him, my whole body pressed against his.

He said in a low, husky voice, "Julia told me the garden bedchamber will be free. Come with me, my love. I will make you happy. I swear I will make you happy."

And I went.

Chapter Thirteen

THAT EVENING IN THE room adjoining Julia's garden, my world changed. Marcus awakened something in me that I hadn't known existed. I was apprehensive at first, but he was so patient and said such beautiful things to me, that I soon lost myself in the fire of passion that leaped between us. I had never dreamed that things could be this way between a man and a woman.

I had to attend Julia's reception the following day, and I was afraid to go. I knew that as soon as I saw Marcus, my feelings would be clear on my face for everyone to see and gossip about. I considered sending a message that I was ill, but in the end I went. I couldn't stay away forever, and I supposed it was best to get the first time over and done with.

I arrived a little late, and Marcus wasn't there. Julia whispered in my ear that he had thought I might be more comfortable if he stayed away, and I was enormously grateful for his tact. It was much easier to laugh and talk and pretend to be the person I had always been without feeling the power of his dark masculinity hovering over me.

I had fallen in love with him. I had fooled myself into thinking that could never happen, but it did. We began to meet regularly, three afternoons a week at Julia's, during the time after lunch when most of the Romans of Sepphoris were taking their daily siesta. Julia took her siesta then as well, and we never once saw her when we were together in her house. Julia was always discreet.

The rains of winter passed into the sunny warmth of spring, and I lived counting the hours from one meeting with Marcus to the next. Seeing the rest of the world through a sort of haze, I was focused on the man who had become the center of my life. When we weren't making love, we were telling each other our life stories. I told him about my father and Judith and about being sent to live in Magdala with Aunt Leah.

I didn't tell him about Daniel. I tried not to think about Daniel, about how physical love might have been between us if we had been together. It was too hurtful and confusing to bring him back into my mind and heart when I knew I would never see him again.

Unsurprisingly, Marcus' life had been very different from mine. He had grown up a treasured son of the Claudian family, and great things had always been expected of him. He spent his childhood at the family villa in the countryside, and I could see that this place, and not the Roman palace, was truly the home of his heart.

His green eyes lit up when he described the beautiful, golden countryside to me, the gently rolling hills, the soft, sweet-smelling air. And he talked about his beloved horses. He had ridden since he was two years old, and he told me the names of all of his own horses and described their different personalities and quirks. I never knew anyone who had such a love for animals.

I didn't tell him that I was afraid of horses. When the Roman soldiers stormed through our towns at a gallop, we were always terrified of being trampled. The horses snorted, tossed their heads, and sidled and backed as if they would kick at any moment. For Jews, horses were a symbol of Rome.

We didn't meet only in Julia's bedchamber. It wasn't long before we were acknowledged in Roman circles as a couple, and together we attended the theatre and chariot races and dined as guests at other Roman homes.

In my heart I knew what I was doing was wrong, but I tried not to think about it. The Jews in Sepphoris, once so tolerant, now thought me a sinful woman and couldn't understand how Aaron put up with my blatant adultery. As for Aaron himself, I scarcely saw him. I stopped going to the synagogue, and when we were home together we were courteous when we saw each other, which we tried not to do very often.

One evening Marcus and I, along with Julia and her current lover, went to the chariot races, which were held in the amphitheatre Herod the Great had built on the edge of the city. Afterward, we were standing outside in the cool spring air, waiting for Marcus to finish speaking with an officer he knew, when a frightening thing happened. A man dressed in Jewish clothing pushed through the crowd and started shouting at me in Aramaic. He called me a whore, a toy of the Romans, a traitor to my people. A group of soldiers descended on him and dragged him away, but he went on shouting at me and shaking his fist all the while, his face twisted with hate. It was horrible, and I turned away.

Marcus put his arms around me, sheltering me from the staring crowd, and shouted for a litter. I could tell from his voice that he was livid. A litter appeared immediately, and Marcus helped me into it and told the bearers to take me to Julia's.

I huddled behind the curtains, shaking like a leaf in a high wind. Such ugliness. Were all the Jews in Sepphoris cursing me like that?

A huge horse stood in front of Julia's doorway when I arrived, and

Marcus was handing the reins to a servant. Then he came over to me, almost lifted me out of the litter, and took me inside. I couldn't stop shaking.

We sat on one of the atrium sofas and Marcus put his arm around me and cradled me against his side. He said grimly, "Don't worry, my darling. That piece of dung won't live to see the morning."

I jerked away from him. "No! No, you must not kill him, Marcus! You can't stain my hands with Jewish blood. Please, please—I beg of you. I couldn't live with myself if you did that."

The atrium fountain trickled gently, forming a peaceful background to my hysterical voice. He didn't answer, and I said again, "Please, Marcus. Don't do anything to him. Let him go."

Lion eyes looked back at me. "He said unforgivable things about you. I can't allow that to go unpunished."

For a moment my mind flashed back to that time in the courtyard, when Daniel had found Samuel touching my hair. I shivered. "Please, Marcus," I repeated. "Let him go. Please." I put my hand on his wrist.

He looked down at my hand, and I could see the physical effort he was making to calm himself. When he raised his eyes again, he looked like Marcus. "He deserves to be killed."

I shook my head. "No one deserves to be killed for what they say."

He stood up. "All right. If that is what you want, I will give the order."

As Marcus went out the door, Julia came in. She rushed to my side and put her arms around me. "I am so sorry, my dearest one." The feel of her arms, the gentleness of her sympathy, released my tears, and I wept into the softness of her breasts.

❧

THE NEXT DAY I was sitting on the side of the bed in Julia's small garden chamber when Marcus came in. He was wearing his military uniform, and I was wearing a thin silk robe that revealed my body.

He sat beside me and asked me how I was.

"All right," I replied, although I wasn't sure that was true. I had stayed awake all night thinking about the words that man had screamed at me. I asked, "Did you find out who he was?"

"He was a Zealot. They're the group giving us the most problems, but I didn't think they'd dare act in Sepphoris, where they don't even have support from their own people."

I had heard of the Zealots, of course. They were an underground Jewish military movement dedicated to throwing the Romans out of our land. The group had started twenty or so years before in a small town north of the Sea of Galilee, and many younger Jewish men had joined it.

Marcus was frowning.

"What did you do to him?" I asked in a small voice.

"We questioned him and let him go with a message to his friends. The next time I catch any of that kind, I *will* have their lives."

I bent my head and said nothing.

"Mary, do you know anything about this *messiah* the Zealots talk of? There's another group seeking him too—a bunch of crazy monks who live in the desert."

"The Essenes," I said, with a catch in my voice.

"Yes, that's the name." He looked down at me. "Who is this messiah?"

"Our scriptures have promised that a great warrior will come to us, that he will defeat the occupiers of our land and rule over us as a great Jewish king. Like David once did."

Marcus bent down to remove his sandals. "This messiah is just a prophecy, then?"

"Yes."

He stood up and pulled his tunic over his head. "It's a nice dream, but it isn't going to happen. The Empire will crush any so-called messiah like a bug under our feet, just as we have done with all rebellions."

He stretched himself out on the bed and pulled me to join him.

Afterward I lay with my cheek pillowed on his chest, listening to the slowing beat of his heart.

"I won't let anyone hurt you again, Mary," he said, stroking my hair. "I'll always take care of you, I promise."

I didn't reply. I had never felt so torn. Was I a Jew or a Roman? Was it possible to be both?

He said, "I'm going to be away for a week or so. Rome has appointed a new procurator for Judea, a man named Pontius Pilate, and I must go to Caesarea to greet him and brief him on the state of the province."

"I'll miss you," I said.

"I'll miss you too," he replied, sounding sleepy.

We were quiet, and when Marcus' arm around me loosened, I glanced at his face and saw that he had fallen asleep. I leaned up on my elbow, so I could look down at him. His lashes—those absurdly long, little-boy lashes—rested gently against hard cheekbones. His hair was too long; he would be getting it cut at the baths today. His shoulders and chest were bare, and I studied the sheer male strength of him as he lay there beside me. I bent and kissed him lightly on the arched bridge of his nose.

I can't give him up.

I curled up next to him and let the finality of that thought sink into my brain. I didn't know what our future would be, but it wasn't in me to give him up.

❧

MARCUS WAS GONE FOR ten days, and during that time I became certain of what I had suspected for a month. I was with child.

All my life I had been regular as the moon, and now I had missed two cycles. I also felt different. My breasts were tender and my stomach not quite as flat as usual. Fortunately I wasn't sick, so Aaron didn't suspect anything.

I should have been happy. This was what I had always wanted—my own baby. Every fiber in me longed to feel my child in my arms, to touch my lips to the warm little head, to inhale the wonderful baby smell I had known when I held other women's children.

But I was worried. I didn't know what Marcus would do when I told him. We had never discussed the possibility of my becoming pregnant. However, I knew all too well what Aaron would do. He would immediately claim the child as his own. He would say that since he was my husband, no one could deny him that right.

I wished with all my heart that I led a normal life, that my child was the child of a husband whom I loved, and that we could celebrate this moment together. But it was not like that. I had lost my first love, I was married to a man I disliked, and I was bearing the child of a non-Jew whom I loved, but wasn't married to.

How had I allowed myself to get into this position?

❧

TREPIDATION SEIZED ME WHEN I received a note from Marcus that he had returned and would meet me at Julia's that afternoon. I wanted so badly to pray for my baby, but I couldn't. I was unclean. I was a sinner. I couldn't ask God to help me when I had done this to myself.

Plutus let me into Julia's as usual, and I walked through the quiet house and out the wide-open doors into the garden, where I found Marcus sitting on a bench by the fountain. I went to sit beside him.

He said, "Do you have any idea how beautiful you are when you walk?"

This comment was so far from my own troubled thoughts that I looked at him in bewilderment. "What do you mean?"

He smiled. "My darling, I love that you really have no idea how beautiful you are. Watching you walk always makes me think of how the old men must have felt when they watched Helen walking on the walls of Troy in the *Iliad*."

I had read a Latin translation of the *Iliad* Julia loaned me, and I wasn't sure I liked being compared to Helen, who had started a war. But he had meant it as a compliment. "Thank you," I said.

Laughing, he took my hand, kissed my palm, and then folded my fingers over the kiss. "I missed you."

"I missed you too. How was your meeting?"

He sighed. "I don't think Pilate is the right choice to be procurator, Mary. He strikes me as the sort who likes to make unimportant gestures just to demonstrate his power."

"What do you mean?"

"I mean gestures that do nothing to further the strength of Rome but only serve to outrage the population. I told him it's always wiser to let an occupied people have their little customs, as long as they don't interfere with the governance of the country, but I'm not sure he agreed."

I nodded.

"Now, before I take you to the bedchamber and show you how much I missed you, tell me about you," he said.

This was the moment. I drew a deep breath, looked up into his hawk face, and said, "Marcus, I am going to have a child."

He didn't answer at first. I felt myself go stiff, preparing to hear something I didn't want to hear. Then his face broke into a boyish smile, and he said, "It was only a matter of time, my darling. How are you feeling?"

My breath rushed out of my lungs. "All right, I think."

"Good." He put his arm around my shoulders and rested his cheek on the top of my head. "I did a lot of thinking about us while I was away, Mary, and mostly I was thinking about what I would have to do to marry you."

I had thought of many things he might say, but this wasn't one of them. I shut my eyes and leaned my cheek into his shoulder. "You can't marry me, Marcus; I'm already married."

I felt his shoulder shrug under my cheek. "You will divorce him. The old man will agree as soon as he hears you are bearing someone else's child."

I pulled away from him. I didn't deserve his love and support. Looking straight ahead, I told him all about Aaron's scheme to get an heir.

When he didn't reply, I glanced at him. The contempt on that proud, aristocratic face made me shiver.

Marcus said, "How could he possibly have imagined that I would allow a son of mine to be brought up as a Jew?"

I raised my chin. "I am a Jew, Marcus."

He put his arm back around my shoulders and drew me to him. "You're going to be my wife, Mary, and that will make you a Roman."

"But don't you understand, Marcus? Aaron will never divorce me. I know a Roman woman can divorce her husband, but a Jewish woman cannot. The decree of divorce must come from the man, and Aaron won't do it. I know he won't. We cannot marry if I am still bound to Aaron under the law."

His green eyes glittered. "In Galilee, I *am* the law."

"Remember what you just said to me about not stirring up the population? Thus far Rome has had the support of the Temple priests because you let them keep their status, but for you to violate our law so blatantly will be something they cannot countenance. You don't want to anger them; it wouldn't be wise."

"Do you really think the Temple priests would involve themselves in the divorce of one Jewish woman?"

"They might. Aaron is a very powerful man in Jewish circles. And he won't give up this child without a fight."

He nodded thoughtfully. "You make a good point. I'll have to arrange it some other way." He gave me a commanding stare. "Don't tell your husband about the child."

I had no intention of telling Aaron, and I agreed quickly.

He stood up and pulled me to my feet. "You aren't to worry yourself about this, Mary. The only thing that matters is that I love you and that we'll be married. Our child will be a Roman citizen and my legal heir. I promise you that."

He began to kiss me and the familiar magic of his touch ran through me like fire. I put my hands behind his head, feeling the crispness of his short black hair under my fingers, and he picked me up and carried me to the room.

Chapter Fourteen

Marcus left for an appointment, and I stayed behind at Julia's. I felt bowed down by the weight of my own emotions. Julia had been like a mother to me these last years, and I needed to talk to someone I could trust. So I waited for her siesta to be over, and then I asked a servant to tell her I was waiting.

She came downstairs, took one look at me, and whisked me back up the stairs to her private apartment. "What has happened?" she asked when we were seated side by side on the white upholstered couch.

I told her about the baby and then I told her what Marcus had said.

She gave me a radiant smile. "He said he wanted to marry you?"

"Yes, he did. But Julia, he seems to be forgetting that I'm already married! I told him that Aaron wouldn't divorce me, that Jewish women cannot initiate a divorce. And Aaron is desperate for an heir. He'll never let me go. I don't know what I should do."

I began to cry. It seemed now that I cried at the smallest thing.

Julia put her arms around me, and I leaned against her, comforted by the maternal warmth she radiated. Julia had the most wonderful scent. She smelled like roses.

She said, "Are you certain Marcus was serious?"

I sniffled. "He seemed to be. He said that I wasn't to worry, that he would arrange things."

Julia patted my back. "If Marcus Novius Claudius wants to marry you, my dear, he will. But it won't be as easy to arrange as he might think. Do you know what has to happen before such a marriage would be possible?"

I straightened up and wiped away my tears with my fingers. "No. What?"

"By law, a patrician cannot marry out of his class, so you'd have to be made a patrician. Such a jump in status requires either the approval of the Senate or the personal approval of the emperor himself."

"But ... how can he accomplish that? I'm a Jew."

"You may have been born a Jew, but in every other way you're one of us. My goodness, you're one of the most sought-after guests in Sepphoris."

Julia looked at me the way a proud mother would look at her daughter. I couldn't meet her gaze. I had certainly not been a good Jew these last few years, but I didn't feel that I was a Roman either.

"Marcus' family must be very highly placed if he thinks he can get the emperor or the Senate to do as he asks."

Julia shifted so she was facing me. "His father will ask Tiberius. Marcus' father and the emperor were old campaigning partners in the Gallic wars. Tiberius, unfortunately, has deteriorated into a licentious drunk, but I think he'll do it—if not to please Marcus' father, then to infuriate all the old men in the Senate who despise him."

I stared at the picture of the goddess Diana on the wall, her hunting bow in hand, a stag by her side. A chasm of doubt had opened in my mind. If I married Marcus, I would have to live with his family. What if they looked down on me?

If only Marcus were a Jew and not a Roman. I immediately realized how absurd an idea that was. Marcus was the epitome of a Roman. Take that away from him, and he would be someone else entirely.

I bit my lip and asked Julia, "What about Aaron?"

"How many times, Mary, have I told you not to bite your lip!"

"Sorry." I immediately closed my mouth over my teeth.

Julia picked up a deep blue silk scarf from the end of the lounge and began to refold it. "Aaron isn't important, my love."

I watched her clever hands as she handled the vivid material. "Don't underestimate him, Julia. He'll go to the Sanhedrin if he has to. The Zealots have made attacks upon tax collectors all over Galilee. So far the Sanhedrin has condemned them, but all that may change if a Roman interferes with the Law of Moses, and that's how Aaron will present his appeal. I don't want to see Marcus risk his career by stirring up a rebellion."

Julia listened to what I was saying, and when I finished, she laid down the scarf and nodded thoughtfully. "I see what you're saying." Then she smiled. "Let Marcus deal with it, Mary. He will get your divorce without stirring up a revolution, I'm sure of it. You will be free to marry the father of your child."

The father of my child. A great surge of happiness swept through me at those words, and I smiled back at Julia. "You're right."

❧

I TOOK JULIA'S ADVICE and didn't ask Marcus any more questions about the divorce. I put my trust in him and did my best to avoid Aaron. The longer I kept Aaron ignorant of my condition, I thought, the better things would go.

One afternoon several weeks after I'd told Marcus about the baby,

I was sitting in my own garden happily reading a new collection of poetry that Julia had ordered from her book agent in Alexandria. The garden was the one place in the house I had made my own. Since I couldn't have replicas of any human form in Aaron's house, I had installed a fish-shaped fountain, with the water coming out of the fish's mouth. The gardener and I had grown roses. Ever since I was a child, I had loved roses, and now I had hundreds of them.

I was just thinking how very peaceful it was here when one of Aaron's assistants, Jonah, burst through the door that opened into the house. I stared in astonishment as he strode across the mosaic floor toward me; Aaron's assistants never came into the garden. Jonah's face was red, and he was breathing heavily. Clearly he had been running hard.

"What is it, Jonah?" I asked, rolling up my papyrus. I wasn't alarmed, just surprised. "What has happened?"

"My lady, I don't know how to tell you this, but . . . my master has fallen down the steps by the colonnade, and he . . . he . . ."

I looked at the young man's sweating face—and I knew. "Is he hurt?"

"Oh my lady, he is dead! The fall broke his neck. I came to tell you that they'll be bringing his body home shortly."

"Aaron is *dead?*" I repeated.

"Yes, my lady. I'm terribly sorry." Then he repeated himself, to make things clear, "The fall broke his neck."

My first emotion was shock. Aaron was an old man, but he was still quite healthy. I had always been certain he would live for many more years. I found it difficult to grasp that he no longer existed, that he had actually died.

Elisabeth, one of the house servants, came into the garden carrying a tray with a cup of water. She brought it to me and said, "Drink this, my lady."

I raised my eyes to her face. "Have you heard?"

She nodded. "My husband was at the market, and he saw it happen. Drink."

My hand shook as I raised the cup to my lips, and she put hers over mine to steady it. I drank.

"Thank you, Elisabeth," I said.

She took the empty cup and stepped away, out of hearing but within my call. I turned to Jonah, who was still panting from his run. "How did he come to fall? My husband is . . . was always steady on his feet."

"I didn't see how it happened, my lady. Jonathan and I had gone ahead of the master, to make sure his litter was ready. He didn't like it if we hovered over him. So we didn't turn to look back until we heard people shouting. Then we saw him lying at the bottom of the stairs. He was dead when we got to him, my lady. We could tell by the way he lay that his neck had been broken."

I wished Jonah would stop saying that. The picture his words conjured up, of Aaron lying at the bottom of the stairs with his neck twisted, made me feel physically sick. My voice trembled as I asked, "They're bringing him home, you said?"

"Yes, my lady."

I struggled to think clearly. What must I do when the body got here? "I'll have to prepare him for burial."

"Yes, my lady," he said again.

I wanted desperately to send for Julia, but of course I couldn't do that. Aaron might not have been the most observant of Jews, but he had never doubted his own identity. He must be buried properly, according to our tradition.

I would have to do this by myself.

I called Elisabeth's name, and she came quickly to my side. "Will you look to see if we have the proper oils for anointing the dead? If there are none in the house, you'll have to send someone to buy them."

"Yes, my lady."

I had never anointed a dead body. I looked up into my maid's calm brown eyes. "Do you know how this should be done, Elisabeth?"

"Yes, my lady, I do. I will help you, if you like."

"Thank you," I said gratefully. "I would appreciate that very much."

"Shall I send for the rabbi?" she asked.

"I suppose we should."

"It would be the proper thing to do, my lady," she said.

"Then send for him."

She gave me a quick, encouraging smile. "I'll help you. You'll be all right."

My eyes blurred with tears, and I nodded. I had always liked Elisabeth and her husband. They didn't live in the house but came to work every morning from one of the outlying villages to the north. She reminded me a little of my Aunt Leah.

Elisabeth left, and I turned once more to Aaron's assistant. "Thank you, Jonah. I think I'd like to be alone for a while."

"Yes, my lady." He backed away, then turned and made a hasty exit. Alone in the quiet garden, I put my hands over my face and wished with all my heart that Julia would put her arms around me and call me her dearest girl and tell me what I should do. Marcus' words, *I'll have to arrange it some other way*, crept into my mind, and I pushed them down. I wouldn't think that way. I wouldn't! I had to concentrate on burying my husband.

WE PUT AARON IN the tomb he had previously purchased in a cemetery garden outside Sepphoris. Then I endured three days of visits from the Jewish wives of Aaron's friends and business associates, the very women whom I had spurned for years in favor of Julia and her circle. I listened without comment to the malicious words these women directed at me, all under the guise of sorrow for poor Aaron, who had been forced to put up with such a sinful wife.

I hadn't seen either Marcus or Julia since the day Aaron was carried home. I wrote to tell them what had happened, of course, but I also asked them to give me time to bury my husband among his own people.

The day after the visiting was finally over, the weather turned chilly, but that didn't keep me indoors. I sat in my beloved garden, wrapped in a light wool cloak, breathing in the cold, clean air. With trembling hands, I rang the small bell on the table. When a servant appeared, I asked to speak to Elisabeth's husband, Jeremiah.

He arrived almost immediately crossing the cold tiles to stand before me. "You wished to see me, my lady?"

"Yes, Jeremiah. I understand from Elisabeth that you were present when the master fell down the colonnade steps."

"Yes, my lady, I was."

"Did you—" I paused, drawing a deep breath. Did I really want to ask this question? Did I really want to know the answer?

"Did you see anything out of the ordinary?"

Jeremiah looked surprised. "How do you mean, my lady?"

"You have no suspicions that the master might have been . . . pushed?"

"Ah." Jeremiah's long thin face was very grave. "There was a crowd of people on the steps, my lady. It's possible someone might have bumped into the master, but I cannot say that I saw anything like that happen."

"And no one has come forward to suggest that it might not have been an accident?"

"No, my lady. No one has come forward."

I forced a smile. "Thank you, Jeremiah. That will be all."

I watched my servant walk away.

It was terrible of me to have such suspicions of Marcus. He was an honorable man, the father of my child. Of course I trusted him. I had to trust him.

I'll have to arrange it, Marcus had said. And now I was a widow, free to marry whomever I wished.

I got up from my chair and went into the house, shivering uncontrollably.

Chapter Fifteen

I DIDN'T THINK I would sleep at all that night, but I slept for twelve hours without stirring. When I finally arose, my body felt rested, and I forced myself to think only of what I would do today. I ate the morning meal and then went out into the garden. Aaron had often scolded me for getting my hands dirty, but I loved to work in the garden. I toiled hard all morning and was just finishing up when Elisabeth came to tell me that Julia was here.

I went in all my dirt to meet her in the courtyard, and as soon as her arms came around me, I began to cry.

Julia patted my back. "There, there my darling. Everything is going to be all right."

It was cold in the garden, and Julia wasn't dressed for the cold, so I took her upstairs to my chambers. These rooms and the garden were the only parts of the house where I had ever felt comfortable.

Roman bedchambers were small, with just the bed and perhaps a couch, but I had the wall between two of the upstairs rooms removed to create a large and comfortable space.

Julia looked around with interest. A number of years ago I had commissioned an artist to paint pictures of the Sea of Galilee on all the walls. She regarded the scenes: glistening blue water with little fishing boats bobbing on the surface, a magnificent sunrise, and a view of the hills from Magdala.

"Very lovely," she remarked when she had looked carefully at everything.

Looking at the paintings myself, I suddenly had a fierce yearning to be back at the lake, to be young and carefree, playing with the children in the garden and waiting for Daniel to come home.

Stop this, I commanded myself. If I kept thinking like this, I would start crying again.

We sat on my green couch, and Julia pushed her scarf away from her perfectly dressed blond hair. "How are you bearing up, my love?"

"Oh, Julia, it was so sad. Aaron spent all his life accumulating money, and what did he get from it in the end? I kept thinking about that as we put him in the tomb. There was no one there who truly mourned him. I was the only person who wept, and that was because I kept thinking of how he had wasted his life. I won't miss him. I don't think anyone will miss him." I sighed and repeated, "It was sad."

"He enjoyed his money. He lived in a nice house, enjoyed many of life's luxuries." Julia was trying to cheer me up.

I refused to be cheered. "He wasn't a happy man. He wanted an heir so badly. I'm almost sorry I didn't tell him about the baby. It would have given him such joy."

"Your child would never have been Aaron's heir!"

"I know that. But if I had let him think that for a little, he would have died happy."

Julia said, "You do know you're being maudlin? Aaron lived as he chose to live, and, if we are to be perfectly honest, it is a great mercy that he died. The way is now clear for you and Marcus to marry."

Julia never flinched from facing reality.

"Yes. It is very . . . convenient."

She nodded. "It will make things much easier for Marcus. He needs his family to stand behind him if he is to have you declared a patrician, and—to be perfectly frank, Mary, the fact that you're now a great heiress will weigh significantly with them. No Roman willingly turns his back on a fortune."

I began to pleat the dirt-stained skirt of my robe. I wanted to tell Julia about my suspicions. I wanted to share this burden. But it wouldn't be fair to Marcus. I should talk to him first. It would be wrong to put such ideas into anyone else's mind if he was innocent.

I looked up from the fingers wrinkling my robe. "The thought of living in Rome frightens me, Julia. Why didn't you return to Rome when your husband died? Why did you choose to remain here, in a foreign land?"

She leaned her head back. Up close you could see the wrinkles in her neck that were invisible from a distance. Those wrinkles revealed her tenderness, her vulnerability. Being beautiful was important to Julia.

She didn't answer immediately, and when finally she did, she didn't look at me directly. "I am going to tell you the truth, Mary. I stayed in Sepphoris because I had a position here. Among this community of Romans, I am an important person, to men as well as women. All the consequential people in the city, both governmental and military, seek me out. They want my notice and my patronage. My reception is the most important social event of every week."

"It is," I agreed.

She turned her head, and the expression in her blue eyes was partly humorous and partly sad. "In Rome, Mary, I would be nothing; a little fish in a sea teeming with big fish. My father is a senator, and my husband was the son of a senator, but there are many families in Rome who can make that claim. Here I am unique. Very few sons or daughters of senators come to a provincial capital like Sepphoris. That's why I decided to stay here. I didn't want to go back to obscurity in Rome."

"Would I live in obscurity in Rome?" My voice was hopeful and I rested my hand on my stomach. "Marcus told me his family had a villa in the country. It sounded like a wonderful place to live and raise a family."

Julia laughed. "I can't quite see Marcus Novius Claudius living in obscurity, Mary."

Nor could I. But I could live in the country with our children, and he could come to visit us. He loved that villa. He would come as often as he could.

I wondered if his mother and father lived at the villa.

"Do you think Marcus' parents will hate it that he married a Jew? Tell me the truth, Julia. I need to know."

"The truth is they will accept you because of the money you bring them. And then they will come to love you, just as we have here in Sepphoris." She picked up my hand and held it. "There is something unique about you, Mary. And I'm not speaking of your physical beauty. You have a talent for listening to people, for making them feel special. It's a rare gift, and it will make you friends wherever you go. You will do fine with Marcus' parents, believe me."

It was nice of Julia to say such kind things about me, but I knew she was prejudiced. There was nothing special about me, apart from my looks. And looks were fleeting. Even Julia was beginning to show the dimming of age.

I smiled at her a little mistily. "You are too good, Julia. But thank you anyway."

She looked around the room. It was crowded with the things that were important to me. The rest of the house bore no imprint of my presence.

Julia said, "Mary, my darling, come and stay with me for a few days. Your memories of this house can't be happy ones. Come to me, and you may see Marcus whenever you wish."

I was tempted, but I knew I couldn't accept her offer. "I can't, Julia, much as I'd like to. There's a great deal of business to take care of, you see. Aaron's estate is vast, and his man of business will not visit a Roman house. I really must stay here."

"Can Marcus come here now that you're a widow?"

"I don't think that would be a good idea. It seems . . . disrespectful, in a way."

She smiled. "You have such quaint ideas sometimes, my darling. But it's of no great matter. You can still see each other at my house."

I walked her to the door. As she turned to leave, she surveyed me from head to toe, frowned, and told me I was too thin.

I sighed. "Julia, you're always telling me I'm too thin."

"But now you're eating for the baby as well as yourself. You can't afford to let your emotions rob you of your appetite, Mary."

"I won't," I promised, and we said good-bye.

Later that day I received a note from Marcus asking me to meet him at Julia's the following afternoon. I replied that I would, and then I began to worry about how I could possibly ask Marcus whether he'd caused the death of my husband. I was almost relieved when Aaron's banker called with some papers for me to look at.

᠊᠊᠊᠊᠊᠊᠊᠊

WHEN I REACHED JULIA'S house late the following afternoon, the sun hung low in the western sky. I walked through to the garden and found a group of workers packing up their gear.

The eldest of them apologized for being in my way.

I smiled. "Not at all. I had forgotten that Julia Tiberia planned to add more mosaic tiles. Is that what you have been doing?"

"Yes, my lady. This is our first day." The man smiled back. He wasn't young, but he looked fit. His face had the deep tan of those who work outdoors. His brown eyes looked intelligent.

"Julia Tiberia said the builders from Nazareth are the best in the country and that you're the best in Nazareth."

He looked pleased. "We are but a small business, my lady, just my sons and me, but we are very conscientious." He nodded to the four younger men, who had finished packing up, and they took their leave.

I wasn't sure if any other workmen might be around, so I went into the garden chamber to wait for Marcus. I stood by the latticework window and looked out into Julia's small grove of fig trees.

Perhaps a half hour passed before Marcus opened the door and came in. He seemed to tower in the small space; I had forgotten just how big he was.

He came to me immediately and took me in his arms. "I'm sorry I'm late, Mary, my love. How are you? I wanted to be with you, but you asked me to stay away. It wasn't what I wanted."

I put my arms around his waist and buried my face in his shoulder. His arms tightened around me, and I felt safe and protected and loved. *He's a good man*, I thought. *He would never do anything evil.*

He put a finger under my chin and lifted my face. The window was on the west side of the house and the sun spilled in behind us.

The light played off the planes of his face in a way that made them seem harder than usual.

He said, "You're too thin."

I laughed. "Are you and Julia in a conspiracy to fatten me up?"

He smiled back. "No. But that is my child you are carrying, and I want you to feed him."

I sighed and stepped away, resolutely pushing back my desire to cuddle against him again. "Marcus, we need to talk."

He glanced over my head at the bed. "Now?"

"Now," I said firmly.

"All right." His tone said he was humoring me. "We'll talk. Come and sit down." We sat on the couch, turning to face each other. "I assume you want to talk about our marriage," he said.

I opened my mouth to say I wanted to talk about Aaron's death, but what came out was "Perhaps we should."

His face grew serious, and he took my hand. "I can tell you now that I was a little concerned about getting permission from my father. It is he who has Tiberius' ear, you see, and I need him to make the formal request to the emperor that will declare you a Roman patrician. Tiberius hardly sees anyone anymore, but he and my father are cousins, and they fought together in the same war. I know he'll agree to see my father."

"But why do you think your father will agree to do this now, if you weren't sure of him before?"

He gave me the smile I loved the best, the one that made him look like a boy, and said, "Your inheritance."

All that money that seemed such a burden to me. I said as lightly as I could, "Are you marrying me for my money, Marcus?"

He took it as a legitimate question. "I have no need of your money, my love. I have plenty of my own. My family has plenty of money too." One black eyebrow quirked. "But they will be overjoyed to get more."

He must have caught an expression on my face because he said, "That's the way of the world, Mary. I know it's not your way. I have never met anyone to whom possessions meant so little as you, but don't make the mistake of judging others by your own selflessness, my love. Money is what runs the world."

I thought of why Lord Benjamin wouldn't allow me to marry Daniel, of the huge bride price Aaron had paid for me, of the way the rabbi in Sepphoris spurned the poor and cultivated the rich. It was hard to deny Marcus' statement.

He leaned forward and grasped my other hand. "Don't look so sad. I wanted to marry you when you didn't have a penny. Not everyone measures value by money. I want to marry you because I love you, Mary. That is my only reason."

I looked into his face, and I knew he was telling me the truth.

I couldn't ask him if he'd killed my husband. There had to be some other way to broach the question of Aaron's death. Then I thought of Jeremiah, and I had an idea.

"One thing is worrying me. One of my servants saw Aaron's accident, and he told me he thought Aaron might have been pushed. Could that be true?"

His black brows drew together. "I've heard no such thing. He fell, Mary. He was old, and he fell. That is all."

I looked at my lap. "Do you think you might make some inquiries? I hate to think that someone might have done this deliberately."

"Look at me, Mary," he said.

I raised my face. His light green eyes locked on mine. "Be sensible, my love. Nothing can be gained by pursuing such an inquiry now. And even if someone did bump into him, it would have been an accident."

"I see," I said in a low voice.

"Don't look back, my love, look forward. The path to our marriage is clear because of the old Jew's death. I no longer have to strong-arm him into divorcing you, and my family will be much more inclined to welcome you as an heiress. We have been very fortunate; I don't want to do anything that could jeopardize our future." He paused. "Do you understand what I am saying?"

I was horribly afraid that I did understand. "Yes," I breathed.

"Good. Then come to bed."

I shivered. "I don't feel very well right now, Marcus. Could you call me a litter?"

He jumped up. "You have no color in your face. Come and lie down."

I let him help me to the bed. I was not pretending; I did feel ill.

"I'll see if Julia is home," he said.

I shut my eyes, but all I could hear was his voice in my mind repeating over and over, *the old Jew's death.*

121

Chapter Sixteen

Julia came into the bedroom, sat beside me, and put her cool hand on my forehead. "What's the matter, my darling?"

"I want to go home," I whispered.

"Mary, if you're ill, you must stay here. I can look after you much better than the servants at your house."

"I'm not ill. I'm upset, and I can't stay here. Please, Julia. Get me a litter."

She gave me a shrewd look. "Did you and Marcus quarrel?"

"No. I just . . ." My voice trailed away, and I looked up at her imploringly.

"All right," she said. "Don't upset yourself any further. I'll get you a litter, but I'm coming with you."

"Thank you." My lips formed the words, but no sound came out.

There was no one more efficient than Julia. She had me wrapped in a warm cloak and bundled into a litter before Marcus even knew what was happening. He wanted to carry me to the door, but Julia shook him off and said this was *women's business.*

Those were always magic words, women's business; men invariably backed away as if they were in danger of catching leprosy. Before

I knew it, I was home and in my own room, with the Sea of Galilee all around me, and Julia ordering Elisabeth to bring me a jug of cool water.

After I drank some water, I looked at Julia, sitting on a stool beside my bed. A few strands of her hair had loosened and hung in feathery locks around her ears. "I'm sorry for putting you to so much trouble," I said in a small voice.

She waved away my apology. "Are you going to tell me what has made you so distraught?"

I shut my eyes. What was I going to say? That four words from Marcus had made me certain he was responsible for my husband's murder? But I had to tell someone; I couldn't carry this burden alone.

I opened my eyes and met hers. "I think Aaron was murdered."

"Murdered?" Her blue eyes were filled with disbelief. "What are you talking about, Mary? Aaron wasn't murdered. He fell."

I pushed myself up, so that I was sitting taller. "Let me tell you a story. It's about the greatest of our kings; his name was David."

"I have been in Sepphoris long enough to have heard the name of David," Julia said.

"He was chosen by God to lead our people, but he didn't always follow the law that God gave to Moses. David was susceptible to women, you see, and one evening, when he was walking around the palace roof, he saw a beautiful woman bathing in one of the palace pools. David sent to inquire who she was and was told her name was Bathsheba and that she was the wife of Uriah, the Hittite, one of David's best battle commanders. But David had been smitten by Bathsheba's beauty, and he sent for her anyway and took her to his bed.

"When Bathsheba found she was pregnant, David didn't want his men to know he was responsible for seducing a married woman, so he sent to the war front to have Uriah report to him immediately. His plan was that Uriah would sleep with his wife, and then he and everybody else would think the baby was her husband's.

"But Uriah was a dedicated leader and refused to take advantage of the comforts of home while his men were sleeping in the open. The two nights he was in Jerusalem he didn't go to Bathsheba's tent; instead he slept with the slaves.

"When David saw his plan had failed, he sent Uriah back to the battlefront with a letter for his commander. In the letter the king ordered the commander to put Uriah opposite the enemy where the fighting was fiercest and then to fall back with his troops, leaving Uriah to meet his death. David's plan worked, and Uriah was killed in battle.

"Bathsheba mourned for Uriah, but when her mourning was over, David took her into the palace and made her his wife, and she bore him a son."

Julia had been listening intently, and now she opened her mouth as if to say something. I didn't give her a chance. "What David did was a sin against God; he took the wife of another and then arranged for her husband's death so that he could marry her." I stared at the lake, so peaceful under the setting sun on my walls. "Does this story have a familiar sound, Julia?"

Julia said, "Mary, look at me." When I reluctantly obeyed, she enunciated with great clarity, "Aaron's death was an accident. There can be no comparison between this old story and you and Marcus."

"'*The path to our marriage is clear because of the old Jew's death.*' That's what Marcus said to me this afternoon, Julia. And I knew, I *knew* with every fiber of my being, that he had arranged for Aaron to fall."

Julia shook her head, stood up, and began to pace back and forth. Finally she halted. "Do you really believe that Marcus Novius Claudius would stoop so low?"

"Julia, even you said Aaron's death was amazingly fortunate. It freed me to marry Marcus and left me with a fortune to smooth the way with his parents."

She stood at the foot of my bed looking at me. "He loves you, Mary. I don't think you understand what a staggering thing he is doing in marrying a Jew. He must love you very much indeed."

Marcus' face flashed before my eyes: the green eyes, the hawk nose, the arrogant mouth. "He did this terrible thing because of me, and I don't think I can live with that."

"Mary, you're making too much of this. It was an accident. But what if it were true? What then? What could you possibly do?" Julia's voice was calm and reasonable. "You're carrying Marcus' child. If you refuse to marry him, then what will happen to the child? Do you want to marry someone else so the child will have a name?"

"No!" I couldn't possible marry a strange man for such a reason. I didn't want a repeat of my marriage to Aaron.

If only Daniel had waited for me.

"Would you lie and pretend the child is Aaron's? No one in Sepphoris would believe you, Mary."

"I could go back to the lake and bring my baby up there."

"You don't think the gossip will follow you? This is a tiny country, my love. Even with all your money, you'll not be able to protect your child from the stigma of bastardry. And besides, Marcus would be a wonderful father. He loves you, and he will love this baby. Do you want to deprive your baby of his father?"

I felt as if I was being torn in two. "I don't know what I should do!

125

I want a family so much, Julia. I want to marry someone I love and bear his children and watch them grow. Time for that is running out. It's just . . . if I marry Marcus, I will always feel that my happiness is stained by Aaron's blood."

"You don't *know* Marcus was responsible. All you have is a suspicion. Don't let a suspicion poison your future, Mary."

After Julia left, I remained in my room, my mind raging with doubt and fear. I pictured the family Marcus and I could make. I pictured his face as he gazed at his firstborn son. I imagined smiling up at him as he tenderly kissed the top of my head.

I finally drifted off to sleep and had a succession of strange and frightening dreams in which Marcus and Daniel and Lord Benjamin appeared. When I awoke the next morning, I still didn't know what I was going to do.

❧

THEN CAME THE DAY of Julia's reception. In all the years I had known her, I had not missed a single one. But today I felt I couldn't face all those sophisticated Romans.

It wasn't that I suspected any of Julia's guests of being a murderer. If Marcus had employed anyone, it would have been an ordinary soldier. *If*—that was the word I couldn't banish from my mind. Julia had said that I shouldn't let a suspicion poison my future, and I needed to think about that.

So I stayed home from the reception and was sitting in my bedroom rereading the *Aeneid* when Elisabeth appeared and said that Marcus Novius Claudius had come to call.

My maid's face was scrupulously blank as she made this announcement. Most of the Jewish servants in my household had long since learned that our ways were very different from the observant religion they practiced in their own families and villages. I suspected that Elisabeth prayed for me to be rescued from my sins, although she never told me so.

I panicked. Julia must have told him what I had said to her; the two of them had always formed an alliance against me.

What was I thinking? I put down the scroll and jumped to my feet. Julia was not allied against me! She just wanted the best for me and believed that meant marrying the father of my child.

The father of my child. The thought was powerful. I longed for him with all my heart—except for a persistent doubt. How could I build happiness founded upon the commission of a murder?

I said to Elisabeth, "Take Marcus Novius into the small reception room, and tell him I'll be there shortly."

"Yes, my lady."

As soon as she left, I snatched up my wool cloak and fled into the garden and then into the street. It was a foolish thing to do. I couldn't run away from Marcus forever. But I was afraid to see him just now; I felt too vulnerable. I needed to know what I was going to say before I could trust myself in the power of his presence.

I hurried along the streets, which were crowded with people on their way home from work. Many stared at me as I hastened by. Roman women rarely walked unaccompanied by a servant. But I pushed on, not knowing where I was heading, just knowing that I had to get away from Marcus. After a while I found myself on the road that led into the poorer part of town, where the craftsmen and day servants and laborers lived. The street was narrow, the houses crowded close together. I didn't look around, I just walked, my eyes straight ahead, my mind preoccupied.

Then I tripped. It was so stupid—a bump in the street I didn't see. I fell forward, unable to break my fall because my hands were tucked into my robe.

People came running to help me. I felt dizzy and embarrassed and kept apologizing for being so clumsy and assuring them that I was all right. But when two men helped me to my feet, I swayed, and they had to hold me up to keep me from falling again.

"Bring her into the house," I heard a woman say, and the men half carried me across the threshold into a cramped, sparsely furnished room. "Put her here," the same voice said, and I was lowered to the floor and a cushion put under my head.

"I'm all right, really." I tried to sit up.

A gentle hand pushed me back. "You hit your head when you fell, my lady. It's best to stay quiet. We've sent to your house; someone will come to take you home shortly."

I squinted as I looked up at the woman kneeling beside me. "How do you know where I live?"

She smiled. "You are Mary, the wife of Aaron, the merchant, am I right?"

"Yes, but—"

"You have lived in Sepphoris for years now, my lady, and you're not easy to forget. Now, I'm going to get you some water."

Suddenly I was desperately thirsty. "Thank you."

I closed my eyes and rested my hands on my stomach. How could I have been so stupid? I might have endangered my baby. Nothing, nothing in the world was more important than my baby.

I felt vastly tired. Julia was right. What would I do with a baby on my own? I had money, but a baby needed more than money. A baby needed a father, a family. A baby needed to belong.

When Marcus came into the room, I tried to push myself to a sitting position, but he called to me to stop and said he would carry me. When he reached my side, I raised my arms to him. He lifted me as if I weighed nothing and carried me to the litter that was waiting outside. I buried my face in his shoulder and felt loved and protected and safe.

"I'm sorry," I whispered into his ear.

"You should be," he returned. "If anything had happened to you . . ."

He sounded angry, but I knew it was because he had been afraid for me. I closed my eyes. Marcus would always take care of us, and that was all that mattered to me now.

Chapter Seventeen

AFTER MARCUS HAD LAID me on my bed, he bent and kissed my forehead. "Trust in me, Mary. Everything will be all right, I promise you."

I smiled up at him. "I know," I said and watched him leave the room.

I nodded off at once. My sleep was deep and dreamless. A pain in my stomach woke me at dawn. I frowned and moved a little, to see if I had been sleeping in an awkward position. It was then that I felt the wetness between my legs.

My heart stopped. Slowly, fearfully, I reached to feel what the wetness was. When I brought my hand back, I saw the blood.

"No!" I said out loud. "No! This isn't happening. I won't let this happen!"

The house was still asleep. The live-in servants would just be getting up, and it was too early for Elisabeth and Jeremiah to have arrived. I was alone.

I grabbed the silk sheet off the bed and stuffed it between my legs to stop the bleeding. It would stop, I told myself. This was just a minor thing; the baby was fine.

But the blood kept coming. I grabbed another sheet. At last my door opened, and Elisabeth peeped in. When she saw me, she cried out.

"It's just a little bleeding, Elisabeth, but I need your help."

Elisabeth came over to the bed and looked at the blood-soaked sheets. She said, her voice infinitely gentle, "You're having a miscarriage, my lady."

I wouldn't believe her. "No, I'm not. It's just a little bleeding. Stop it, Elisabeth. Make it stop!"

She grasped my hand in hers. "There is nothing to be done, my lady. I am sorry."

My stomach cramped again, and more blood gushed out. I doubled over but not from physical pain. "Noooooo!" I wailed. "Not my baby. Noooooo!"

Elisabeth put her arms around my shoulders to support me. "You must be brave, my lady. There will be other children. This will be over soon. Be brave."

The cramps and the flow of blood began to slow, and finally she took the bloody sheets away and put on new ones. She helped me back into bed and put another compress between my legs. "You will need to stay in bed for a few days, but then you'll be fine," she assured me. I nodded, and she left to get me something to eat and drink.

I knew I wouldn't be fine. Something terrible had happened to me with the loss of my child. God was punishing me, as He had punished David by taking his son. And, like David, I deserved to be punished. Marcus might have ordered the murder of Aaron, but he would never have had the opportunity to do such a thing if I'd remained true to my marriage vows. I was as guilty as he was.

Two deaths now separated me from Marcus, an impenetrable barrier, and I could never marry him. Giving him up was part of my punishment, and I deserved it.

❧

I SAW MARCUS ONE more time, three days after the miscarriage. He called at the house to see how I was doing.

I watched him come into the garden. He was dressed in his military uniform, and somehow that symbol of battlefields and death made it easier for me to say what I had to say.

He tried to change my mind, of course, but I was adamant.

He was angry and hurt. "You've tried and convicted me in your own mind. And now you dismiss me. I never thought you could be so unfair, Mary. Unless you've been lying to me all this time, unless you never loved me at all."

"I love you, Marcus. I'm not saying I don't love you. I'm just saying I can't marry you. I know this isn't all your fault. I had a hand in Aaron's death as well. You would never have done it if it hadn't been for me."

"You are so sure I was responsible?"

I looked into his angry green eyes. "Tell me you didn't ask one of your men to follow Aaron and cause an accident. Swear that to me, Marcus, on your honor as a Roman. Will you do that?"

We had been sitting side by side on the stone bench that gave the best view of the roses. I saw a muscle twitch in his jaw, and he stood up. "I wouldn't have to swear anything if you truly loved me."

He wouldn't swear to a lie on his honor as a Roman.

"I'll miss you," I said, the tears beginning to seep down my cheeks.

"Mary!" He extended a hand to me.

I shook my head and looked down at my lap. Then I listened to the sound of his footfalls as he walked out of my life forever.

~

For the first time ever, I had no one to answer to but myself. I could make my own choices. I had the money to do whatever I wanted to do. I was free.

And I was inconsolable.

I don't know what I would have done if Julia hadn't stood beside me. She moved in to live with me while I tried to sort out all of Aaron's business. Her advice was invaluable. Julia had been handling her own money for years; she knew what she was doing, while I most certainly did not.

In all those weeks I never left the house, going outdoors only to visit the garden. I didn't want to risk meeting Marcus. And in all the time we were together, Julia never once tried to get me to change my mind about him. All she said was "The loss of a child is the worst thing that can happen to a woman. But you still have a life to live, Mary, and you're going to have to make some decisions about where and how you want to live it."

I couldn't remain in Sepphoris. It wasn't just my fear of meeting Marcus. It was the realization that Sepphoris was a place of sin for me. I needed to get away, and the only refuge I had was Bethany, with my brother and sister.

I wrote to Lazarus. Instead of writing back, he came to fetch me. I left the day following his arrival; I couldn't ask my observant brother to remain in my unclean house. Elisabeth packed a few items for me, and Julia said I should write and let her know what I wanted to do with the things I was leaving behind: my clothes, my jewelry, the furniture, the kitchenware, the decorations, the very house itself. I said I would do so, and I also told her to keep all the servants employed until they could find other positions.

Jeremiah packed my limited belongings on one of the donkeys Lazarus had brought. I was to ride on the other one; Lazarus would walk.

Julia and I exchanged an embrace in the middle of my courtyard before I left. "Will I see you again?" I whispered into her ear as we clung together.

"You're not coming back to Sepphoris, are you?"

We released each other. "No. I don't believe I can."

She smiled at me. "Then I will come to visit you. Take time to heal, Mary. Don't make any rushed decisions. And write to me."

I kissed her cheek. "Thank you for everything, my mother."

Her blue eyes glistened with tears. "Go."

I nodded and went out to join Lazarus in the street.

THE JOURNEY WASN'T DIFFICULT. We took the road through the fertile and beautiful Jezreel Valley to the Jordan River, turned south to Jericho, and were soon at Bethany. The weather was beginning to heat up, and the grain harvest was still under way. I had made this journey many times during my years with Aaron, when we went to Jerusalem for Passover, but I had always traveled in a litter. I found it far more enjoyable to be on foot.

Bethany looked tiny to eyes that were accustomed to Sepphoris, but I was glad to be there. When I saw my little sister running to meet me, I felt a surge of happiness for the first time since I'd lost my baby.

She flung herself into my arms, like a child herself, and I hugged her hard. She was much smaller than I; the top of her head only came to my nose. I had always thought she was adorable.

She hugged me back. Then she pulled away and gave me a stern look that sat strangely on her round, innocent face. "You're too thin. It's a good thing you came to us, Mary. You need some good Jewish cooking to fatten you up."

Martha was a wonderful cook. I grinned at her. "I invite you to try."

She laughed and said, "Come into the house for some refreshment. You must both be hungry and thirsty after your journey."

Meekly, both Lazarus and I followed her inside.

❧

NO BETTER PEOPLE EXIST in the world than my brother and sister, Lazarus and Martha. I burrowed into their lives like a fox burrows into its den, seeking safety from the pain of the world outside.

There was another reason to keep to the house. In the eyes of the townspeople I was a sinner from Sepphoris, and they knew they should shun me. Although everyone in Bethany loved my brother and sister, still they suffered, dutifully ignoring me and thus offending Lazarus and Martha. The easiest way out of this difficulty was for me to avoid the town, which was no hardship. I was busy trying to figure out what to do with my life.

My mind and heart were such a chaos of warring thoughts and emotions that it was hard for me to think. Being back in an observant Jewish household, with its regular round of prayers and careful attention to ritual cleanliness, struck a chord I thought I'd put behind me. It had been a long time since I had prayed. I didn't know if I could anymore. I didn't know if I even wanted to.

But every day I saw Lazarus reciting the *shema*. Every day Martha prayed over the food she was preparing. In almost everything they did, they sought the blessing of God. They were good people.

I was not a good person.

It was true that I had been forced into a loveless marriage. But, much as I wanted to, I couldn't blame Aaron for pushing me into Marcus' arms. I chose to become Marcus' lover. And I *had* loved him. I had loved him, and I had made him do a terrible thing.

And God had punished me by taking my baby.

I could tell all this to only one person, and so I spoke to my brother. He was deeply compassionate, because that was his nature. Lazarus would never judge me, but he urged me to reconcile myself to God.

Part of me wanted to do this. Part of me wanted to become the old Mary, with her unquestioning faith in the goodness of the Lord. But too much bitter hurt lay between that girl and me. I couldn't go back to synagogue, as my brother wished. I just didn't know what I believed anymore.

It might seem odd that I would speak to my brother and not my sister, but I didn't want to upset her with my troubles. She had enough to worry about with Lazarus' illness. I didn't want to add to her burden.

Until I returned to Bethany, I didn't know that my brother had a sickness in his brain. The headaches had begun around the time of his Bar Mitzvah and had tormented him ever since. They were so agonizing that he couldn't do anything but lie in bed and wait for them to go away. Sometimes two came in a week; sometimes he would go for months without one. He had told me once that his greatest fear was that one day the headache would not go away and he would go mad from the pain.

This was why he had never married. He didn't want people to know of his illness because he was afraid they'd say he was possessed by a devil; nor did he wish to burden a woman with a husband who might become permanently incapacitated.

Of course, no one in the village could understand why my handsome, financially comfortable brother was still unwed. An unmarried man of twenty-two was almost unheard of among Jews—except for the Essenes, of course, and everyone knew they were strange.

Lazarus' illness was also the reason why Martha hadn't married. She was a pretty girl, small and bright-eyed, with two deep dimples in her cheeks. Lazarus had received offers for her, but she refused to leave him. The two of them were inseparable, and I was grateful for their great kindness to me.

❧

I REMAINED IN BETHANY for almost a year. After I was able to think clearly enough to focus on my future, I wrote to Julia. She wrote back, telling me first that Marcus had gone back to Rome. This news made me feel safer. The greater distance between us put him at a greater emotional distance as well. I could picture him in Sepphoris, but I couldn't picture him in Rome.

Julia also gave me encouragement and sound advice. She had once been in my situation, and she had built her own house and lived in it by herself. Couldn't I do the same?

I knew exactly where I wanted my house to be: on the Sea of Galilee. I had always loved the lake, and it would make me happy to wake every morning to the sight of the sun coming up over those clear blue waters.

Martha and Lazarus tried to persuade me to stay with them. The very idea of me, a single woman living by myself, horrified them. But I was adamant. I wanted to be alone. I wanted my own house where I could have my own things and do as I pleased. Men had ruled my life for too long. I wanted to be free.

Winter was coming when I journeyed to Galilee in search of a house. Martha and Lazarus accompanied me, as did a builder I hired from Jerusalem. I wanted his opinion before I made a purchase. I could tell he thought I was mad, but he came highly recommended, which was all I cared about.

I didn't want to go back to Magdala, and Herod Antipas' new city of Tiberias was too much like Sepphoris, so we looked first in Gennesaret, but I couldn't find anything that suited me. I didn't want to live in a Roman city, but neither did I want to live in a small village. I was growing discouraged by the time we reached Capernaum, but it turned out to be just what I had in mind.

Capernaum was the most important town on the lake, a regular stop on the great caravan route that ran from Egypt to Damascus. The busy traffic made it a center of news, business, and commerce. A Roman garrison was posted there, but it was not at all like Sepphoris. It was a sophisticated Jewish town, and I liked it immediately.

As with most of the lake towns, fishing was Capernaum's chief commercial occupation, but just outside the city lay great fertile fields of wheat and olive groves and vineyards. There were certainly houses for sale but not on the lake. My frustration was rising again when a local man came to our inn and told me about a lake property he had heard was for sale. The house itself was nothing, he said, just a tiny mud brick dwelling, but the land was big enough to accommodate something much larger. The elderly woman who lived there had just died, and her sons, who were farmers, wanted to sell the property.

Lazarus, Martha, and I went immediately to see the scribe who was representing the family. When he learned I was the would-be purchaser, he looked at the plain wool tunic, robe, and veil I was wearing and shook his head regretfully. "I am sorry, madam, but the owners are asking far more than any individual can pay. Someone from the fishing industry will be sure to buy it; in fact I have had several inquiries already. The family wanted to sell the land for years, but their mother refused to give it up. They're looking to make a small fortune on it now, and they will get it. Property on the lake is like gold in your hand."

"How much do they want?" I asked.

He looked at Lazarus who looked placidly back and said nothing.

The scribe wearily quoted me a price.

"I'll pay it," I said calmly. "I can draw the money from my bank immediately, and the family will have it by the end of the week."

The scribe looked back at my brother, clearly wondering if I was delusional.

Lazarus said, "My sister is a very rich woman."

At these words, a canny look came into the scribe's close-set eyes. "Well then, of course I will present your offer to my clients. They may surprise me, however, and ask for even more."

"Whatever your clients are paying you to represent them, I will double it—if I get the property," I said crisply. I had learned more than I realized from Julia over the years.

The canniness was replaced by the gleam of greed. "Certainly, my lady. I'm sure I can convince them to take your offer. It will be in their best interest, after all."

"Yes, it will," I said, noticing that I had gone from *madam* to *my lady* once he had learned the depth of my purse.

We went to look at the property, which was unkempt but beautiful. I would knock the house down, of course, and build my own.

Suddenly I was excited. I pictured a house and a large garden. I knew exactly what I wanted. I walked around the property, showing the builder what I envisioned here and there, and he agreed it would be suitable.

I stole away for a moment and stood alone on the rocky beach gazing out across the lake at the hills on the other side, suddenly aware I was looking forward to the future. My life wasn't over. I would begin a new life here on this beautiful lake where as a girl I had once been so happy.

Part 3

Jesus of Nazareth

Chapter Eighteen

THE ARCHITECTURAL STYLE I chose for my house combined the Jewish sense of closed family space with the openness I loved about Julia's house. While the house was being built, I made monthly visits to watch its progress. The workers didn't quite know how to deal with me. They hadn't known many women employers. It was an awkward situation for them, and I did my best to be pleasant and encouraging and hoped they would say nice things about me to their wives.

When it was finished, the house was perfect. I hadn't been able to include an open roof like the one in Julia's house—it was colder and rainier around the lake than it was in Sepphoris—but I hired an artist from Jerusalem to paint pictures of the lake and the countryside on the walls of a large atrium-style room, and the effect was lovely. I had the traditional Jewish courtyard, with the kitchen and storage rooms. And I planned to plant a garden on the land that ran down to the lake behind the house.

The one thing I didn't have yet was a library. Aaron had no book collection for me to inherit, so I decided I'd create one of my own. Julia had given me the name of a seller in Rome, so I put together a list of the works I liked the most and sent it off to him. The room with its cabinets was ready and waiting, and I expected my shipment shortly.

The thought of having my very own books made my heart glow with joy.

I made the move to Capernaum two weeks after Passover. I had always thought spring was the most beautiful season in Galilee, and this year was even more spectacular than I remembered. The hills were blanketed with brilliant flowers, and the shining lake water reflected back the blue of the sky.

The week after I moved in I held a party in the courtyard for the workers and their families. Word had gotten around town about me, so everyone knew I had lived in Sepphoris, and I was fearful they might not come. I took great care to assure the men that all the food would come from a ritually clean Jewish kitchen.

They came, and the party was a success. The men were proud of their work and anxious to show it off to their families. Many of them brought friends. I made certain to speak to everyone, including the children, and by the time the courtyard had emptied, I was exhausted but happy.

I had hired Elisabeth and Jeremiah from Sepphoris to be my live-in servants. They had accepted my offer immediately. I was happy to know that I would have such kind people living in my house in this city I hoped to call my home.

I had always known my position in Capernaum would be uncertain, but every day that passed made it clearer that I was an outsider. The successful party wasn't a portent of things to come. I received no invitations. When I walked through the marketplace, dressed like an ordinary housewife in a plain linen tunic and a simple veil, people avoided me. I felt as if the words *Sinner from Sepphoris* were painted on my forehead.

I was feeling lonely and discouraged, afraid that I had made a grave mistake in coming here, when by chance I encountered my cousin Ruth in the marketplace. We met in front of one of the fruit stalls and stared at each other in amazement.

"Mary?"

"Ruth?"

We laughed and hugged, looked at each other, and laughed and hugged some more.

"Don't tell me you're the rich lady from Sepphoris everyone is talking about?"

I managed a rueful smile. "I'm afraid I am."

"It never crossed my mind it could be you. Why haven't you come to see me?"

I laughed. "How would I know you were living in Capernaum?"

She smiled. "True. But I'm so glad to see you!" She shook her head. "You look more beautiful than ever, you wretch."

"Oh Ruth, how I would love to talk to you. Do you think you might be able to come visit me?"

"Of course I'll come visit you! I can't wait to see this house everyone is talking about. How about tomorrow?"

I smiled with my whole heart. "Tomorrow would be fine."

❧

SEEING RUTH WAS LIKE touching real earth again. She looked older, but she was still Ruth, and it didn't take long for us to feel as if we'd been parted for months instead of years.

The first thing I did was show her around the house. She was almost as amazed as I was when first I went to Julia's.

"It's so big," she said.

"Not as big as the house in Magdala."

"Yes, but the house in Magdala housed two large families. As far as I can see, this house is only for one person—you!"

One of the things I always liked about Ruth was that she spoke her mind. "It may be a bit extravagant," I admitted, "but I got used to a large house when I lived in Sepphoris."

"My house looks like a hovel in comparison."

"I don't believe that."

She grinned. "Well, maybe not. But I have a husband and four children."

"Do I know the man you married?"

"I don't think so. His name is Nathaniel bar Simon, and he comes from one of the villages outside Capernaum. He owns some large olive groves, so we do well enough."

The courtyard where we sat lay between the side of my house and the fence that separated my property from my neighbor's. The day was fine, and the breeze off the lake delightful. Elisabeth had provided us with wine and a tray of fruit and bread. We ate and drank as we talked comfortably.

"So," I said, "what do the people in town think I've done, to make them treat me like some kind of pariah?"

She sighed. "The word is that you led a wicked life in Sepphoris."

"That's all?" I asked cautiously. If they knew about Marcus, I would never be accepted.

"That's enough, don't you think?"

"But Ruth, if these people don't know anything about me, why should they think I'm a sinner?"

She waved her hand. "For one thing . . . well, just look at yourself, Mary. You might be one of those pagan goddesses. You certainly don't look like any of the wives in this town!"

I looked down at my perfectly correct clothing. "What do you mean? I was very careful to buy clothes that would be appropriate for a Jewish woman of my age." I gave her an injured stare. "My clothes aren't any different from yours, Ruth."

Ruth tilted her head. "It's the way you hold yourself. That authoritative air you have."

I had been as mild as a lamb in all my dealings with the people here. I said, "It's because I lived in Sepphoris, isn't it?"

"That too, of course," she replied.

I looked at my hands. "I didn't ask to live in Sepphoris, Ruth. I went against my will."

Ruth covered my hands with hers. "I know, dearest. I saw your face when they married you to that old man. I was so sorry for you, Mary. So very sorry."

My throat closed down. I nodded, unable to speak.

Ruth changed the subject. "Did you know that Lord Benjamin is dead?"

I nodded. "Yes. I heard from my brother."

"And Samuel has eight daughters. Can you imagine?"

I stared in amazement. "Eight girls? And no son?"

"Not a one."

"Poor Naomi," I said. The woman was always held accountable for the sex of her child.

"How about you?" Ruth asked gently. "No children from that old man?"

I froze. After a long minute, I managed to shake my head.

"Three wives and no children. It's clear whose fault that was."

I picked up my cup and took a long swallow of wine.

Ruth said, "Have you heard about what Daniel did?"

I hadn't heard his name spoken out loud for years. I took a slow breath and let it out. "I heard he went to the Essenes."

"Yes. It was a great shock to us all. I think it's what finally killed his father."

"Has . . . has anyone heard from him?"

"So far as I know, no one has heard anything from him since he left."

Jeremiah approached quietly and asked if he could get us anything else. Ruth shook her head, saying she had to leave. I said to Jeremiah, "You must make certain that in the future we get all our olives and oil from Ruth's husband, Nathaniel bar Simon."

"I will remember, my lady," Jeremiah said. He picked up the plate of fruit and went inside.

Ruth said, "I think I should warn you, Mary, you have already made a dangerous enemy."

My eyes widened in surprise. "How can that be? I don't know anyone."

"One of the Pharisees, Ezra bar Matthias, has taken against you. Apparently he saw you once when you came to check on your house. When he learned you'd lived in Sepphoris and had your own money, he decided you must be a walking embodiment of all seven of the deadly sins. He denigrates you every chance he gets."

"Pharisees think all women are unclean. He probably hates me because I have money and can do as I like."

Ruth looked thoughtful. "Your position is certainly unusual among Jews," she said.

I changed the subject. "I would love to see your children."

"We will all come and visit you. Nathaniel too. And you must come to us."

"Nothing would make me happier," I said.

She smiled. "Don't worry about that Pharisee. I have plenty of friends in Capernaum who will be happy to make your acquaintance. You can meet them at the synagogue."

The synagogue. I knew it would come up sooner or later.

Ruth saw the look on my face. "I know you haven't been going to synagogue, Mary, and that is another mark against you with the people of the town. If you truly want to be one of us, you *must* go to synagogue."

I rubbed my eyes and wondered how to explain. "I haven't been in years, Ruth. The kind of people who went in Sepphoris . . . I just couldn't bear them. They were only interested in money, and the rabbi was the same. Just sitting under the same roof with them made me feel unclean."

"Did your husband go?"

"Yes. He was one of the ones I couldn't bear. Aaron was not a good man, Ruth." I thought of how he had pushed me into Marcus' arms. "Not a good man at all."

"Listen to me, Mary." Ruth took my hand and spoke slowly and clearly, "If you wish to be accepted in Capernaum, you must go to synagogue. It's different here from what you describe in Sepphoris. Our rabbi is a good man, a kind man. The people who attend are mostly fishermen and merchants from the city. Nathaniel and I always come into Capernaum because we like it better than the synagogue in our own small village."

I bit my lip. "I don't know if I can."

Her hand on mine tightened. "If you don't come, you will be isolated from the entire Jewish population of Capernaum. Do you want that?"

"No!"

"Then you must put Sepphoris and everything that happened there behind you. I'll have Nathaniel take you to see the rabbi first, and he will welcome you and invite you to join us. You'll see."

Perhaps he will, I thought cynically. *I'm sure he knows all about my money.* But I had to take Ruth's words seriously. I hadn't come to Capernaum to live in isolation. I missed Julia terribly, and I wanted to make friends with the local women.

"Do you think Nathaniel would do that?" I asked.

"Of course he will," Ruth replied.

The synagogue wasn't the Temple, I told myself. The synagogue was for teaching, not for sacrifice. I suspected I would disagree with much of what I heard, but I didn't have to listen, I just had to be present. I inhaled deeply and took a giant step.

"All right. I'll go to synagogue."

Ruth's smile was radiant. "It will all be fine, Mary. I'm sure there won't be trouble. The rabbi doesn't like Ezra bar Matthias either."

I walked Ruth to the courtyard door, trying to resign myself to what I knew I had to do.

"Make sure Nathaniel lets the rabbi know I have a lot of money," I said as she walked through the gate.

Our eyes met, and then Ruth nodded. She might be a good Jewish woman, but she wasn't ignorant of the ways of the world.

Chapter Nineteen

Ruth was as good as her word and produced her husband a few days after our conversation. Nathaniel bar Simon was a man of average height with steady, thoughtful brown eyes, a slightly crooked nose, and a quick smile. He looked around the atrium and said simply, "Very nice."

I liked him at once. "Thank you for doing this for me. I haven't been to synagogue in a long time."

"So Ruth has told me. She has also told me what dear friends you once were and how pleased she is to have found you again."

Ruth said, "I hope you don't mind, Mary, but I also told him all about Daniel and how dreadfully Lord Benjamin treated you both."

I inhaled sharply. "It was a long time ago."

"Yes, it was," Nathaniel, said. "Now it's time to concentrate on the future. I have asked the rabbi for an appointment, and he's waiting for us. Shall we go?"

I was ridiculously nervous as we walked along the narrow streets that led to the synagogue. I was afraid that this rabbi would be just like the one in Sepphoris.

The synagogue itself looked like the synagogue in Magdala, not the grandiose one in Sepphoris. The rabbi was a small, gray-haired man with a wrinkled face and humorous eyes.

He said, "Nathaniel has told me about you, Mary of Magdala, and I am happy to welcome you to our synagogue in Capernaum."

My smile was a mixture of pleasure and relief. I was Mary of Magdala again, and I liked that very much.

≈

I ATTENDED A SABBATH synagogue service three days later with Ruth and her family. Once inside, we separated, women and girls to one side of the central aisle, men and boys to the other. I felt the eyes of the congregation upon me as I followed Ruth, but I looked forward, my back as straight as a plank of wood.

The interior of all synagogues followed a similar plan. The places of honor were in the front, facing the congregation. Local Pharisees, scribes, visiting dignitaries, officers of the synagogue, and the rabbi usually occupied these benches. On a high platform behind them was the table where the scrolls of the Torah reposed.

The first part of the service consisted of prayer, which we began with the *shema*, the prayer that all Jewish men were required to recite twice a day:

Hear, Israel, the Lord is our God, the Lord is One.
Blessed be the Name of His glorious kingdom forever and ever,
And you shall love the Lord your God with all your heart and with all
your soul and with all your might.

My lips moved, following the words I had known by heart since I was a child. When we had finished, I shivered a little. It felt so strange to be back in familiar surroundings with familiar sounds and smells. Ruth's youngest daughter looked up at me and I smiled at her reassuringly. She smiled back.

The second part of the service consisted of readings from the Torah. The words were first read in Hebrew and then translated by one of the synagogue officers into Aramaic so the congregation could understand.

During the third part of the service the rabbi would invite a distinguished person to speak, and today he called upon a visiting scribe who talked about the time when our people were slaves in Egypt and the Canaanites occupied our land. He spoke of how Joshua had been led by the Lord to reclaim the Promised Land for His people. He spoke of David, our great warrior king. And he spoke about the present time, about how the Roman occupation was like those that had gone before. He said we must be prepared to do as Joshua and David had done—go to battle for our country. A great commander-king was coming to lead us, he said, and we must pray for the Messiah to arrive soon. Once he showed himself, the Romans would be defeated just as surely as all the other pagan armies had been defeated all those years ago.

I was stunned by the fiery words. I had become accustomed to a city where Romans and Jews lived together peacefully.

The path to our marriage is clear because of the old Jew's death.

Marcus' words leaped into my mind in all their callous indifference. Aaron's murder had not caused a ripple of guilt to disturb his conscience. In Sepphoris, Jews and Romans might live without animosity, but the Romans believed themselves vastly superior. The Roman Empire ruled with an iron fist, and even if the iron was disguised, as it was in Sepphoris, it was still there.

After the service was over, the men gathered in the synagogue courtyard, talking excitedly about what the visiting scribe had said. Most of the women were interested in meeting the exotic stranger in their midst—me. I smiled and talked about my girlhood in Magdala and how happy I was to be back on the lake among good Jewish people once again.

A number of the older women held back, shooting baleful looks my way, but on the whole I was pleased with my reception. I gave the women around me a severely edited version of my life in Sepphoris, and they listened eagerly. I had been right to return to the lake, they told me, where the people followed the Law of God and of the elders who had gone before us.

The women said nothing about the scribe's speech, but it was in my mind the whole time I walked home. *The Messiah*, I thought. It is the hope of a messiah that sent Daniel to the desert. I saw his face in my mind as I turned down my street—not the Daniel who had come to me in Sepphoris but the Daniel I had known in Magdala. Happy. Young. Loving me.

I missed him. I missed him so much.

⤳

I HADN'T YET MET my nearest neighbors. A high mud brick wall separated our houses so we couldn't see each other, but I often heard the sound of children's voices. Since they were Ruth's friends, she volunteered to introduce us, and the day after the Sabbath we went together to knock on the door.

The rambling house, made of the same mud brick as the wall, belonged to a man named Simon Peter bar Ezekiel. Ruth told me he was a fisherman in partnership with his brother and that they had their own boat. Owning your own boat was significant on the lake. It meant you made all the profit off your catch. The men who had to hire someone else's boat made much less.

A serving girl answered our knock and bade us come in. The front room was just large enough to accommodate a clean but scuffed wooden table with benches on either side.

Footsteps sounded, and then Rebecca, Simon Peter's wife, came in. She gave me a warm smile when Ruth introduced me. "I'm sorry I haven't called on you, but the children have been sick one after the other. I couldn't go to synagogue yesterday, so I missed seeing you there as well."

When a woman could not go to synagogue it was usually because she was having her period and was considered unclean. She had to remain at home until it was finished.

The day was warm, and Rebecca invited us into her courtyard, which had the usual fig tree and outdoor oven. We sat on a circular stone bench and chatted while the serving girl went to fetch some juice.

Rebecca was older than Ruth and I, but her hair was still a dark brown. For some reason, she reminded me of Julia. I couldn't imagine why, since they didn't look at all alike, but there was something similar about them.

We sat in the sun and talked. I sipped my juice and thought how pleasant it was to be here, with these attractive, modestly dressed women who talked about their husbands and their children and their household problems. Rebecca had a wry sense of humor that set us laughing more than once.

Rebecca's youngest daughter toddled out into the courtyard, seeking her mother. She was a beautiful child, about three years of age, and she told me her name was Leah.

"Leah," I said softly. "I had an Aunt Leah once. It's a lovely name."

"She missed you very much, Mary," Ruth said, patting my hand.

"And I her." I turned to Rebecca. "She was my mother's sister and so kind to me. I was very sorry I didn't get to see her before she died."

Rebecca's daughter had climbed into her mother's lap and was looking at me out of big, solemn eyes. "Pretty lady," she said.

I replied just as solemnly, "Thank you. You're pretty too, Leah."

She nodded, accepting the tribute as her due.

Rebecca said ruefully, "Peter is always telling her how pretty she is. He spoils her dreadfully."

Leah rested her head against her mother's shoulder and put her thumb in her mouth. Rebecca removed it and said to Ruth, "Did you know that Seth bar Nathan broke his leg and can't work? Hannah is beside herself. The baby is due in a month. We'll have to do something to help them."

I listened as the two women spoke about the unfortunate family, and an idea that had been germinating in my brain for some time suddenly blossomed. "Are there many people in Capernaum who need money to take good care of their families?" I asked.

"Enough," Rebecca said. "The fishermen who hire themselves out to work on other men's boats have the most problems. If they get hurt and can't work—as Seth has done—then the family is in trouble. My husband and his brother own their own boat and work as partners, so our situation isn't quite so dire. There's always someone to back the other one up. And if need be, we can hire help. But the poorer men don't have that luxury."

"And these men for hire . . . they can't afford their own boats?"

"Not on the wages they earn. They barely manage to keep their families fed, and it doesn't help having to pay such outrageous taxes to Rome." Ruth nodded in agreement.

I asked, "Can't they get a loan?"

Rebecca and Ruth looked at me, eyebrows raised. Ruth said, as if she was speaking to a child, "Only the rich can afford to give loans, Mary, and they would never take a chance on a man like Seth. His ability to pay back the money is virtually nonexistent."

"Hmmm," I said, thinking hard.

Leah sneaked her thumb back into her mouth, and once more Rebecca removed it.

I said, "You may already know this, but my husband died with no male heirs, so I've inherited all his money. It's far more than I will ever need for myself, and I want to use it to help people in need. Like Seth."

Ruth said gently, "Mary, that's kind of you, but Ruth is right. Seth will never be able to pay back that kind of loan. If he used it to buy his own boat, he would be in a much better position to provide for his family, but how he would be able to save enough—"

I interrupted, "You don't understand. I don't care if the loan never gets paid back. I would like to give the money free and clear, but"—here I raised my eyebrows—"I know how proud Jewish men can be."

Rebecca laughed. "You're right about that. My husband would beggar us all before he'd take charity, but if we were in serious trouble, he would probably accept a loan."

Ruth agreed.

Rebecca shifted Leah, who had gone to sleep, to her other shoulder. "Times are hard," she said. "Taxation is draining money from us all. We pay taxes to the Romans, and then we have to pay more taxes for the upkeep of the Temple and the priests." Her eyes flashed with indignation. "Almost half of what Peter makes goes to taxes!"

I had heard Aaron complain enough about the double taxation of Jews to know how unfair my people thought it. There was nothing I could do about the taxes, but I hoped I could help in other ways.

"Do either of you have an idea about how I should make these loans? I would rather people not know I was giving them."

"If I were you, I'd speak to the rabbi," Ruth said.

I nodded slowly. It was a good idea. If the rabbi would agree to authorize and distribute the loans, then I could keep my name out of it.

"I'll do that," I said.

"The Lord will bless you for your kindness, Mary," Rebecca said.

I shook my head. "All this money is a burden to me. I will be delighted to find a way to get rid of some of it."

Leah woke up with a start, hitting Rebecca in the chin with her head. The little girl began to cry. Ruth and I stood up, ending the visit so Rebecca could see to her daughter. As we walked up the street toward my house, Ruth told me she would have Nathaniel make another appointment with the rabbi so I could discuss my idea of loans.

I was happy as we parted and I went indoors. Thanks to Ruth I thought I could make friends in the community, and I felt very good about giving Aaron's money away to deserving Jewish families. I was humming as I went in to see Elisabeth in the kitchen to ask what she was planning for supper.

Chapter Twenty

OVER THE NEXT FEW months I met and became one of a circle of very nice Jewish women. Even though Ruth never said so, I was certain she had regaled them with the "tragedy" of my separation from Daniel and forced marriage to Aaron. I didn't like my private life being spread around town, but I recognized the advantage my story gave me.

Because they felt sorry for me, my new friends were able to overlook my years of living in Sepphoris. Deep in their hearts, most women adore a love story. Especially a sad one. All my Roman friends had grieved their hearts out for poor Dido when Aeneas deserted her.

I had loved two men and lost them both, and I didn't want to read about or live through a love story ever again.

I had my enemies in the town, however. Some women wouldn't speak to me and told their children loudly to "keep away from that shameless woman." I tried not to show my hurt, but I felt it nonetheless. The fact that these women were right about me made their sneers even worse. I often thought that if my new friends knew the whole truth, they would snub me too.

Ezra bar Matthias remained my worst enemy. He was a Pharisee, part of a group that devoted itself to the strictest interpretation of the Mosaic Law. Over the centuries men like Ezra had broken down the Ten Commandments into hundreds of minute rules that covered even the smallest aspect of Jewish life. They not only endeavored to live perfect lives themselves, but they thought everyone else should be just as strict.

Ezra bar Matthias considered himself purer than pure, and whenever I happened to pass him, he would draw his robe away as if he was afraid I might contaminate him. He told everyone I was a filthy whore, a woman who had practiced every one of the deadly sins, and that just speaking to me would make the speaker unclean.

Then, one day at the market, as Ruth and I were standing in front of the cheese maker's stall, I learned the Pharisee was not so pure after all. I felt someone's eyes on me and turned my head to look. It was Ezra bar Matthias.

If he had been glaring at with me hatred, I would have turned back to the stall. But I saw the look in his eyes clearly, and it was a look I had seen before in the eyes of other men. I knew it well. Not hatred—lust.

I stared straight back at him, and he flushed and turned quickly away. But he knew that I had caught him, and after that he kept away from me.

❧

SOON THE CHILLY WINTER rains set in, and I was forced to spend most of my time indoors. Sepphoris, an inland city, had mild winters, but here the wind was bitterly cold as it swept off the stormy, wave-tossed lake. Everyone moved inside.

I had more time to think than I wanted. I read a new book that Julia had sent me, but just thinking about Julia made me miss her more. She was a faithful correspondent, and I enjoyed her lists of the new clothes she had bought at the colonnade shops, what horses had won at the races, and what new plays were being performed at the theatre.

Part of me missed the sophisticated Roman life I had known in Sepphoris, but when I sat in my house, with the cold rain pounding against its tightly closed roof, I knew I could never live among Romans again.

Time away from Sepphoris had helped me see clearly. The whole of Roman life was corrupt because it had no moral center. If Marcus had been raised a Jew, if he had been taught the commandments of the Lord, he would have known it was wrong to have Aaron killed. But he had flicked Aaron's life away as if he was an annoying insect.

That winter, for the first time in years, I started to pray. I asked the Lord to help me learn to be a good woman. I asked Him to help me know Him better. I took my first step on the path that I hoped would eventually bring me to some kind of peace.

⟳

THE LOAN PROGRAM I had arranged with the rabbi kept me happily occupied. Winter was a hard time for hired laborers. Farm and fishing work was scarce, and many people took advantage of my offered money.

Toward the end of winter Julia wrote to tell me that a Roman officer I knew from the gatherings at her house had been appointed commander of the garrison in Capernaum. She had told Fulvius Petrus that I was in Capernaum and that he should call on me.

My heart sank into my stomach when I read this. Fulvius Petrus had been one of Marcus' lieutenants, and he knew all about our affair. If he should mention it to someone in Capernaum, all the goodwill I had gained would be lost. I thought of what Ezra bar Matthias would say, and I shuddered.

I was still standing with the unrolled letter in my hand when Elisabeth came in to say that Rebecca was at the door. I hastily rolled up the scroll, even though Rebecca would not be able to read it, and told Elisabeth to bring Rebecca in.

I was standing in one of the small rooms that opened off the atrium that I had fitted up for winter. It had a big charcoal brazier, thick rugs, and two couches. The walls were painted the color of the lake in summer.

Rebecca came in, loosened all her warm scarves, and sank onto a couch. She sighed. "It's always so peaceful here, Mary."

I smiled. "That's because I don't have five children running around."

She smiled back and unwrapped another scarf. "Do you ever get lonely here?" she asked. There was genuine concern in her voice.

Dear Rebecca. Perhaps this was why she reminded me of Julia, always concerned about my welfare.

"Occasionally." I hesitated, then I said something I had hardly even admitted to myself, it sounded so self-important. "I have a feeling that this is a time for waiting, that something enormous is going to happen to me and I must just be patient and wait for it. I don't know what it could be, but . . ." I shrugged and laughed. "I suppose that sounds arrogant."

"No, I don't think so, Mary. There is something about you—and I don't mean your looks—that is different. You seem . . . significant in a way we other women aren't. I can't explain it, but I can feel it. And I'm not the only one."

I was so surprised that I couldn't answer.

She smiled. "Have you thought of marrying again? You love children. Anyone can see it from the way you are with mine. It's not too late for you to have your own children, you know."

I stared at the charcoal brazier that was keeping the room so snug and warm. I'd once had thoughts of marriage, and the baby I had lost was still an open wound in my heart. But I couldn't imagine anyone who could put the faces of Daniel and Marcus out of my mind.

Before I could answer, we heard a knock at the door. Then Elisabeth came in again, this time announcing the arrival of Rebecca's husband.

I had come to know Simon Peter rather well. He was a big man, with a huge chest and shoulders and a deep, resonant voice. There wasn't a subtle bone in his body; he was always straightforward and to the point. I liked him. He was a good man.

"What are you doing here?" Rebecca asked. "I thought you and Andrew were going to work on the boat."

"The wind is whipping off the lake, and Andrew has a cough and a runny nose, so we decided to wait until tomorrow. When I heard you were over here, I decided to come along to enjoy the quiet and warmth of Mary's salon with you."

He grinned at me, and I smiled back. "You're very welcome, Simon Peter."

His hair and beard were wet, probably from the spray off the lake. He sat close to the brazier, and I sent for more wine. We settled down to chat.

⤳

FULVIUS PETRUS ARRIVED IN Capernaum toward the end of winter, and I sent Jeremiah to the commander's house with an invitation for him and his wife to visit me.

They came the following afternoon. It was one of the few days the sun was shining, so we sat in the atrium. Elisabeth served wine and a bowl of our best olives. I was thankful that Fulvius Petrus was dressed in a plain white tunic and red wool robe. His wife, whose name I remembered was Portia, had also dressed simply. It would have been dreadful if the whole town had seen him marching down to my house in full uniform or—even worse—if he had come on horseback.

Fulvius was a nice-looking man, with the dark hair and eyes of Rome. I had spoken to him many times in Sepphoris, but I had no feel for what kind of man he was. In those days all other men had paled into insignificance beside Marcus.

He said, "I was delighted when Julia Tiberia told me you were in Capernaum. Portia and I have been looking forward to renewing our acquaintance."

I smiled.

"This is a lovely house," Portia said. "So different from what one usually sees in a Jewish city."

"Thank you."

The two of them exchanged a glance, clearly wondering why I had invited them if I wasn't going to talk with them.

I sighed. "I must be frank with you. After my husband died, I came to Capernaum to start a new life. I grew up on the lake, in the town of Magdala, and I have always loved it here."

I paused.

Portia said, "The lake is lovely."

"Yes, indeed," Fulvius said.

I bit my lip. "You see, no one here knows anything about my life in Sepphoris. I have returned to my Jewish roots. I have made friends. I go to the synagogue." I waved my hand in a helpless gesture.

Fulvius nodded slowly. "And you don't want anyone to know about Marcus Novius Claudius."

I looked directly into his eyes. "No, I don't."

Portia said, "There's no reason for us to mention his name. He has gone back to Rome, you know." She gave me a reassuring smile.

The relief I felt was immense. "Thank you," I whispered.

"Dismiss him from your mind," Fulvius said briskly. "What I would really like to discuss with you is the state of things in Capernaum. This is the first time I've been put in command of a Jewish city. Would you share with me what you know?"

"I'd be happy to," I said.

They remained with me for an hour, and when they left, I felt as if I had pushed another rock up against the door to my past.

Chapter Twenty-One

THE WINTER STORMS GAVE way to the warm sunshine of spring and suddenly it was time for Passover. The people of Capernaum usually traveled to Jerusalem for the holiday in a caravan, and when Ruth and Nathaniel invited me to travel with their family, I accepted. Bethany was only a few miles from Jerusalem, and it would be a good opportunity for me to visit my brother and sister.

When I wrote to tell Lazarus that I was coming to visit, he also invited Ruth's family to stay. I had known he would do that, and Ruth and Nathaniel were happy to accept the invitation.

The trip brought back memories of the Passover journeys I had made from Magdala—and memories of Daniel. Was he happy in his celibate life out in the desert? Did they ever hear news of the outside world? Could he possibly know that I was a widow?

Stop it, I told myself. *That part of your life is over.* I bent to pick up Ruth's youngest child, who was lagging.

The road from Capernaum to Jericho was thick with caravans. Ruth said she had never seen the road as congested as it was this year, and we soon found out the reason. A prophet was preaching in the region of the Jordan, and many of these people were traveling to see him.

Nathaniel discovered this when he fell into conversation with a man from Bethsaida on the first evening we stopped to camp. He brought the news back to our group while were still sitting around the fire.

"Prophet?" one of the men said. "I've heard nothing of a prophet."

Murmurs of agreement came from the rest of the men.

"Did you get his name?" someone asked.

Nathaniel said, "They call him the 'Baptizer' because he is baptizing people in the waters of the Jordan."

The man across from me grunted. "There are always prophets. It's an easy life, if you ask me. All you have to do is talk a lot of rubbish, and people are happy to feed you and house you as if you were the Messiah himself."

Ruth said, "What does 'baptizing' mean, Nathaniel?"

"According to the man I spoke with, the prophet pours river water over people's heads and tells them to repent and their sins will be forgiven."

Silence reigned as we all thought about this. I would certainly like to have my sins forgiven, but I didn't see how someone pouring water over me could accomplish that. I said, "I thought only the Lord could forgive sins."

"Mary's right," someone agreed. "It's not for mere men, even if they are prophets, to forgive sins. Only the Lord can do that."

The man across from me grinned through his massive beard. "It sounds like a good show, though. It might be interesting to take a look."

Ruth's eldest son, Eli, turned to Nathaniel. "Can we go, Papa? I've never seen a prophet."

The rest of the children added their voices to Eli's. They had been born on the lake, and the idea of having water poured over their heads didn't frighten them. From the looks on their faces, they thought it would be great fun.

Nathaniel looked sternly at his own children, who were sitting between him and Ruth. "We're not going to waste time gawking at any so-called prophet. We've made this journey to celebrate Passover in Jerusalem, and that is what we're going to do."

The children bowed their heads in acceptance of the paternal decision, but Eli didn't look happy.

❧

IT WAS LATE AFTERNOON by the time we arrived in Bethany. As soon as Martha saw us coming up the road, she ran to greet us. We hugged and I introduced her to Nathaniel, Ruth, and the children. Martha clucked over them and told them she had food and drink in the house. They flocked after her like little chicks following their mother.

"Lazarus is in the courtyard," she called over her shoulder to me, so I invited Ruth and Nathaniel to come and meet my brother.

He was sitting at the long table under the fig tree, and he stood as I introduced my cousin and her husband. I looked closely at Lazarus' fine-boned face and was relieved to see that the pain lines that so often marked it were absent. His color was good, and he looked healthy.

He invited us to sit, pouring cups of water and offering a plate of figs. After we had been served, he asked about our journey.

Nathaniel said, "The road was even more crowded than usual this year. I heard that there is some self-proclaimed prophet preaching in the region of the Jordan, and many of the people were going to see him."

"Yes, we've heard about him here in Bethany," Lazarus replied.

I said, "Supposedly he is forgiving sins by pouring water over people's heads. I thought that only the Lord could do that."

"That's true, Mary. But John—that's his name—isn't saying that he's forgiving sins. He's saying that if people repent, then the Lord will forgive them."

"Where did he come from?" Ruth asked. "We've heard nothing of him in Capernaum."

"One day he just walked out of the Judean desert. I've heard he was an Essene."

I put my cup down so hard that water splashed onto the table. "An Essene? I thought they could never leave their settlement."

"A few of them do. There is a house in Jerusalem where some of them live."

All three looked at me. They knew about Daniel, of course.

Lazarus said gently, "The men who live in Jerusalem are older, Mary. I think perhaps that desert living became too harsh for them."

I nodded, picked up my cup, and took a long drink. *Daniel and I are finished*, I told myself. *Too much has happened for us to be as once we were.*

Lazarus turned to Nathaniel. "He's made quite a stir, this prophet. Some people are saying he's the Messiah. Even some of the Pharisees and Sadducees from Jerusalem have gone to him to be baptized."

"Really?" Nathaniel said in amazement.

This was truly stunning news. The Pharisees and Sadducees hated each other. The Pharisees weren't a class; they were individuals who resided in the towns and villages of the country. They followed the Law to the letter so they would go to heaven when they died. The Sadducees were priests and aristocrats. They lived mainly in Jerusalem and thought a person's reward came in this life. They were immensely powerful because they controlled the Sanhedrin, the highest legislative and judicial body in the country.

I heard youngsters' voices and turned to see Martha shepherding Ruth's children out to the courtyard. They sat at the table with us and were quiet, as well-brought-up children always were in the presence of adult conversation. But when Lazarus said something else about the Baptizer, Eli couldn't contain himself.

He tugged on his father's sleeve. "Please can't we go to see him, Papa? I may never have the chance to see a prophet again."

Nathaniel frowned at the interruption.

My brother said, "I've been planning to go see him myself. It's amazing the effect this man seems to have on people. Anyone who can impress both Pharisees and Sadducees must have some unusual powers."

Nathaniel's lips twitched into a small smile. "That is a true word."

Eli had enough sense to keep quiet.

I said, "I would like to see him too."

Eli shot me a grateful look.

"We could go tomorrow," Lazarus proposed. "He's preaching just south of Jericho. If we start early enough we can be there and back before dark."

Nathaniel looked at his eldest son's hopeful face and sighed. "All right. Passover doesn't begin for another day. Let's go to see this prophet, John the Baptizer."

⁓

MARTHA REMAINED AT HOME with the two youngest children, and Lazarus, Nathaniel, Ruth, and I started off the next morning with the two oldest. We went by the well-traveled merchant's route and reached the ford south of Jericho by noon.

There was a mass of people crowded on the riverbanks and we heard the prophet's voice before we were able to see him. He was repeating the same words over and over: *"Repent. The Kingdom of God is upon you. Repent and believe."*

I had expected a big booming voice, like Simon Peter's, but this voice was high-pitched, nasal, and piercing. We threaded our way through the crowd, Nathaniel and Lazarus in the lead with the rest of us right behind them. Finally we were close enough to the river to see what was happening.

Hundreds of fully clothed people were wading in water up to their thighs to where the prophet stood. He was thin, to the point of emaciation, with wild black hair and a flowing, unkempt beard. He appeared to be dressed in some kind of animal skin, which he had cinched about his middle by a rope. His skin was deeply browned, and even from the shore, I could see the glint in his dark eyes. He looked quite mad.

I watched him pour water out of his cupped hands over the heads of the people as they came to him. Each time, his thin, piercing voice commanded them to repent of their sins and make themselves clean for the coming of the kingdom.

I had no desire to wade into the river, no belief that the prophet could forgive my sins. But there was something riveting about that solitary figure. The whole scene seemed unreal, yet all of us watching were enthralled.

Eli and his brother Moses had taken their father's hands. Nathaniel asked, "Do you want to go into the river?" Both boys shook their heads vehemently that they did not.

Moses asked in a small voice, "Is that what a prophet is supposed to look like?"

All of a sudden the crowd, which had been well behaved, began to push and shove. Nathaniel pulled his sons close to his side, and Lazarus put protective arms around Ruth and me.

"What's happening?" Ruth asked.

I stood on tiptoe and saw that the pushing crowd had created a pathway and two men were walking through the opened space. Their immaculate white garments shone in the bright spring sun. The pristine tunics and their arrogant manner told me that they must be Temple priests.

They stopped just short of the water's edge, making sure their spotless sandals stayed dry.

The crowd was eerily quiet. Even John's nasal voice had fallen silent as he looked at the two men standing on the shore.

One of the priests called out, "You. Who do you think you are? Is it true that you have been telling people that you're the Messiah?"

John took a step toward the shore, the water eddying around him. "You want to know who I am?"

"Yes. That is precisely what we want to know."

A harsh, rusty-sounding laugh came from John, and then he raised his voice. "Who am I? '*I am a voice crying aloud in the wilderness.*'" He took another step toward the priests. "I have been sent to prepare the way of the Lord. That is who I am."

I looked at Lazarus, and he looked back at me, raising his eyebrows. There were murmurs all around us from the crowd.

The priest's voice reverberated with anger. "Don't dare quote scripture to me. We have come here to find out if you are the Messiah. If you're afraid to answer us, then you must be a fraud."

John bent and cupped some water in his hand. He watched it as it trickled through his fingers. Then he looked up and this time his voice was quiet, "I baptize with water for repentance; but I tell you there is one coming after me who is mightier than I, and he will baptize with the fire of the Holy Spirit."

Even from a distance I could see the priest stiffen. "What man? Of whom are you speaking?"

John's face contorted with fury. He began to wade toward the shore, yelling as he came, "You viper's brood! Do you really think you will escape retribution for what you do?"

The priests backed away. Then, as John continued to come toward them, they turned and hurried back up the path. John shouted insults after them until they were out of sight.

The crowd was buzzing with excitement.

Moses said in a trembling voice, "I'm not sure if I like prophets, Papa."

"We'll go," Nathaniel said. Holding his sons' hands, he nodded to Ruth to join them, and they began to retrace their steps to the road.

Lazarus remained where he was, his eyes fixed on the figure still standing in the river.

"What are you thinking?" I asked.

"I'm wondering who he is. And I'm wondering who he might be speaking about."

He turned away and put a hand on my arm. "Come along, Mary. We had better go with your cousins."

Chapter Twenty-Two

I HADN'T BEEN TO THE Temple for Passover in years. As I waited for Ruth to come out of the house with her family, I chatted with Lazarus and tried not to show how uneasy I was. I had come a long way from the girl who had stood on the Mount of Olives and regarded the beauty of the Temple with awe and respect. It might still be a beautiful building, but now I had serious doubts about what went on inside its walls.

The Temple had driven Daniel away, and he was the most deeply religious person I knew. Daniel loved the Lord with all his heart, yet he had turned his back on the heart of Jewish worship. I still remembered every word he had said to me: "Our religious leaders have been corrupted by money. Animal sacrifice, and the money it brings in, is the business of the Temple these days, not prayer. We need to be saved from ourselves as well as from the Romans."

During the years I dutifully accompanied Aaron to the Temple, I had seen the truth of Daniel's words for myself. I hated the selling of animals. I hated the stench of the burned offerings that engulfed the city as the priests, for a price, slaughtered hundreds of thousands of lambs and burned their entrails and fat in supposed sacrifice to the Lord.

I spoke none of these dangerous thoughts to my companions. Instead I kept them to myself as I accompanied them along the well-worn road from Bethany to Jerusalem. Then I remained with Ruth and her children in the Court of the Women while Nathaniel and Lazarus took the lambs they had purchased up to the Court of the Priests.

We returned home well before sunset so Martha could have supper ready when the light died and Passover officially began. Martha took the basket of lamb's meat from Lazarus, saying, "The rest of you, go to the courtyard and let us begin to prepare the meal."

Martha and Ruth started toward the kitchen, and I took a few steps after them. Martha saw me, stopped, and said kindly, "Go along to the courtyard and help with the children, Mary. Ruth and I will be fine. I have two girls coming in to assist us."

I was hurt. "But I want to help with the meal."

Martha smiled. "You haven't been inside a kitchen since you left Magdala, Mary. You'll only be in the way."

Ruth said to Martha, "She didn't do much cooking in Magdala either. But she was always good with the children." She looked at her girls. "Do you want Aunt Mary to go with you?"

Adah took my hand and beamed up at me. "Yes!"

I had no choice but to turn and go with the men and children into the courtyard. But I felt rejected.

By the time the sun had set and supper was ready, I had gotten over my ruffled feelings. We sat in the front room, where tables had been arranged in a square, with one side of the square left empty. Lazarus, as our host, sat at the top of the square, with the rest of us filling in the other two sides.

The Passover meal is long, with many hand washings and prayers between courses. I sat through it all with a warm glow of happiness at being here with my family.

I listened as Lazarus told us about the evil deeds of Pharaoh and about the Israelites' escape from captivity in Egypt. The ancient story of the lamb's blood marking the doors of all Jews, so the angel of Death would pass them by, always made a chill run up and down my spine.

As I looked around the table, I felt deeply and profoundly that this was where my life was meant to be rooted. These good and kind people were my people. Impulsively, I leaned over and kissed Martha on the cheek.

She smiled at me, showing her dimples. "What was that for?"

"It's to thank you for this wonderful meal and because I love you."

Her dimples deepened. "I love you too, Mary. We're so happy to have you here with us on this holy night."

"I'm happy to be here," I said. And I meant it with all my heart.

⋙

I HAD BEEN BACK in Capernaum for a few weeks when I heard talk going around the marketplace that John the Baptizer had named another man as his successor. John had baptized many of the people in town, and they were agog at this news. Everyone wanted to know who the new prophet might be.

A few weeks later, news came to Fulvius Petrus that Herod Antipas had arrested John. The Romans were always the first to hear any news of importance because it came by horseback via the Roman Messenger Service.

Fulvius immediately informed the rabbi of John's arrest, knowing it would be of great interest to the town. Sharing of information wasn't common among Roman commanders, but in the short time Fulvius had been in Capernaum, he had reached out to the Jewish leaders, even donating money to the synagogue. If a Roman could ever be said to be popular in a Jewish community, Fulvius was popular in Capernaum.

He came in person to tell me about John. I took him to sit in my garden, which sloped down almost to the lakeshore. It was a sunny day, and Jeremiah brought us wine and a plate of olives.

Fulvius waited until we had been served before he told me about the arrest. "It all dates back to Antipas' seduction of his brother Philip's wife, Herodias," he said as he rolled an olive in his fingers before popping it into his mouth.

Everyone in Galilee knew about that scandal. Philip was the Tetrarch of the region north of Galilee, and he and Antipas were both sons of Herod the Great. Even worse than the seduction of a brother's wife was the fact that Antipas had proceeded to marry her while his brother was still living.

This action went directly against Jewish law, and Antipas had been denounced by virtually every Jew in Galilee. The situation—the seduction of a married woman and the subsequent marriage—hit too close to my own life for me to be comfortable discussing it, and I avoided it whenever possible.

Fulvius continued, "John made the mistake of publicly accusing Antipas of committing incest by marrying his brother's wife."

I said, "I don't imagine Antipas cared to be reprimanded by a prophet everyone was listening to,"

"Not at all. John was safe enough while he remained in Judea, which is under Roman rule, but once he crossed into Galilee, he came under the jurisdiction of Antipas, who had him arrested and thrown into the fortress of Machaerus."

I felt a rush of pity as I thought of that wild figure standing in the river. How terrible it would be for such a man to live without fresh air and light.

Soon after the news of John's imprisonment, rumors came to Capernaum about his chosen successor. Instead of baptizing, he was preaching in all the towns around the lake.

Again, Fulvius Petrus was the one who brought me the information. I knew the local Pharisees were outraged that I should entertain a man who wasn't a member of my family—and a Roman!—but I ignored them. I enjoyed Fulvius' visits too much to put a halt to them, and my friends, and the families to whom I had loaned money, all stood behind me.

I was still officially an anonymous donor, but the recipients had figured out where the money was coming from. We kept up the pretense of anonymity to save face, and the rabbi continued to be the official dispenser of funds.

The pleasure I took in Fulvius' visits made me feel slightly guilty. Like Julia, he was a connection to a life I had renounced, but it was enjoyable to talk to a well-read person about poetry and philosophy. I had bought quite a number of books for my new library, and I still ordered books from Julia's bookseller in Rome. I had tried to get a Greek translation of the Hebrew Scriptures, but the bookseller had informed me it was impossible. There was no such translation. To read Jewish scripture you had to know Hebrew, and the only people trained to read Hebrew were the Jewish hierarchy.

This disturbed me. I had wanted very much to read the Word of the Lord for myself.

On one pleasant afternoon Fulvius and I were sitting in my garden, looking out at the lake with all the fishing boats bobbing on its rippling surface.

Fulvius took a sip of wine and said, "The new teacher's name is Jesus of Nazareth. He's creating a frenzy all along the lake because he is supposedly working miracles."

Miracles, I thought. Miracles always made me skeptical. "What kind of miracles?"

"He is said to have cured many sick people."

I shrugged. "Sometimes sick people get well on their own, especially when they believe they'll get well. I've seen it happen more than once."

"True, but I must confess I'm curious to see him. He's working his way around the lake, so he's sure to come to Capernaum soon. Then we can judge for ourselves."

I smiled, but I didn't share Fulvius' curiosity. Nothing any prophet could say or do would bring back what I most longed for—my baby.

Chapter Twenty-Three

Aweek later Jesus of Nazareth came to Capernaum. He preached at synagogue on the Sabbath, but I wasn't there to hear him because I was menstruating. Rebecca wasn't able to go either, as her mother, who lived with them, was very ill. Simon Peter came home sparking with excitement about the new teacher, and Rebecca stopped by to tell me about it after their Sabbath meal.

She brought along her two youngest daughters, Leah and Deborah, because she knew I loved the little girls. I gave them the dolls I kept for them, and Rebecca and I settled at the table in the courtyard where we could keep an eye on the children as they played.

"I needed a rest," Rebecca confessed, as she sipped fresh pomegranate juice. "Andrew's wife volunteered to sit with my mother for a bit, and I wanted to tell you what Peter said about the wonders of this new teacher."

"What is so wonderful about him?"

"Quite a lot, according to my husband. He started off as usual, reading a passage from scripture, and then he spoke to the congregation about what it meant."

I nodded. This was indeed the synagogue procedure. The rabbi could ask anyone to read the scripture and give the address. Often it was a scribe or a Pharisee, but the rabbi could call upon any Jewish man who had a message. Our rabbi had called upon this new teacher.

Rebecca continued, "Peter said that what made Jesus' talk so different was that he never once called upon the rabbinical rules to back up his teaching. You know how it is when the scribes preach. They say something, and then they tell you about all the scripture and rabbinical references that support their comment. Jesus spoke as if he were the authority, as if he needed no one else to testify to the truth of what he preached. Peter said he was exhilarating."

I knew what it was like to endure lengthy lists of citations, and I could understand why everyone found this refreshing. But was that enough to have created such enthusiasm in Peter? True, he was an emotional man, but—

"Mama!" Leah called.

We looked at the girls. Deborah had both the dolls. Rebecca said, "Deborah, give your sister's doll back to her, and play nicely."

After Deborah had restored the doll to Leah, Rebecca turned to me. I said, "It must have made a nice change, to have someone speak out directly, but is that all?"

"No," Rebecca said. "Listen to this. There was a man in the synagogue possessed by an evil spirit. When he heard the words of Jesus, his demon cried out, 'What have you to do with us, Jesus of Nazareth? I know who you are, you are the Holy One of God.'"

My eyes widened. "What happened after that?"

"Jesus said to the demon, 'Be silent and come out of him.'" She paused.

"Rebecca! Don't tease. What happened next?"

"The man threw himself to the floor and rolled around. The

demon howled and then—it came out! The man was himself again, and the demon was gone."

I was silent. This was truly an amazing story. Jews believed there were many demons in the world, malignant beings that hated God and took possession of people's bodies to do their evil work. There were special people who had the power to lure the demons out with charms, rituals, and incantations. Sometimes this ceremony worked; often it did not.

However, for a demon to be vanquished by one simple command was certainly extraordinary enough to make people take notice.

❧

I WAS STILL UNCLEAN the following day, but the day after that I was able to go to the marketplace. The name of Jesus was on everyone's lips. I hadn't heard such passionate interest in a single topic since the Baptizer's arrest.

It was a hot day, and when I got home I asked Jeremiah to bring some water to the garden. I wanted to sit by the lake, where there was always a breeze. I pulled off my veil and pushed up the long sleeves of my tunic, wistfully remembering the light silk sleeveless Roman clothes I used to wear. When I heard Jeremiah's steps I turned to ask him something and saw that Rebecca was following him.

She looked furious.

"What is it?" I asked as she came up beside me.

"You won't believe what has happened!" Her cheeks were red, and she was out of breath.

I pointed to the bench beside me. "Sit, before you collapse in this heat. Jeremiah, put the water on the table, and bring another cup, please."

"Yes, my lady."

I filled the single cup and passed it to Rebecca. "Drink this."

She shook her head. "I don't want to drink your water."

"Jeremiah is bringing another cup. Drink this, and then you can tell me what has upset you."

She accepted the cup and drained it. As she put it down on the small table in front of us, I said, "Now, what is it?"

The words exploded out of her. "That man, that Jesus of Nazareth, has k-kidnapped my h-husband!"

She was so furious that she stuttered as she spoke.

"What are you talking about?"

"Simon and Andrew were fishing from the shore this morning, and this teacher, or whatever he calls himself, came walking down the beach. And he took them! Just like that. He took them!"

She wasn't making sense. "How did he take them, Rebecca? He didn't drag the both of them away by himself."

"Don't be funny," she snapped.

"I'm not trying to be funny. I'm trying to understand what happened."

Her face went from furious to frightened. I reached over and put my hand over hers, as they lay clenched in her lap. "Tell me."

She nodded and shut her eyes for a moment. Then she opened them and looked at me. "This is what I heard from old Isaac. You know how he's always hanging around the lake?"

I nodded.

"He saw it happen. He said Peter and Andrew had cast their nets into the water and were slowly dragging them back to the shore, when this man, this Jesus of Nazareth, went up to them and told them to follow him, that he would make them fishers of men."

"Fishers of men?" I repeated.

"Yes. And they went, Mary! They dropped their nets on the shore, with whatever fish they had caught still in them, and wandered off after this man as if he were King David."

Her anger had burned itself out, and now her lips began to tremble.

"When did this happen?" I asked.

"Yesterday." A tear rolled down her cheek. "I haven't seen Peter since. He asked old Isaac to tell me he wouldn't be home for supper, and he hasn't come back yet." She sniffed.

I was having a hard time believing this story. What could the man have meant, *fishers of men*?

I had another thought, which I didn't share with Rebecca. Why would a learned man, who could read scripture and preach in the synagogue, want Simon Peter as a follower? It's not that Peter wasn't a good man. He was a very good man. But he was a man who thought with his heart, not his head. He was a simple fisherman, not a scholar.

"And you don't know where he is?" I asked.

"No. I have five children and a sick mother at home, and he's off following some golden-tongued stranger." She stood up. "Well, if Peter thinks I'm going to sit at home with his supper, waiting for him to decide when he's ready to join us, he's mistaken. I'm going down to the shorefront now to see if I can find him. I was hoping you would come with me."

Simon Peter would be furious if his wife showed up to drag him back home as if he was a runaway child.

"Do you think that's wise? Perhaps it would be best to wait. He'll come home eventually, Rebecca. You know he will."

"I don't care if it's wise. I'm going. If you don't want to come with me, I'll go alone."

I stood up. "Of course I'll come with you."

For the first time that day I saw her smile. "I knew you would," she said.

I sighed, rolled down my sleeves, put on my veil, and led the way down to the shore.

⊗

THE SUN WAS HIGH in the sky as we walked along the shingle beach that lined the lakeshore. The sun-bright water was dotted with fishing boats, and two or three men were casting their nets from the beach. They stared at us as we walked by. The lakeshore belonged to men; women had no place here. We ignored them and walked on.

We quickly came upon Peter's boat. It was pulled up on shore with the sea fishing nets neatly stowed in the bow. Someone had emptied the fish from the shore nets and hung them on the side of the boat to dry.

This was truly an astonishing sight. Peter and Andrew treated their boat as if it were made of gold. It represented their livelihoods; it fed both their families. To see it sitting there, uncovered and neglected, was a shock.

As we stared at the abandoned boat, old Isaac shuffled up to join us. "That teacher man took them," he said. "He took Zebedee's two boys too."

We looked at the old man, whose skin was a nest of leathery wrinkles from perpetual exposure to the elements. "He took James and John too?" Rebecca asked.

"Yep. Just like he took your man. They got right out of the boat and left their poor old father alone."

"But where did they go?" I asked.

185

He shrugged. "Away."

Something very strange was going on, but we weren't going to solve it by standing here. The sun was blazing off the water, and I was sweating under my veil and tunic. I put my hand on Rebecca's elbow. "Come along, Rebecca. Let's go home. Simon Peter is sure to show up sometime, and you can give him a piece of your mind when he makes his appearance."

She pinched her lips together. Then she nodded. "All right. I suppose that's the only thing I can do."

❧

BEFORE I WENT HOME, I paid a brief visit to Rebecca's sick mother. Rebecca was worried about her and with cause. I had seen fevers like that carry off many elderly people.

I took Rebecca's daughters home with me to give her more quiet time with her mother. Leah told me when we reached my courtyard that they wanted to go into my house to play. I knew what they really wanted was a treat from Elisabeth, so I took them into the kitchen, where Elisabeth obliged with slices of almond cake. Then we went into the front room and were playing a word game that had them both in giggles when Jeremiah escorted Rebecca's oldest son into the room.

Abram was breathless from running. He looked like his mother, with curling black hair and bright brown eyes sparkling now with excitement. "Father has come home, and I'm to bring my sisters back. Mother wants you to come too, Mary."

I didn't want to find myself in the middle of what I feared might be a domestic squabble, so I smiled and said, "You don't need me to bring the girls home, Abram. You're perfectly able to do that by yourself."

He shook his head vigorously. "No, they *want* you to come. Father has brought the teacher with him—the one who spoke in the synagogue—and he has cured Grandma of her fever!"

Chapter Twenty-Four

THERE WAS A GATE in the fence between my property and Peter's, and Abram led us through, directly into the courtyard where his family was gathered.

"Grandma!" Leah called, running to the woman who was sitting on a bench under the fig tree.

I stood just inside the gate and stared at Hannah as Leah went to kiss her. She had been burning up with fever only an hour and a half ago; now she was sitting in the shade of the tree, her face rosy with health, a toothless smile on her face.

My eyes moved to the stranger who was sitting beside Peter. Jesus of Nazareth looked back at me.

He was an ordinary-looking man, slim, with medium brown hair and a close-cut beard. He was not handsome like Daniel, nor did he have the dominating presence of Marcus. But his eyes were a clear, amber brown, and they looked into mine as if he knew me.

Simon Peter said, "Master, this is our neighbor, Mary of Magdala."

I immediately noted that Peter hadn't used the Jewish word that means "Teacher." He chose instead the Greek word for "Master."

Jesus of Nazareth said, in the unmistakable accent of Galilee, "I am pleased to meet you, Mary of Magdala."

There was something in those eyes that held me captive. I sought for something to say. "I'm sorry I missed your talk at the synagogue."

"There will be others," he replied.

He had a wonderful voice. People would listen to him just to hear that voice. But he was making me feel unsure of myself, a feeling I didn't often experience and didn't like. I said, "You speak as if you come from Galilee."

"Yes. I am originally from Nazareth, but I spent most of my adult years with the Essenes."

The Essenes! My back stiffened. I burned to ask if he knew Daniel.

Rebecca said, "Mary, the Master healed my mother!"

I broke eye contact with Jesus and went to kiss Hannah. "I'm so glad to see that you are better."

"It was a miracle," she said, casting adoring eyes at Jesus. "The Master came to my sickbed, took my hand, raised me up, and I was cured!"

Rebecca said, "I had to drag her out of the kitchen, she was so determined to get back to work."

I remembered Hannah's sunken, suffering face and didn't know what to say.

Rebecca held out a hand. "Come and sit beside me."

I crossed to sit on the bench next to her and rested my hand on Leah's small round head as she sat on the ground before us.

Simon Peter said proudly, "The Master has been performing miracles like this in all the towns around the lake."

I looked at Jesus. "Have you always had this power . . . Master?"

His eyes were calm. He sat quietly, with his hands in his lap, yet

189

all of us in the courtyard, even the children, were completely focused on his slender figure.

He said softly, "I do miracles now because it is the time for them."

Simon Peter, always a direct man, said, "Why is this the time, Master?"

Jesus looked from Peter to Andrew, who was sitting on Peter's other side. "I have begun my father's mission, and I work miracles so that you might believe in me and in what I have come to bring to you."

The men gazed back at him, their faces filled with awe.

My father's mission? What can the man be talking about?

"Just what is it you have come to bring us?" I asked in my most neutral voice.

Simon Peter scowled at me. "I'm sorry, Master. Mary isn't like other women. She is her own mistress, which sometimes makes her forget her place."

I glared at Peter. How dare he apologize for me?

Jesus said, "Do not chastise her, Peter. She wishes to learn." He looked at me directly, as if I were the only person in the courtyard, and said, "I have come to bring you the Kingdom of God."

❧

BEFORE I COULD BEGIN to take in what he had said, a group of men surged into the courtyard from the house. I recognized Simon Peter's fellow fishermen, James and John, and their father Zebedee; Ruth's husband, Nathaniel; and a number of other men from the synagogue. They crowded around Jesus, eagerly asking questions.

Rebecca said in my ear, "Do you think all these men will expect to stay for supper?"

She sounded anxious, and with good reason. She didn't have the means to feed so many people without notice. I whispered back, "Don't worry. I'll have supper for everyone at my house. Elisabeth always has plenty of food, and my house is bigger than yours."

She gave me a relieved smile. "Thank you, Mary."

"I'll slip out now and alert Elisabeth."

She nodded, and I made my way to the gate between our properties.

When the heat of the day began to wane, Peter brought the men over to my house, where the table was laid and the food already cooked. Rebecca had come earlier to assist Elisabeth, who had not been able to get her usual girls on such short notice.

The men sat down, with Jesus at the head of the table and Simon Peter in the seat of honor at his right. We left Elisabeth to work in the kitchen, and Rebecca and I served the meal.

For the next two hours the two of us ran back and forth between the dining room and the kitchen, changing dishes and filling cups. Part of me wished that I could be sitting with the men, listening to Jesus, but the other part thought it would be wisest to keep my distance from someone I perceived as possibly dangerous. I didn't need another charismatic man in my life.

Night had fallen, and Jeremiah was lighting the lamps when we heard the noise of many people outside. This was unusual. There were only two houses on this little road, and it was always very quiet.

Jeremiah went to the door, and when he opened it, we could clearly hear loud voices calling for the Master. *Heal me!* they were crying. *Heal my son!—Heal my daughter!—Heal my mother, my father, my aunt, my uncle!*

Jeremiah came back into the dining room and said, "I think every sick person in Capernaum is gathered outside our door, my lady."

Jesus stood up. "I will go out to them."

Peter jumped up as well. "Not alone, you won't! We will all come with you, Master."

"Go to the door and tell them the Master is coming," I said to Jeremiah. I didn't want an unruly crowd of frantic people storming into my home.

Rebecca and I followed behind the men as they filed into the small front garden, which was being thoroughly trampled by the noisy crowd. Jesus pitched his voice to be heard by all: "There is no need to push. My father's mercy is for all. Wait, and I will come to you."

He waded into the crowd, moving among them, laying his hands on the sick and speaking quietly. Cries of incredulous joy and heartfelt thanksgiving followed wherever he went.

I turned and went back into the house. Rebecca followed.

"Who is this 'father' Jesus speaks of?" I asked her as we went into the atrium to wait until the crowd had dispersed. "Nazareth is a village of artisans. People in Sepphoris used to employ them all the time. There are no priests or holy men in Nazareth."

"I don't know what he means," Rebecca said. "But he has amazing power, Mary. He was healing people out there. And he certainly healed my mother."

I couldn't deny that. But men with power were dangerous, and often, the greater the power, the greater the danger. I learned that in Sepphoris. Powerful men would stop at nothing to get what they wanted.

Keep yourself safe, Mary. Stay away from that man.

❧

THE FOLLOWING MORNING SIMON Peter came to see me. Jesus had spent the night at his house, but Peter told me the Master had risen early and gone out alone into the countryside. Peter and Andrew and the sons of Zebedee followed him, begging him to return to Capernaum. He said that he would return but that he needed time alone to be with his father.

There it was again. His father. There was something peculiar about the way he spoke of his father.

Peter found me in my garden, working on the roses. It would be a few years before they would look like the roses I had grown in Sepphoris, and I tended to them with painstaking care.

I stood there silently with the garden scissors in my hand, waiting for Peter to get to the reason for his visit.

He said, "The Master is determined to travel to all the towns he hasn't yet reached in Galilee. He wants me and Andrew and James and John to go with him, Mary. He's chosen us to be his followers."

I put my scissors down to study Simon Peter's face, trying to see something in it I might have missed. But I saw nothing more than the man I knew. A following that included Peter and other common men like him hardly seemed an auspicious way to start a ministry.

I said, "Do you want to go with him?"

"We all want to go. Very much. Jesus of Nazareth isn't like anyone we've ever seen before, Mary. He has come to us as an emissary from the Lord. I'm sure of it." Peter's brown eyes were glowing. His whole face was glowing. He said, "I think he might be the Messiah."

My head snapped back. "Are you serious?"

"I've never been more serious in my life."

And I had never heard him sound so serious. "Andrew wants to go as well?"

"Andrew, James, and John, we all want to go."

Andrew was a surprise. Peter could be volatile, but Andrew was steady, a man who could be relied on to rein in Peter's more far-fetched enthusiasms. And Zebedee's two sons were another surprise. Zebedee owned a number of boats, and his sons looked to inherit a thriving business. James and John were well aware of their worth and didn't seem the kind of men who would turn their backs on their inheritance to follow an unproven teacher, or prophet, or whatever Jesus of Nazareth was.

"How long would you be gone?" I asked.

Peter looked anxious. "That's just it . . . I'm not sure. The Master wants to preach in all the towns. We could be away for a month, maybe more."

I was beginning to understand why he had come to me. "And your wife? Your children?"

Peter's face had flushed scarlet. He mumbled, "We were hoping that perhaps you could take care of them until we returned."

He was looking down at his sandals, unable to meet my eyes. It impressed me that this proud man could feel so strongly about Jesus of Nazareth that he would humble himself to ask for money.

I couldn't let him humiliate himself any further. "Of course I'll take care of your families, Simon Peter. Consider it my gift to your Master."

Tears glistened in his eyes. He took my hand and pressed it. "Thank you, Mary. You are a good woman, and the Lord will bless you for your many kindnesses."

"I certainly hope so," I replied with a smile.

My attempt to defuse his emotion worked, and he smiled back. "I'll speak to Rebecca now."

"Tell her I'll be by to see her later this afternoon."

"I will."

I watched as he strode across my garden, an ordinary fisherman transformed by a preacher from Nazareth.

Chapter Twenty-Five

GALILEE HAS ITS OWN system of spreading news from town to town, so Capernaum received regular reports about Jesus of Nazareth and the miracles he was performing around the province.

This information was delivered in various ways—by people who had seen the miracles themselves, by a family member of someone who had seen the miracles, and by our rabbi, who received news from other synagogue leaders about the amazing things that were happening.

Jesus cast out demons. He cured a man with a withered hand. He cured a man who was paralyzed. He cured a leper.

This last was the most unsettling miracle of all. Jews believed that leprosy was God's punishment on those who had sinned gravely. If this was true, it must follow that only God can cure a leper, because the sin must be forgiven before the body can be healed. And only God can forgive sin. Consequently there was great division in town about this supposed "cure." The Pharisees didn't believe it, and even the rabbi was uncertain.

Then one day a stranger came to our synagogue and told us the most astounding story. It was brutally hot on that particular Sabbath, and I was crammed between Rebecca and Ruth on the synagogue benches. The service had almost finished when the rabbi invited the stranger to step forward and address us.

When the tall, thin man took his place before us, my only thought was *I hope he doesn't talk too long.* I was anxious to get home to my garden and the cool breeze off the lake. The restlessness that ran around the congregation told me I wasn't the only one eager to escape from the broiling synagogue.

Then the speaker introduced himself as Joshua bar Isaac, "the brother of the leper whom Jesus of Nazareth cured."

Suddenly every eye was glued to the man in front of us. He looked around at all our faces and said, "I am here to testify to the truth of this miracle."

Ezra bar Matthias stood and objected, but the rabbi told the Pharisee to let the man speak.

Joshua said, "My brother was a leper for many years. Everyone in our village knew him. Every day he stood with his begging bowl on the road that led in and out of town. I saw with my own eyes the progression of his illness. I saw how the white patches of dead skin grew to cover his face. I saw the tip of his nose begin to crumble. I left him food and spoke to him every day, and it broke my heart that I couldn't approach him, that I couldn't take his hand or give him the kiss of peace.

"On this particular day, my brother was at his usual post, and I was standing as close as I dared, telling him some news about our sister, when we both saw the teacher approaching with his following. As I watched in horror, my brother ran past me onto the road and threw himself at the teacher's feet.

"Everyone began to back away, shouting at my brother to get away from them, saying they would kill him if he dared to touch the teacher."

I glanced at Rebecca to see how she was taking this. Her gaze was riveted to the speaker's face.

Joshua paused. I had never heard the synagogue so silent. "The teacher didn't back away from my brother. Instead, he reached out and touched his cheek."

I felt a chill of horror run up my spine. How could Jesus have done such a thing? To touch the dead skin on a leper's face? How could he?

Joshua paused again, to allow us to take in the full power of what he had just described. His voice became a trifle louder, "Then the teacher said to my brother, '*Be made clean.*'"

I don't think anyone in the synagogue was breathing, so intently were we listening.

Joshua stretched out his arms. "And my brother was cured! It happened, my friends, under the eyes of us all. The dead skin on his face dropped away, leaving healthy skin in its place. His nose, his hands . . . everything that had begun to crumble was made whole again! My brother was cured!"

For a moment, there wasn't even a rustle of clothing in the synagogue. Then Ezra bar Matthias leaped to his feet. "You lie!" he shouted. "The Nazarene has paid you to go around telling this tale to boost his reputation!"

Joshua's face set into hard lines as he answered Ezra's accusation: "I tell the truth. That is why I have come here—and will go elsewhere— to testify to the truth. After the cure, the teacher told my brother to go and show himself to the priests so he could formally be declared clean. The priests knew my brother. They knew that he was a leper. They knew what they saw when he came to them. Talk to them, why don't you?"

Ezra turned to face the congregation. "This is a lie and a trick! Only God can cure a leper, because only God can forgive sins."

Suddenly, talk erupted among the listeners as they turned to each other to express their feelings about this story.

Rebecca said, "Let's go outside. It is stifling in here."

As I followed her up the aisle, I wondered: *If this man's story is true, then who is Jesus of Nazareth?*

SHAVUOT CAME AND WENT, and the reports about Jesus of Nazareth continued to flow into Capernaum. There were too many cures to question their validity. This teacher had the gift of healing.

I began to think about Lazarus. If Jesus could cure a man with leprosy, surely he could cure my brother of his headaches. So I wrote to Lazarus and begged him and Martha to come visit me. I didn't mention Jesus; I only said that I missed them and wanted them to see my house, now that it was furnished and the gardens were growing.

They arrived two weeks later, hot and dusty from the road. I sent Martha to my room so she could luxuriate in the Roman bath, and Lazarus dipped into the lake to cool down.

We met at the table in my garden. I had built a level stone patio into the sloping land so I could sit comfortably and enjoy the breeze. The lake was calm today, and all the fishing boats were out. I never tired of that scene.

We chatted for a while about what was happening in Bethany, and then I asked if they had heard about Jesus of Nazareth. They had.

Lazarus said, "He has angered many of the scribes and Pharisees in Jerusalem. They say he doesn't obey the cleanliness laws, that he and his disciples eat their food without the ritual washing of hands.

He even went to dinner in the house of a tax collector—and then he called the man to be one of his followers. A tax collector, Mary! People were outraged."

Tax collectors were universally hated and despised by the ordinary citizens of Galilee, and they were never allowed in the synagogue because they collected taxes for Rome.

"I hadn't heard about that," I said. "But he did cure a leper. The man's brother came to our synagogue and testified to the truth of the miracle. Ezra bar Matthias was livid."

Martha asked, "Have you seen Jesus, Mary?"

"Once. He came to dinner in my house, but I was so busy serving food that I never got a chance to listen to him."

"I would like to meet him," Lazarus said. "Everything about him sounds extraordinary."

Martha met my eyes, and I knew she was thinking the same thing I was.

"Is he coming back to Capernaum?" she asked.

"I believe he is. Many of his disciples are from here, and they'll want to visit their families. If you stay for a while, I'm sure you'll have a chance to meet him."

"Good," said Martha, and we both looked at Lazarus, who was turning his cup in his hands and gazing peacefully at the lake.

A FEW AFTERNOONS LATER Fulvius Petrus came calling. I invited him into the house, where Lazarus and I were sitting in the cool of the atrium. The sun in the garden had been too bright for Lazarus; he was afraid it might bring on a headache. Martha was in the kitchen with Elisabeth, planning dinner.

I had been relieved that my sister and my housekeeper got along so well. Elisabeth was my friend as well as my servant. She had taken over the kitchen as her private space, and I never interfered with her. There would be no keeping Martha out of the kitchen, however, and I was nervous that Elisabeth would be upset. To my enormous relief, she and Martha had taken to each other like sisters.

I introduced Fulvius to my brother and invited him to join us. "Is something wrong?" I asked, when I saw the expression on his face.

He sat on one of the benches around the table. "I received a message an hour ago from Jerusalem." He regarded me somberly. "Herod Antipas has executed John the Baptizer."

I stared back at him, stunned.

Lazarus was the first to speak. "Why? Why would he do such a thing now? The Baptizer has been a prisoner for months. There have been no uprisings, no public demands for his release. Why would Antipas do something that might cause the population to riot?"

Fulvius said, "The written notification I received simply announced his death, but the courier gave me the details. Apparently there was a court feast, and the daughter of Herodias—I believe she is named Salome—danced for Herod. He was so enamored with her dancing that he promised to give her anything she asked for." There was a disgusted look on Fulvius' face. "He was drunk, needless to say."

Lazarus and I stared at him, waiting for him to say the unbelievable.

He said it. "She asked for the head of John the Baptizer."

I couldn't speak.

Lazarus' voice was incredulous. "He beheaded a man because a girl pleased him with her dance?"

"Yes," Fulvius said.

I thought of that wild, memorable head, pictured it separated from its body, and felt sick to my stomach.

Lazarus said, "This was Herodias' doing. She hated John because of what he said about her leaving Philip for Antipas."

Fulvius agreed. "I'm sure she had something to do with it."

We sat in silence for a while. Then Fulvius said, "If Jesus of Nazareth isn't careful, he could find himself in danger too."

"From Herod?" I said.

"Herod won't like being pushed into the shade by a wandering miracle worker."

I shivered. "Have you met Jesus, Fulvius Petrus?"

"I heard him preach once. He doesn't only preach in the synagogues, Mary. He preaches on the hillsides—even from a boat on the lake. People follow him wherever he goes."

Lazarus asked, "What did you think of him?"

The Roman said, "I think he's a messenger from your God."

He couldn't have said anything that surprised me more.

He stood up. "I must go. One of my servants is ill, and I've called for the physician. I want to be there when he comes."

"Thank you for bringing us this news," I said.

Fulvius said farewell to me and nodded to Lazarus. Then Jeremiah, who had been hovering near the door, showed him out.

Lazarus said, "This is ill news, Mary."

"I know."

His eyes narrowed as he looked at me. "The Roman seems like a good man—to be concerned about a servant is unusual."

"It must be his old tutor who is ill. He taught Fulvius all through his boyhood. I hope he's all right. Fulvius is very fond of him."

Lazarus massaged the back of his neck.

"You have a headache coming on, don't you?" He made a face and nodded. "Come along to your room and get into bed. Martha will have cold cloths for you before you know it."

"I'm sorry to be such a trouble."

"Don't be silly. You're no trouble to us. You're the one who does the suffering." I put my hand under his arm and led him back to the house under the relentless sun.

Chapter Twenty-Six

MARTHA AND I SAT silent over supper, too aware of Lazarus' empty place to do more than nibble at the meal. Fortunately, he seemed better the next morning. He didn't want to go outside, but at least he came into the dining room and let Martha bring him some food. We hoped the worst had passed.

I was in my garden when Abram came rushing through the gate. His young face was red with excitement.

"Mama sent me to get you, Mary. Jesus has been sighted on the road into town! She says for you to come with us. Father must be with him."

"I'll be right over." I raced into the house to get my brother and sister. Lazarus didn't feel well enough to go out under the sun, but he persuaded Martha he was well enough for her to leave him. Rebecca and Abram were waiting outside my front door when we came out, and the four of us joined the throng of people who were pouring out of Capernaum to greet the miracle worker.

The Roman soldiers who kept guard along the road to Chorazin were on the alert. I wondered if they had ever seen such an exodus of people before. A crowd of us surged along the road until we came upon another crowd coming toward Capernaum. Jesus was at the head of the mass of people, and Peter, Andrew, James, and John walked on either side of him.

The great miracle maker looked so ordinary as he walked along that hot, dusty road. He wore an ordinary brown cloak over an ordinary brown tunic. On his feet he wore rope sandals, the same kind worn by the poorest of the poor.

And yet there was something about that slender figure that drew the eye, that demanded attention. Even if we had known nothing of his miracles, still we would be looking at him.

Abram pushed his way through the crowd, telling everyone he had to get to his father. Rebecca, Martha, and I followed close behind. The crowd from Capernaum had halted on the road, waiting for Jesus to reach them, when Abram finally shoved his way into the front line.

Behind us voices began to shout, "The rabbi is here! Move aside and let the rabbi through!"

Rebecca put her arm around Abram's shoulders to move him out of the way, and we made a path to allow the rabbi through. He went up to Jesus with great dignity, gave him the kiss of peace, and said, "Teacher, I have come to you at the request of the Roman commander in Capernaum. His servant is ill unto death, and he asks that you go to him. I have come because he is a good man who has been kind to our people and contributed money to our synagogue."

Simon Peter scowled and said something to Jesus in a low voice that I couldn't hear. Jesus shook his head and said to the rabbi, "Show me the way."

As Jesus and the rabbi moved toward us, the crowd parted to let them through. Jesus passed close to us but didn't glance our way.

Simon Peter saw us, however, and Abram ran to greet his father. Peter gestured for Rebecca, Martha, and me to join him.

When Jesus and the rabbi reached the gate into Capernaum, the Roman guards stepped in front of us to lead the way. I said in Rebecca's ear, "Fulvius Petrus must have given orders."

The Roman commander's house was in the center of the town, a fine stone building with a small barracks built behind it. Most of the soldiers in Capernaum were quartered in a garrison just outside the city itself.

The house had barely come into view when I saw Fulvius Petrus himself open the door to stand on the front steps. When he saw Jesus and the rabbi coming, he came to meet them.

I was next to Peter, right behind Jesus and the rabbi, so I saw and heard everything that happened. Fulvius walked up to Jesus and bowed his close-cropped Roman head.

Jesus said, "I am here."

"Lord." Fulvius used the Latin word as an address, although he spoke in Greek. "I am not worthy that you should enter into my house. You have only to say the word, and I will know my servant is healed."

Jesus answered him in Greek. "And how do you know that?"

Fulvius straightened to his full height. "I am a man with authority myself. I have many soldiers under me, and when I say to one, 'Go,' he goes; and to another, 'Come,' and he comes. You don't need to come into my house, Lord. You have only to speak the word, and it will be done according to your command."

Jesus was silent. Then he turned to face the crowd, which by now must have encompassed every living creature in the city. He raised his remarkable voice so he could be heard by all. "I tell you, I have not seen faith like this among my own people, Israel."

The crowd was perfectly silent. Jesus turned back to the Roman. "Return to your home. Your servant is healed."

Slowly, deliberately, Fulvius went down on one knee. "I am not a Jew, Lord, but I would like to be your follower."

At this the crowd roared into life. Protests filled the air. I heard words like uncircumcised and swine all around me.

Once more Jesus turned to face us, and this time he was angry. In a voice like the lash of a whip, he said, "Listen to what I say, and then answer me. There was a man going from Jericho to Jerusalem when he fell victim to robbers. They stripped him and beat him and left him lying in the road, half dead. A priest passed by soon after, and when he saw the beaten man lying there, he crossed to the other side of the road. A Levite did the same. But a Samaritan traveler who came upon the injured victim was moved by compassion and offered him help."

At the hated word *Samaritan* there was a rustle from the otherwise silenced crowd.

Jesus continued, "This Samaritan poured oil and wine on the injured man's wounds and bandaged them up. He lifted the man onto his own beast, took him to an inn, and cared for him. The following day he paid the innkeeper and instructed him to take care of the unfortunate man, assuring the innkeeper he would pay more if necessary on his return home.

"Now for the question." The anger was still there, sharp and stinging in his voice. "Which of these three men acted in a way that pleased God?"

The answer came back, grudging but clear: "The Samaritan."

Jesus turned to Fulvius and said, "Anyone who does likewise is my follower."

I found myself shivering. Who was this man? All thoughts of comparisons between him and Daniel or Marcus were futile. He wasn't like them. He wasn't like anyone I had ever known.

Fulvius' front door opened again, and a man came running down the stairs, shouting to Fulvius that his servant was better.

Jesus beckoned to Peter and spoke into his ear. Peter nodded and said to Rebecca, "Come, the Master and disciples will go to our house. We can all use some food and rest."

⤙⤚

I WENT WITH REBECCA to help her, and Martha went to my house to see how Lazarus was faring. Eventually the disciples managed to get Jesus away from the crowd and back to Peter's.

The men sat thankfully in the shade, and I helped Rebecca and her serving girl carry out wine, water, and some hastily prepared food.

Jesus was quiet. He ate quickly and neatly, as hungry as his followers. As they ate, I looked around at the others.

"Who are these men?" I asked Peter's brother Andrew. I liked him. He was a quiet man, always second to Peter in the family and the business, but he had a kind heart.

He smiled at me, his face radiant with pride. "There are twelve of us, Mary. Twelve of us picked by the Master to go with him everywhere and be his disciples."

I tried not to show my surprise. They were men who worked with their hands. They weren't peasants, but they were far from being what I would consider educated. They knew only what had been taught to them when they were boys—that is to say they had memorized parts of the Jewish scripture and learned to say the *shema* twice a day.

I asked Andrew to tell me who they were, and he went around the circle. Peter, James, and John I knew. The others were called Philip,

Bartholomew, Matthew, Thomas, another James, Thaddaeus, Simon, and Judas.

Judas was the one who stood out. He was younger than the others, with a finely drawn face and intense, dark eyes. Something about him reminded me of Daniel.

"Judas is the only one of us who isn't from Galilee," Andrew said. "He's from Judea, and he studied for a while at the Temple. Since he's the most educated, we elected him to hold the common purse."

As we were speaking, Martha slipped through the fence gate and came over to me. She bent and said, "He's worse, Mary. I found him in bed again." Her eyes flicked toward Jesus. "Do you think . . . ?"

Jesus had finished his food and was listening to Judas. I said, "We can only ask," and stood up. I crossed the courtyard, and then I dropped to my knees, bowed my head, and said, using the Greek word by which his disciples called him, "Master, my brother lies next door suffering from a painful sickness in his head. He is a good man, Master, and my sister and I ask that you heal him."

I looked up and was caught in his eyes. For a moment it seemed as if time stopped, and there was no one in the world but the two of us. I felt strangely peaceful. I felt . . . loved.

Then he looked beyond me to Martha, who was standing at my shoulder. "I will come," he said.

I remembered the faith of Fulvius, how he had not needed Jesus' presence, only his word. My faith was not as strong; I wanted him to go to Lazarus.

"Thank you," I whispered.

"Shall I come with you, Master?" Judas asked.

"It is not necessary," came the answer, and he rose and moved toward the gate in the fence.

Martha and I led him to Lazarus' room. When we moved to accompany him inside, he held up one hand. "I will go alone."

Martha and I looked at each other, nodded agreement, and remained in the hallway while he disappeared into the suffering silence within.

Once the door had closed, Martha and I heard nothing from within. We stood together, not speaking but silently praying for Lazarus.

At last the door opened, and Lazarus himself stood before us. His fine brown hair was ruffled, and he looked pale, but he was smiling.

"You're better!" Martha cried joyously.

"Jesus of Nazareth healed me," Lazarus said and opened his arms to embrace her.

I looked over my brother's shoulder to the man still inside the room. "Thank you, Master. With all my heart, I thank you."

He nodded. "Perhaps next time you will trust me, Mary."

My mouth fell open in astonishment as I remembered my moment of doubt. Those eyes kept watching me. I said, "I will, Master. I will never doubt you again."

Chapter Twenty-Seven

Martha invited Jesus to stay for something to eat and drink. He accepted, and I showed him and my brother and sister into one of the small salons off the atrium and asked Elisabeth to serve food and wine.

In simple, subdued words, Lazarus told Jesus the story of his headaches. When he finished, Jesus smiled. I had never seen him smile before; it transformed his face. He said, "The headaches will not trouble you again."

Lazarus' eyes glistened with unshed tears. "You have changed my life, Master. Whatever you ask of me I will do with all my heart."

Jesus nodded and sipped his wine. "I will remember that."

"One thing you should know," Lazarus said with urgency. "You have enemies, Master. Many priests, scribes, and Pharisees are speaking out against you. Some of what they say could be dangerous. One of our local Pharisees calls you a 'spawn of Satan.'"

Jesus' eyes narrowed. "They are my enemies because they reject the truth. The scribes, the Pharisees, the priests of the Temple, they are all hypocrites, loving the honor and plunder of their positions while they ignore the judgment of God. They may look clean on the outside, like well-kept graves, but inside they are full of rottenness and decay."

I thought of Ezra bar Matthias here in Capernaum and the way he had looked at me. I thought of all the priests in the Temple collecting their money, and I said heatedly, "What you say is true, Master. The Temple has become nothing but a treasure chest for the priests and scribes; and the Pharisees, who are supposed to be examples of God's law, are nothing but arrogant hypocrites. They know nothing about the truth of God!"

Lazarus and Martha stared at me, shock in their eyes. Jesus merely lifted his eyebrows and asked gently, "What do you think is the truth of God, Mary?"

"You showed us the answer today, Master, with your story of the traveler who was beaten and left on the road. The priest crossed to the other side because the man might be dead, and touching the dead would make him unclean. The Levite did the same. They obeyed the rules of man, not the truth of God. It was the Samaritan who did the work of the Lord."

He gave me a faint smile. "I see you are a thinking woman."

The approval in his voice broke through the dam that had long been restraining my deepest thoughts, and they burst forth like the floodwaters of the Jordan in springtime,

"I have read the Greek philosophers, Master, and they were trying so hard to find the truth. The Truth and the Good—that's what they sought constantly in their writings. But they were unlucky, Plato and Aristotle and their like. They didn't know the one true God. He didn't reveal Himself to the Greeks; He revealed Himself to us, to the Jews. He chose us, and we have betrayed Him. We have lost the meaning of what He wants from us. I think we've become so ensnared in the rules we have made that we've lost sight of the way the Lord wishes us to live. We had the truth once, but we lost it."

There was a long silence. I could feel my heart thudding all the way up in my head. What had possessed me? What would the Master think of me for saying such things?

He leaned toward me, his expression serious. "I am the truth, Mary. I am the truth and the way and the light. Believe in me, and the Kingdom of Heaven will be yours."

I was so caught up in his gaze that I didn't hear Elisabeth announce the arrival of Peter and Rebecca. It wasn't until she spoke in my ear, saying Rebecca wished to see me outside, that I came back to my surroundings.

I tore my eyes away from Jesus and walked into the atrium. Peter and Rebecca were there, looking anxious. Rebecca spoke, but she had to repeat herself before I could focus enough to understand.

Their problem was simple enough. They needed housing for some of the disciples who were still at their house.

Rebecca explained, "James and John are from Capernaum, so they can sleep at home, but the other eight are far from home. If you were by yourself, I would never ask this of you, but your brother is here so . . . do you think you could do this, Mary?"

"Of course I can," I replied.

"The Master and Nathaniel and Thomas can stay with us, but the others . . ."

I smiled at her. "Don't worry, between the upstairs bedchambers and the downstairs salons, I have plenty of room."

"Thank you, Mary," Peter said with a relieved smile. "I knew we could count on you. Is the Master inside?"

"Yes, he's sitting with Lazarus and Martha."

Peter disappeared into the salon, and Rebecca hugged me. "You are such a good friend." She looked toward the salon and shook her head in disbelief. "To think I was once so angry that Peter followed him."

"He is . . ." I searched for a word to describe Jesus, but there were no words . . . "a remarkable man," I ended lamely.

"He has been sent to us by God, Mary. I truly believe that. He is a messenger from God."

Rebecca had been more accurate than I.

Peter's booming voice came to our ears, and Rebecca smiled. "We'd better go inside."

As I followed her into the salon, I said cheerfully, "I knew I built this big house for some reason. I just didn't know what the reason was until now."

Jeremiah and Elisabeth distributed sleeping mats among the spare rooms for the disciples. Since many of the rooms already had thick rugs, and these were men not accustomed to living a lavish life, everyone was pleased.

As I lay on my comfortable Roman bed, I thought about all that had happened that day. Jesus cured the servant of a Roman military commander. He cured Lazarus. I poured out my thoughts to him, and he told me he was *the truth and the way and the light*. I had looked into his eyes and seen such love in those amber depths. Not just love for me, but love for us all.

I closed my eyes and prayed: *Dear Lord, please show me what I should do, the path I should take. I feel such anticipation, as if something is waiting for me that will change my entire life. Is it Jesus of Nazareth I am waiting for? Who is this man, Lord? He is not a king or a warrior, but . . . can he still be the Messiah? Could it be true that this is the man the Jews have been praying for? I don't want to make another mistake with my life, so I beg you to guide me in the choices that I make. Amen.*

❧

Jesus and his disciples remained in Capernaum for several weeks, traveling to local villages and returning each evening. Judas told me that the Master was attracting such large crowds that he had been forced to preach out in the countryside because the villages were too small.

I wanted desperately to travel with Jesus, to listen to him, to understand him. But it wasn't possible. Jesus' listeners had women and children among them, but I knew well that listening to a teacher or prophet with your husband at your side was very different from traveling with him as his disciple. I still had detractors in Capernaum who would seize on my slightest misstep to label me a sinner.

I wrote a long letter to Julia, pouring out my heart. I had seen my friend only twice since I left Sepphoris, both times at my brother's house in Bethany. Lazarus and Martha had been welcoming, but I had seen how difficult it was for them to relate to a Roman woman. I hadn't yet invited her to Capernaum because I knew it would be considered scandalous to have a Roman woman, dressed in thin linen garments and with her hair uncovered, staying with me. Julia would have been as uncomfortable in Capernaum as I would be to have her.

But I missed her. I had made good friends in my new home, but Julia was more than a friend. She was the mother I had never known.

I was curious to find out how she would respond to my letter about Jesus.

The more I saw of him, the more I listened to him, the more convinced I became that he was indeed a messenger from God. Judas, the youngest of the disciples, believed he was the Messiah, and I was coming to believe the same.

Judas was an interesting man. Before he became Jesus' disciple, he was one of the Zealots dedicated to ending the Roman occupation by the use of force and the military. Judas believed that Jesus had been sent by God to lead our people to triumph over the Romans.

His passion reminded me very much of Daniel. I had to admit to myself that I had a soft spot for Judas.

However, the more I listened to what Jesus was preaching, the less convinced I was that he had any interest in worldly power. He never mentioned Rome. When he talked of his kingdom, it was clear to me he meant something spiritual, a gathering of people who believed in him and in what he preached: kindness, forgiveness, the sharing of wealth.

Every evening, as we all joined for supper at my house, Rebecca and I would sit with the men and listen to the Master talk. I did notice that he appeared careless about the ritual washing Jews were supposed to perform between the various courses of the meal. In Sepphoris I had done as Jesus did, washing my hands only before I ate. I found it a distinct relief not to have to interrupt the meal and the conversation every time a new course was served.

I looked forward all day to those dinners, with Jesus sitting at the head of the table and the rest of us gathered on either side of him. I rarely joined in the conversation, content to listen, though often impatient at the denseness of some of the men.

On a night I'll never forget, it was John who was being particularly thick. He complained that Jesus spent too much time at my house. Why did the Master not come to the house of Zebedee? James and John were among the first disciples called, but the Master had never been to their house. John's mother and father were upset by the slight. John wanted the Master to have dinner at his house for once.

Jesus, who was looking weary, merely nodded and continued to eat.

Then James began. The Master must come to dine at the house of Zebedee. It was only fair that he do so since he spent so much time at Peter's and Mary's.

Jesus briefly shut his eyes. When he opened them he said, "Enough from the two of you. If it will quiet you, I will come to dinner at your home tomorrow. Now, no more of this bickering. Let us eat our meal in peace."

As soon as Elisabeth had served the last course, Jesus stood up and turned to Peter. "I am going to sit in Mary's garden for a while. Do not wait up for me."

"Yes, Master," Peter said.

Once Jesus had left the dining room, Judas turned to John and said furiously, "You tire him out with your concerns about who is first and who should have the greatest honor. We are all disciples together, here to support and learn from him!"

A thundercloud descended on John's forehead, and he began to reply, but Andrew put his hand on John's arm. "You got what you wanted, John. Say no more. The Master doesn't like it when we quarrel."

"Andrew is right," James said to his brother and, after another fierce look at Judas, John subsided.

By the time Elisabeth and her staff cleared the table, all the men had retired to their beds. I went out into the courtyard. The garden, where Jesus had chosen to go, was situated behind the house, facing the lake.

I sat for a long time in the warm night air, thinking. Jesus often referred to his father and his father's kingdom. Andrew had told me Jesus' father was a builder in Nazareth, but when Jesus spoke of him, it was as if he was speaking of some great king. It didn't make sense.

The moon was out when I decided to walk down to the garden. I understood his need to be by himself, away from all the people who didn't understand him, but I couldn't let this chance to be alone with him escape.

He was standing at the end of the garden, looking out at the lake. The moon had risen, casting a white sheen upon its smooth surface, and tiny waves lapped against the shore—a soft, calming sound. I looked up at the heavens, which were sprinkled with starry points of light. Then I went to join him.

He must have known I was there, but he kept his eyes focused on the lake. The moonlight showed me his profile, the thin, arched nose, the defined cheekbones. The scar above his eyebrow was white against his tanned skin.

I said, "They love you, Master. They believe in you. They just don't understand."

Still he didn't look at me. "No, they don't understand."

"They believe you are the Messiah."

"I know."

I gathered all my courage and asked the question that was burning in my heart. "You were with the Essenes for a long time. A boy I once loved joined them in order to pray for the coming of the Messiah. Did you know him? His name is Daniel bar Benjamin from Magdala."

He turned his head to me. "I know of him. He is a highly regarded scholar, but we were in different communities."

"I want so much to understand, Master. If you are indeed the Messiah, why did you join the Essenes to pray for your own coming?"

He turned back to the lake. "I joined the Essenes to learn. I needed to know the scriptures, to be able to read them and speak of them. I needed to know everything if I was to bring the truth of my father to the world. There was no opportunity for me to do that in Nazareth, so I went where I needed to be."

There it was again. *My father.*

"Is it true that you can forgive sins?" I could hear the trembling in my voice, and I clasped my hands together tightly.

Finally he turned to look at me. "Do you need to be forgiven, Mary?"

Suddenly I felt bowed down by the burden of my guilt. I began to cry. "Yes, Master, I need forgiveness. I have been a bad woman. I betrayed my husband, and because of that he died. I have lived a life of godless luxury. I cut myself off from who I was and became someone else, a harlot, a murderous harlot!"

My legs wouldn't hold me and I sank to my knees, weeping. I hadn't realized that I possessed these thoughts, but I knew what I had said was true.

"Can you forgive me?" I sobbed. "Can you forgive my sins?"

"Mary." He bent, pried my hands apart and held them. He tugged gently, and I stood up.

He looked into my eyes. "Mary, you have sinned, it is true, but are you sorry for those sins?"

"Yes, Master." I could hardly get the words out through my sobs. "Yes, I am sorry!"

We looked at each other for a quiet moment. Then he said softly,

"You have sinned, but you have also loved greatly. Your sins are forgiven, Mary of Magdala."

I gazed into his eyes and suddenly felt engulfed by the glory of his presence. His love encompassed me, and I knew that no one on this earth could ever love me as he did. Only God could love like this. I felt his love coursing through all my being, and I knew. "You aren't just God's messenger, are you? You are His Son."

His hands were still clasping mine lightly. "You have said it. You are the greatest of all my disciples, Mary of Magdala, for you have seen the truth."

I wanted this moment to go on forever. "Why me?" I breathed.

"Because yours are the eyes that see and the ears that hear. Yours is the heart that understands."

We stood for a long moment looking at each other, and I felt the perfect unison of my spirit with his. The garden, the lake, the physical world faded, and nothing but profound joy and peace filled my heart. It was the greatest moment of my life.

Then he dropped my hands and turned toward the house. "Come, we must go in."

I didn't want to go, but I knew he had work to do.

"Yes," I said and went with him toward the house.

Chapter Twenty-Eight

I WANTED TO STAY awake so I could hold onto what I had felt, but I fell asleep almost instantly. I awoke when Martha came in to see if I was all right, I had slept so late.

The disciples had already left, going with Jesus to the lakefront where he often taught. I took Lazarus and Martha into the courtyard and told them what had happened. I could never tell anyone else, but I knew that I could tell my brother and sister. They, too, had eyes that could see, ears that could hear, and hearts that could understand.

"The Son of God," Lazarus said, wonderingly. "How did such a thing happen? He was a child once. We know that he grew up in Nazareth. Did God create him and place him in the trust of a human family?"

Martha, ever practical, said, "But he's human too. He gets tired and hungry, just like we do. He gets annoyed when people are stupid, like John was last night."

We went back and forth for a while until I said, "I don't know how. All I know is what happened to me last night. If I could have died at that moment, I would have died with joy. All we need to know is that

Jesus of Nazareth is from God, and he has come to teach us the way God wants us to live. Our part is to listen and learn."

Jesus kept his promise to dine at the house of Zebedee. All the disciples had gone with him, so dinner was quiet at my house. Martha, Lazarus, and I were sitting comfortably over our fruit when Jeremiah came into the room. "My lady, a woman is here who says she is the Master's mother. There are two men with her, and they're looking for him."

I put down the fig I was holding and said, "Please bring them to me, Jeremiah."

The three of us waited in wondering silence until Jeremiah reappeared, accompanied by my visitors.

Jeremiah said, "I will bring water, my lady," and left, closing the door behind him.

I stood up and went to greet the woman. She was small—the top of her head only came to my eyebrows—and her features were a delicate replica of Jesus' face. She smiled, and it was the same smile that I saw so rarely on her son.

Her voice was gentle. "I am Mary of Nazareth, and these are my sons James and Joses. We are looking for my other son, Jesus. I understand he stays with you."

James was looking around the room with a frown. He was a tall, broad-shouldered man, with deep squint lines at the corners of his dark eyes. "Is he here?" he asked abruptly.

"I'm afraid he's not. He's taking dinner at the house of Zebedee today."

The door opened again, and Jeremiah came in with a pitcher of water and three cups on a tray. I said, "Please, won't you sit and have a drink. You must be thirsty."

Mary looked at James and shook her head slightly. He said, "Thank you, but we'd like to go to him now. My mother has something important to tell him."

"Of course. I'll have Jeremiah take you so you don't get lost," and I rang the bell for my servant.

❧

"HE LOOKS SO MUCH like his mother," Martha said as soon as the small family had left the house.

Lazarus and I agreed.

Elisabeth came in and asked if I wanted her to clear away our food. I nodded, and Lazarus, Martha, and I went out into the courtyard, where it was growing cool. We hadn't been there long when Jeremiah appeared again.

"Did you get them there all right?" I asked.

"No, my lady." He looked upset. "I managed to push through the crowd around the house and get into the dining room, but when I told the Master that his mother and brothers were outside, he refused to see them."

I was stunned. This was so unlike Jesus. He might show anger at hypocrisy and stupidity, but to reject his own mother? "Are you sure you heard him correctly?"

"Yes, my lady. I heard him right because he turned to the others at the table and said, 'My mother and brothers are those who hear the word of God and follow it.'"

I couldn't believe what I was hearing.

Lazarus asked, "Have you brought them back here?"

"Yes, they're in the atrium."

"Bring them out here into the cool, Jeremiah, and bring some water and fruit as well."

Jeremiah went back into the house, and shortly the three from Nazareth joined us at the big courtyard table.

James' dark eyes were flashing with fury. "If that isn't Yeshua all over again," he said to his mother. "He never cared about the family, Mother. All he ever wanted was to go his own way."

Mary looked tired but calm. "He was teaching, James. Yeshua is always teaching. It is his calling from God. He knows where we are. He will come after he finishes dining."

Jeremiah appeared with the water, and my guests drank thirstily. Then Lazarus said to James, "If you and your brother wish, I will take you down to the lake to cool yourselves."

James and Joses were sweating profusely and readily accepted Lazarus' offer. Martha rose and said she would send Jeremiah to the lake with some towels. I was left alone with Jesus' mother.

"I'm so sorry that this happened," I said. "It isn't like the Master to be hurtful."

"Yeshua is not like other people." Her voice was warm with love. "The other boys never understood him. They are not his blood brothers; they are the children of my husband's elder brother, Aaron. They came to us when they were small, after Aaron and his wife died of the fever. Yeshua and James were the same age, and James adored him. We used to tease him about being Yeshua's shadow. He was deeply hurt when Yeshua left to join the Essenes. He can't forgive him for deserting the family. You see, James loved Yeshua, but he never understood him." She smiled. "Well, none of us ever understood Yeshua."

She looked at me with the clear amber brown eyes that were so like her son's. After a moment's pause, she added, "How could we understand him? After all, we are but ordinary people, and he is the Messiah."

My breath caught. Spoken in that soft voice, the words were yet filled with authority.

"I know." My voice was scarcely a whisper.

"My husband and I never said anything to anyone else, not even the boys. We didn't know what it would mean, you see. But when Yeshua went away to the Essenes, I knew it was because he was starting on his journey."

The men came back, having bathed in the lake and dressed in clean garments. Elisabeth brought out more food for the visitors from Nazareth. The sun was beginning to sink in the western sky when Jesus came into the courtyard. He was alone, and he went immediately to where Mary was seated. "You wished to see me, Mother?"

"Yes, I did, Yeshua. I'm sorry to have to tell you this, but Joseph is dead. It happened quickly. He caught the fever and was gone in two days."

The words fell like stones into the quiet pool of the courtyard. Jesus sank to his heels so that his face was on a level with his mother's. "Then we should rejoice, for today he is in paradise."

"I know." Her voice quavered a little. "But I miss him."

"He was the best man I have ever known."

She reached out and smoothed his hair. She nodded, seeming unable to speak.

James' angry voice shattered the quiet. "How good of you to finally agree to see us, Yeshua. We've been hearing about how you're curing all sorts of people around the lake. If you had bothered to come home, you might have cured our father before he died."

Jesus stood to face his brother. "James, James, do not be so angry.

Mother understands. I am no longer part of your family. My family now is all of humanity."

James slammed his hand down on the table, making me jump. "Stop talking like you're some gift from God! I know who you are. You were six years old when I came to live with you, and you were a child just like me."

Jesus didn't answer, but the look in his eyes as he regarded his brother was sorrowful.

James went on, "No, I'm wrong. You weren't like me. I was normal, and you were different, always wanting to go off by yourself. But this business of preaching and miracles . . . it makes no sense. You're my brother, Yeshua! You're one of us."

"Enough, James," Mary said. James met her eyes, then looked away. Mary turned to Jesus. "My son, no one knows better than I who you are. Why you are here is for you to know."

They were looking at each other as if no one else was present. "I know it now, Mother. I searched for a long time, but now I know. That is why I can no longer be as a son to you."

"I let you go, my dear, when I sent you to the Essenes. You have learned what you needed to know, and now you must fulfill your mission. I know that, and Joseph knew it too. His last words were that I should give you his blessing."

Joses said quietly, "They're saying you are the Messiah, Yeshua."

"Yes," Jesus replied, "I know." His face was calm and unreadable. He flicked a quick glance in my direction.

I said, "How long are you planning to remain in Capernaum, James?"

"We leave tomorrow. We have work to do at home." He glared at Jesus. "We have a big job in Sepphoris, and we need all the men of the family to complete it on time. But Mother wanted to bring you this sad news herself, so Joses and I came to protect her."

Hidden in James' words was an implication that they had come to protect Mary from her wayward son as much as from any robbers they might meet on the road.

"Then you must stay the night with us," I said. I turned to Jesus' mother. "Would you like to remain as my guest a little longer so you can hear the Master teach?"

Mary's lovely, delicate face lighted. "I'd like that very much."

James said, "We won't be able to come back for you, Mother, until the job in Sepphoris is done."

"That will be fine with me," I told him.

Mary looked at her son. "Yeshua, is it good?"

He gave her his rare smile. "It is good."

And so it was arranged.

Chapter Twenty-Nine

F<small>OR MOST OF THE</small> time that his mother was with me, Jesus remained close enough to Capernaum for us to hear him preach. But he couldn't remain in the area forever; he needed to reach people in the other parts of Galilee.

He said as much one evening when we were dining at my house. Since the disciples—now called the Twelve—were eating at the home of friends, it was just the five of us.

As Elisabeth served the sweet cakes, Jesus said, "My Father sent me to bring heaven's reign to everyone. I have to leave Capernaum to do this, Mother."

"I know, Yeshua. I understand you must go, but I fear for you. So many men of authority hate you. Look at what Herod Antipas did to your cousin John!"

Lazarus said, "She's right, Master. The scribes and Pharisees have been spreading their poison all over the province. I'm afraid you'll find many of the village synagogues closed to you."

Jesus shrugged. "If I am no longer welcome in the synagogues, I must live like the fox who has no lair—out in the open, so that all who wish to find me can do so."

"Why are they saying such things? You aren't dangerous, Master!" It was Martha, whose love was so open, so simple, so clear that she could scarcely imagine evil.

Lazarus answered, "The Master is very dangerous, my sister. He tells people that there's no such thing as clean or unclean. He says that everyone is the same before God and they should be the same before men as well. He tells us to treat the lowliest person, the outcast, as if he were the Master himself. He tells us to love our foes, never to judge, and always to forgive, no matter the injury."

Lazarus turned to Jesus. "You're very dangerous, Master. Kings, priests, scribes, Pharisees, they all rightly see you as a threat to their power, which lies in all the things that you tell people to reject."

Jesus' eyes narrowed. "These so-called religious leaders are hypocrites, a blight upon my Father's kingdom. They will never enter it themselves. But what is even worse, their teachings keep other people out." He closed his hand into a fist. "I tell you, prostitutes and tax collectors will enter God's kingdom before they do!"

Lazarus was right. Everything Jesus said and did was a threat to the religious establishment. Like his mother, I was afraid.

Mary didn't argue. "If you're not going to be here, Yeshua, I think I'd like to go home." She turned to me. "Mary, do you think you could get a message to my son James for someone to come for me?"

Lazarus said, "I will see you safely to Nazareth. Martha and I must return home as well. The dates and summer figs are ready for harvest and I must be there to attend to business."

"But Nazareth is nowhere near Bethany," Mary protested. "I cannot ask you to go such a long way from your own route."

"Nonsense." Martha's small, round face was shining. "We would be happy to go to Nazareth with you. It's a part of Galilee I have never seen. And now that Lazarus is well"—a quick grateful glance here at Jesus—"we can travel with free hearts."

Jesus smiled. I think he smiled at Martha more than the rest of us put together. "Thank you, Martha. My mother will be happy to accept your offer."

~

THE FOLLOWING DAY, AFTER my guests had left, I was sitting alone in my garden, feeling sorry for myself, when Jeremiah brought me a letter. It was from Julia.

Her response to my thoughts about Jesus of Nazareth was temperate. She thought he sounded "interesting" and "certainly very different from Marcus Novius Claudius." But what perked me up immediately was this paragraph:

If you wish to be a disciple of this man, then be one. You are far more intelligent than his other followers, and you should be allowed a chance to know him so you can make up your mind whether or not he is who he seems to be. You write that there are other women in your town who feel the same way you do. Well, why not organize a group of women and travel together? From what you tell me, none of his other followers has any money—they will probably be delighted if you offer to finance them.

Julia, ever pragmatic, had come up with the perfect answer.

I invited a group of my friends, and we sat for hours in my garden, enjoying the breeze from the lake and talking about my proposal. Everyone wanted to do it; the question was would their husbands allow them to? Once again I found myself deeply grateful that I had no husband.

My hope had been to collect twelve women disciples to match the twelve men. We didn't quite make that number, but we got ten, which was remarkable in view of the outrageous thing we were proposing. Susannah came; Jesus had cured her son and her husband was happy for her to be a disciple. Another Mary joined us whose husband, Clopas, Jesus had healed of a chronic sore. Four women whose families had been recipients of my loans came. My cousin Ruth and my good friend Salome came. I wanted Rebecca to come, but she felt her family was too young for her to leave, especially since their father was away as well.

The only one to come who wasn't a friend of mine was Joanna. She had been born in Capernaum and was visiting family when she heard about our plans and asked to join. I didn't want her, but I couldn't find a way to keep her out. She was married to King Herod Antipas' steward, and I had a suspicion that her husband had asked her to spy on Jesus for him. I agreed to let her join us, but I determined to keep a close watch on her activities.

✍

MEN CAN MOVE QUICKLY, but women work differently. We needed to organize our clothes, our food, and our houses before we could leave Capernaum. I also needed to make sure I had enough money with me if we couldn't find free lodging. It was a Jewish tradition that people offered to house a prophet when he visited their town, but I had a strong suspicion they wouldn't be so willing to house a group of women for free. In fact, we would probably have to pay dearly for a roof over our heads. Jesus had been pleased when I told him about his new disciples. To give us a few days to prepare, he crossed the lake to preach to the people on the other side.

They returned in three days, and as usual, the news of their arrival sped around the town, drawing a crowd along the road to greet them.

I walked up my small street to the main road and waited until Jesus reached me. As I stood there, I cast my thoughts back to similar times when I had waited for Daniel or Marcus.

This feeling was similar in that my heart was pounding, but I felt no urge to run and throw myself into his arms. I didn't need to feel his arms around me to know he loved me. I didn't need to press my body against his for him to know I loved him. What I felt for him was the greatest love of my life. I would have turned my back on Daniel and Marcus in a second to follow this man. He offered me everything I had ever wanted in my life—love, belonging, a rule to live by, eternal life, peace.

As Jesus came into view, flanked as usual by Peter, Andrew, James, and John, a man slipped through the crowd to throw himself at the Master's feet. The scene was uncannily like the one when Fulvius' servant had beseeched Jesus to come to his house. Only this was no servant; it was Jairus, one of the officials of our synagogue.

Jairus had never declared himself a follower of Jesus, nor had he condemned him. I had always thought he was waiting to see which side would benefit him most by joining. He was a cold-blooded sort of man, so it was startling to see him on his knees.

I was close enough to hear him say, "Teacher, my little daughter is at the point of death. Come and lay your hands on her, so that she may live."

I was horrified. Not Hannah! Jairus doted on his only child, a lovely girl just on the brink of womanhood.

Jesus said something to Jairus, and then the two of them began to walk down the street with the disciples following. The crowd parted to let them through.

I moved quickly into the midst of the disciples. Judas looked at me and nodded gravely. We continued on into town.

We were almost there when we heard the weeping and wailing. We all knew what the sounds meant—Hannah was dead. Jairus, the most dignified of men, let out the cry of a wounded animal. The howl went straight to my heart.

Jesus took the man's elbow and began to walk him toward the house. I could see his lips moving as he spoke quietly to the bereaved father. They disappeared into the house.

Peter explained later that Jesus had told the weeping parents their daughter was not dead but sleeping. Then he had gone over to where Hannah lay, taken her limp hand into his own, and said, "Child, arise."

"And she sat up," Peter said. He said it almost matter-of-factly, he had become so used to Jesus' miracles. "I had to tell *you*, but the Master instructed us to keep it quiet. It's not wise to provoke his enemies any more than is necessary. He still has work to do."

Jesus had raised the dead before, but this time he had raised a girl. A twelve-year-old girl had been important enough for him to risk another major miracle that might increase the vitriol of his opposition.

As I listened to Peter, I remembered my words to Aunt Leah when she had told me I must marry Aaron. *I have a soul too. Surely the Lord thinks I'm just as important as a man.*

"I don't think He does," Leah had answered me sadly.

But Jesus, the Son of God, didn't seem to think that women were of no importance. He had cured Peter's mother-in-law, and he had raised Hannah from the dead. And he was allowing a group of women to follow him as disciples, a world-shattering event in the Jewish tradition.

Before the day ended, he gave me another reason to believe that he meant what he said about everyone being equal before God. It happened right in front of my house. I was standing inside the front gate, watching as Jesus went among the people who had gathered there begging to see him. He had comforted and cured a few people and was returning to the house for dinner when he halted, turned, and asked, "Who just touched my cloak?"

The crowd, which had begun to disperse, stopped and looked around. Peter, James, and John, ever-present, came to attention like soldiers, glaring all around them. No one came forward.

Finally a small figure darted out of the crowd and fell in a heap at Jesus' feet. An angry rumble arose from the gathering as her veil fell back, and we all recognized her. It was Bathsheba.

Everyone in town knew Bathsheba. For twelve long years she had been cursed with a perpetual flow of menstrual blood. This problem affected not only her health but every other part of her life. One fixed belief of Judaism was that women were unclean during menstruation. During that time of month we couldn't be with men; we couldn't prepare their food or wash their clothes. Everything we touched was unclean—the bed we lay on, the chair we sat on—and any man who might touch us became unclean as well.

For twelve years, Bathsheba lived as a pariah. She sought all kinds of doctors, tried all kinds of remedies, begged the purifiers of the unclean to help her. Today, in her desperation, she was defying the law to come in contact with people. Even worse, she had touched the Master, making him unclean.

The crowd's anger toward the little woman was building. Peter made as if he would dare impurity himself and drag her away when

Jesus held up his hand for silence. He looked down at the trembling heap at his feet.

I had to strain to hear Bathsheba's voice. "You have healed me, Teacher. As soon as I touched your cloak, I could feel the blood stop flowing. You have healed me." And she began to sob.

Jesus bent toward her and said, "My daughter, your faith is what healed you. Go and be in good health."

Bathsheba scrambled to her feet and looked around, as if she was confused and didn't know what to do next. Jesus looked to me and nodded slightly. I opened the gate and went to kneel next to the little woman. "Come with me, Bathsheba. I will take you home."

"Mary!" she said, and tried to smile.

My heart had always ached for Bathsheba. I had visited her regularly since moving to Capernaum, something I had kept hidden even from Ruth. "Come along." I put my arm around her shoulder and led her away.

Chapter Thirty

Jesus and his disciples, including the women, left Capernaum right before the olive harvest began. I loved this time of year. The punishing hard blue sky of summer had grown softer and cooler. The autumn rain was gentle and warm. It was the best time of year for traveling the countryside, and travel we did.

Galilee is a land of small villages, all quite close to each other, and each village was filled with people eager to see the new miracle-working teacher. Jesus spoke occasionally in the village synagogues, but often they were too small for the vast numbers of people who wanted to listen to him.

They came from the villages, the farms, and the hill country, bringing their wives and their children with them. Often they didn't bring enough food, and Jesus had to perform one of his miracles to feed them.

Those two months of traveling through the countryside, among people Julia would consider mere peasants, was the fulfillment of a dream. I had never felt so exhilarated, so useful, so alive. The eager response of the crowds gave me confidence that Jesus would be successful in his mission, that he would bring the Kingdom of God to us, and that he would change the world.

We women grew very close during this time. The men, unfortunately, didn't get along nearly so well. James and John, whom Jesus had called the "Sons of Thunder," lived up to their stormy names. They were particularly jealous of Peter, chosen by Jesus to be the leader of the Twelve.

As the weather grew colder and the crowds more demanding, I could see Jesus was tiring. Day after day he had to extend himself, pour out his precious truths to crowds who listened, but did they understand? He, who had been slim to start with, lost weight. I wasn't surprised when one night he finally lost his temper.

It was growing dark when we managed to escape from the day's crowd by following a sheep track over the hill. Once we were on the other side and safely on flat ground again, Peter asked me, "Where are we staying tonight?"

Judas and I were usually the ones to find places to sleep in the small villages. I said, "Back on the other side of the hill, unfortunately."

We were standing on a grassy plain, with the hill we had just climbed between the Master's followers and us. I thought Jesus looked exhausted, so I said to him, "Perhaps we should camp here for the night, Master. It's quiet, and if we make a fire we'll be warm enough. We can easily wait until morning for our next meal."

Some of the strain left his face. "A good idea, Mary. Let us do that."

Andrew and Thomas collected wood from under the scattered small patches of trees nearby and built a big fire. We assembled around it, grateful for the heat, women on one side, men on the other. The fire was hot enough to keep us warm, and I was contemplating wrapping myself up in my cloak to sleep when Jesus' voice, sharp and impatient, disturbed the silence. "What is it you want to say to me?"

I looked across the fire to see what was wrong. Jesus' eyes were on James and John, who were exchanging uneasy glances. Finally John thrust his chin forward and said, "We have a request to make, Master."

"Yes?" I could see the temper in Jesus' eyes from all the way across the fire. Unfortunately, John did not.

"It is this. When you come into your glory, will you have James and me to sit beside you, one on your right hand and one on your left?"

I heard the hiss of Peter's breath, but he was sensible enough to keep quiet.

Jesus closed his eyes. I could see him struggling to remain calm. Finally he opened them, saying in a level voice, "In the world of earthly empires, the rulers lord it over the common people. But among you it must not be so. Whoever wishes to become great among you must act as a servant, and whoever wishes to be first among you must be a slave to all."

James and John looked down at the ground in front of them and said nothing.

Jesus stood up. "I will spend this night on the hillside by myself. In the morning we will start back to Capernaum."

We were silent as he turned away from the fire and began to walk toward the hillside. I understood that he needed to be by himself sometimes, that he needed to commune with his Father. But this was different. Tonight he looked so alone as he walked away. He must be bitterly disappointed in James and John.

I got up and walked after him.

He must have heard me coming, for he stopped to wait. I looked up at his shadowy profile and said, "They do try. It's just that they can't help thinking that your kingdom will be administered like an earthly state. It's what they know."

"You understand. Why can't they?"

I sighed. "Because they're men. The lust for power is part of their nature."

"And it's not that way for women?"

"For some women, perhaps. But I think we have a greater understanding of what's important in life than men do. We have no earthly power to quarrel over, you see. Our lives revolve around our parents, our husbands, our children. It's not so hard for us to understand that the kingdom you speak about is a kingdom of love."

He was silent for a few beats. Then he turned and flashed me a smile. For the briefest moment I caught a glimpse of what he must have looked like when he was a boy. "Perhaps that is why I like women so much," he said.

We both laughed.

I said, "I heard something today in the village when I was looking for rooms. There are rumors going around that Herod wants you dead. This tour has been too successful. Too many people are calling you the Messiah. He thinks you're dangerous."

"That old fox." His voice was weary. "His father tried to kill me when I was a baby. He didn't succeed then, and his son won't succeed now."

I said, "He killed John the Baptizer."

"It's not Herod I have to fear, Mary."

There was a note in his voice that made me shiver. He saw it. "You're cold. Go back to the fire and warm yourself. I shall see you in the morning."

"Yes. Good night, Master."

He didn't answer but moved off, his slim figure agile as a mountain goat as he went up the hill. I watched him until I couldn't see him any longer and then I went back to the camp.

I prayed. I prayed with him all night, even though he was on the mountain and I was not. I prayed to God to keep His Son safe. He had sent Jesus into the world to bring us the truth, but the world could be deaf and ugly and dangerous. If even the men he had especially chosen didn't understand him, how would the men who stood to lose their worldly power react to his words?

I couldn't keep the image of John the Baptizer out of my mind.

⁓

JESUS DIDN'T REMAIN LONG in Capernaum but moved north, into the territory of Antipas' brother, Philip. It was too difficult for most of his women followers to take more time away from their families, so we remained behind. I would miss him terribly, but I was relieved to see him go. He would be safer in the north.

The campaign against Jesus increased while he was gone. The scribes and Pharisees preached in the local synagogues against the Master's "crimes." These so-called crimes came down to the simple fact that Jesus opposed many of the ritualistic rules that for centuries had defined our religion.

He was against ritual cleanliness and purification. He opposed animal sacrifice, fasting rules, eating codes, priesthoods, and the Temple. What Jesus preached was an inner purity of the heart and soul. It was this purity that would allow the believer to share in the union he himself had with his Father in heaven.

The scribes and Pharisees didn't understand that, for Jesus, love was the test. All he asked was that we treat everyone, high and low, as if they were Jesus himself. A simple rule indeed, but terrifyingly hard to follow. He wanted us to love our enemies, to care for the poor, and to pray quietly by ourselves to the Father, who would then hear us and reward us.

I often worried if I was up to the demands he was making on me and on the rest of his followers. It was true that I didn't seek power. But his call to forgiveness . . . that was something else. He had forgiven me for my sins more than once. Over the course of the last few months I had told him the whole story of my thwarted love for Daniel and about my relationship with Marcus, and he had understood the guilt I felt and had forgiven me.

He believed I had forgiven those who had wronged me, but I wasn't certain I had managed to do that. Like John and James, who couldn't let go of their dream of power, I was having a difficult time letting go of my anger against those who had hurt me.

Sometimes I thought it was easier to follow the myriad rules of the Jewish Law than to follow the very simple requirements of Jesus.

⁓

I MADE PLANS TO spend Hanukkah with Lazarus and Martha, and when Jesus arrived back in Capernaum at the beginning of the month, I asked him to join us. I feared what might happen to him in Galilee and was greatly relieved when he agreed to join us. He wanted to preach in Jerusalem, and Bethany was only two miles away from the city.

I thought Judea, and even Jerusalem, would be safe for him. Judea was under the command of a Roman procurator, and Rome had no reason to fear Jesus. He never spoke of political matters, even though he was often asked questions about the Romans. He had no interest in the empire of Caesar. His mission was the Kingdom of God.

Where Jesus went, the Twelve went too. Rebecca, Ruth, and Nathaniel also came, leaving their children in the care of grandparents. Martha would have her hands full with such a crowd, but we would manage somehow.

We set off a few days before Hanukkah, taking the road through Samaria. The Samaritans and Jews had hated each other for centuries, and I was concerned about trespassing into enemy territory, but Jesus insisted. He wanted to preach to the Samaritans, and I couldn't argue with him about that. It was what I loved about him—that he excluded no one from the kingdom.

It was an unusually warm winter day when we first set foot in Samaria, and by mid-afternoon everyone was thirsty. Thomas was the first to spot a well beside the road, but when we reached it, we found a Samaritan woman was already there. Jesus walked right up to her and asked her to draw him a cup of water.

Judas was standing next to me, and I could see his shock as the Master took the unclean cup from the unclean woman and drank from it. The woman was surprised as well and asked why Jesus, a Jew, would consent to take water from a woman of Samaria.

I listened to their conversation. Jesus told her that once Samaritans drank of the living water, they would no longer worship on Mount Gerizim, and when Jews drank, they would no longer worship in Jerusalem. As true believers, Jews and Samaritans would worship the Father together, for the water he offered was the water of eternal life.

This comment was truly a test for some of the disciples, especially Judas, who still believed that he could convince Jesus to lead a Jewish army against Rome. All the centuries-old enmity between Jews and Samaritans sounded when Judas gasped.

However, the woman's face filled with wonder. "Only the Messiah could accomplish what you say."

And Jesus replied, "I am he, I who tell you this."

At this point the woman whirled around and began to run back toward the village, forgetting even to take her water jar.

Judas immediately said, "You cannot mean to include the Samaritans in your kingdom!"

Jesus turned and looked at Judas. The rest of us held our breaths. Judas had made no secret of the fact that he wanted Jesus to be the Messiah who was prophesied in Scripture: a king, a freedom fighter, a great military leader who would lead the Jews to conquer the world.

Jesus said, "You must listen to me more carefully, comrade."

His use of the word *comrade* caught my attention. He had never used that word to describe his relationship with the other disciples.

He continued speaking to Judas, "My kingdom is not of this world. How can you have listened to me for all this time and not realize that? How many parables have I used to explain this to the people? It is true that I came for the Jews, but my kingdom is open to all those who understand my words. I am the way, the truth, and the life. Entry into my Father's kingdom comes through me."

He stopped speaking but continued to look hard at Judas, who bent his head and mumbled, "Yes, Master."

"So be it," Jesus said, and sorrow and resignation sounded in his voice. "Let us continue on our journey."

Chapter Thirty-One

I HAD BEEN CONCERNED that Martha might not have room for all the people heading to Bethany, but I shouldn't have doubted her. She had made sleeping arrangements for everyone. The disciples were to stay with local friends while Jesus and I, Rebecca and Peter, and Ruth and Nathaniel were to remain with her and Lazarus. Jesus had his own room, Lazarus shared with Peter and Nathaniel, and Martha shared with Rebecca, Ruth, and me. My two months of following Jesus had weaned me from my soft Roman bed and accustomed me again to floor mats. I slept well under my cloak and the blanket Martha provided.

It rained the first day of Hanukkah. Jews were accustomed to warm weather and sun, and we huddled in our houses around charcoal braziers in the winter when it got too cold. Since the feast of Hanukkah lasted eight days, we felt no urgency to walk to Jerusalem in the freezing rain, deciding instead to wait for the next day to make the trip.

Daniel always slipped into my thoughts during Hanukkah. The feast celebrated the triumph of Judas Maccabeus, the hero Daniel had admired so greatly. I hadn't been to the Temple for Hanukkah in years, and that night I lay upon my sleeping mat, listening to the rain beat against the roof and thinking of my lost love. I finally slept and woke to a fine morning. We left for Jerusalem immediately after breakfast.

The air was still cool but the sun felt good on my head as we walked along the road that led into the city. Other people walked with us, but the crowds were nothing like those at Passover. Still, the disciples took no chances. They formed a circle around Jesus so that he walked in the midst of them. A bodyguard, I thought, with approval.

No one seemed to take any special notice of the composed, slender figure in the white wool robe as we entered through the gate. The Roman guards gave me their usual rude stares, which I ignored. We made it to the Court of the Gentiles without Jesus being recognized.

The Court was crowded. The merchants were loudly hawking birds and oxen and sheep for sacrifice, while the money changers were occupied exchanging Roman coins for shekels. As always, the atmosphere was that of a marketplace, not a place of prayer.

I felt a flutter of fear in my stomach as I saw the Master look around the Court. I recognized the look in his eyes, and I prayed, *Please don't let him lose his temper. Don't let him give the priests any cause to arrest him.*

Animal sacrifice was the heart and soul of the Temple. It was how the priests made their money. If Jesus preached against animal sacrifice, the priests and high priests of the Temple would see him as a threat, and he didn't need any more enemies. The scribes and the Pharisees were enough.

I was beginning to wonder if there was any place in the country where I would feel he was safe.

We left the Court of the Gentiles quickly, climbing the stairs to the Court of the Women. The scholars were holding forth in their various posts, and Jesus circled the area, stopping to listen here and there. I watched as people naturally parted to let him through, giving way without being asked. It was always like that. He burned with an energy that radiated beyond the slender body that housed it.

After all, I thought, he was the Son of God walking among humankind. He couldn't entirely disguise this truth.

He had reached the Portico of Solomon when a scribe finally recognized him. He said something sharply, and Jesus turned to face him. Immediately a group of people began to gather, and I heard the scribe say again, "Are you Jesus of Nazareth, the man who is calling himself the Messiah?"

Jesus didn't answer immediately, just regarded the scribe thoughtfully. The scribe said again, his voice sarcastic, "Don't keep us in suspense. If you are the Messiah, tell us so."

I looked around me and saw that the crowd was composed mainly of scribes and Temple priests. My hand went to my throat.

As Jesus began to reply, someone behind me said my name. I turned and looked directly into the face of the man who had spoken.

It was Daniel.

⤚⤙

THE BREATH WAS KNOCKED right out of me. After ten years, here he was—Daniel, the one I had thought lost to me forever.

He frowned. "Are you all right? You went white as frost. Please don't faint on me."

I inhaled deeply and lifted my chin. "I never faint."

For a long moment we stood, just looking at each other. I heard Jesus' voice in the background, but for once I didn't listen. Daniel said, "Let's get away from this crowd."

I nodded and followed as he threaded his way through the Master's growing audience. We found a place that was quiet and sat on an empty marble bench. I turned to look at him again.

His youthful face had been hammered into maturity. I could see it in the set of his mouth, the look in his eyes. He wasn't a boy any longer.

"What are you doing here?" I asked.

He said, "I thought I remembered how beautiful you were, but I see now that I didn't."

I laughed self-consciously. "I'm a lot older now, Daniel."

"I knew you the moment I saw you. I didn't even have to see your face, I knew you from the way you held your head. No other woman carries her head as proudly as you do."

Tears stung behind my eyes. "I thought I would never see you again. I almost don't know what to say to you now that you're here."

He gave me a crooked smile. "I feel the same."

"Did . . ." I bit my lip. "Did you know that I'm a widow?"

He looked at his hands. "I heard about a year ago. We have little contact with the outside world, but someone who came through with supplies mentioned your name in connection with Jesus of Nazareth. He said you were a rich widow and one of his chief followers."

So he knew.

"The report you received was correct. I am both a rich widow and a supporter of Jesus." I repeated my earlier question: "What are you doing here? Have you left the Essenes?"

He shook his head as if to clear it. "No, I haven't left them. I'm here on a mission." He shot me an ironic glance. "I was sent to discover if Jesus of Nazareth is indeed the Messiah we wait for."

"Ah."

"What do you think, Mary?"

The sound of my name on his lips made my heart leap. I waited a moment before I answered. "There's no question in my mind that he is the Messiah. But surely you must know about him from the Essenes. He was with you for many years."

He shrugged. "We have many communities scattered around the Judean desert, and he and I never met. I am at Qumran, in charge of inscribing our scriptures in Hebrew, Greek, and Aramaic. I once invited Jesus to join us, but he refused."

I didn't know that. "He told me once that he admired your work tremendously."

Daniel's lips tightened. "We wanted him to join us at Qumran. He knew nothing when he first came, but he amazed his teachers by how quickly he learned. They said he never forgot anything that was said to him—a precious gift for a scholar. But he refused my invitation."

I tried to explain. "He couldn't join you, Daniel, because he is the Messiah. His mission is out here in the world, preaching the word of God."

"Or perhaps he was tired of the strictness of our lives. Monastic life and scholarship are not something many men wish to do, Mary. Walking the world amid the adulation of thousands might have seemed more attractive."

My back stiffened. "He does miracles! No one, no holy man or prophet before him, has done the things he has. He's raised people from the dead, Daniel! And I have seen with my own eyes the most extraordinary healings. Yes, he is the Messiah, but he's even more than that." I paused, wondering if I should continue. I decided to be honest. "He's the Son of God come to bring us back onto the true pathway to his Father in heaven."

Color flushed into Daniel's face. "Son of God? How can you believe such a thing? His father was a builder, a carpenter in Nazareth. He worked with his father until he came to join us. How dare you speak such blasphemy, Mary? Jesus of Nazareth most certainly is not the Son of God!"

"His mother says he is."

Daniel jumped up, paced a few feet away from me, and then swung around to come back. "Listen to me, Mary. The scriptures say the Messiah will be a great man, a man of power, of authority. A prince among men. He must be all these things if he is to defeat the forces of darkness in this world and bring us into the light. This Jesus may be a successful preacher, but he is none of those things I just mentioned. None of them!"

I grabbed his hand and saw his eyes widen with surprise and something else I couldn't read. His hand felt so familiar. I had a tremendous urge to hold it to my cheek, but I knew that was forbidden. I said, "Don't judge before you hear him, Daniel. He is the light you are seeking. Just listen to him, I beg you. Don't be like those scribes you despised when you studied in Jerusalem. Listen to him with an open mind and an open heart. Then make your decision."

He removed his hand from mine.

Suddenly I felt overwhelmed. *This is Daniel I am talking to. Daniel!*

He said, "That's what I was sent here to do."

We were looking at each other silently when I heard a commotion coming from Solomon's Portico. "What can be happening?" I asked nervously. "I had better get back."

Then I saw Lazarus running toward us. "We have to leave immediately, Mary. The priests have sent for the Temple guards to arrest our Master."

"Oh no!"

"It's all right, the disciples are getting him away. But we had better return to Bethany immediately."

"Yes." Then I remembered Daniel and hurriedly introduced him to my brother.

"You must forgive me for hastening away," Lazarus said, "but things have gone a bit beyond our plans here."

"I understand," Daniel said.

"Where's Martha?" I asked.

"She's all right, she's with Ruth and Nathaniel, but we must leave now."

Lazarus put his hand under my elbow and urged me forward. I threw Daniel a quick smile and went with my brother.

The Temple guards didn't pursue Jesus beyond the Temple grounds, and Lazarus and I caught up with the others on the road. I walked the two miles to Bethany with my face down, my eyes trained on the road. We were almost to Bethany before I understood what the churning in my heart and stomach meant. I was angry. I was angry with Daniel. Perhaps I had been angry with him for a long time and had not recognized it.

I needed to think about all of this. I needed to talk to the Master.

WHEN FINALLY WE REACHED the house, Ruth said she was tired and wanted to rest, and the disciples gathered in the winter room around the charcoal brazier, speaking in low voices about what had happened in the Temple. Rebecca had family in a neighboring village, and she and Peter had gone there to have their meal.

I wrapped my cloak around my shoulders and said I was going out into the clean air of the courtyard to get the stink of Jerusalem out of my nose. Jesus, who had just come to the door, said, "I'll go with you."

We went outside and sat at the courtyard table to watch the sun as it slowly sank behind the Judean hills. It was cold enough for our breath to hang in the air.

"Lazarus said the priests called the Temple guards to arrest you," I said. "Now you have even more enemies."

He said, "That's not what has upset you."

I shot him a sidelong look. He seemed perfectly calm sitting there, with his hands folded before him on the table.

I told him about meeting Daniel.

"Ah," he said.

"He's on a mission for the Essenes, to discover if you are truly the Messiah."

He didn't say anything.

I stared at the table in front of me. "I've been thinking about that parable you tell about the son who took his inheritance from his father and spent it on dissolute living."

He was quiet.

"After the money was gone, he was forced to go home. He asked his father to take him on as a servant, but instead his father welcomed him as if he were a prince. The father forgave him even though the son had deserted him and squandered all his money."

"Yes," Jesus said. "That is what that parable is about. Forgiveness."

"You forgave me my sins. I told you all about them, and you forgave me."

"Yes, I did."

I said in a rush, "I thought I had forgiven those who hurt me, Master. I forgave Lord Benjamin. I forgave my father. I forgave Marcus. But . . ."

"But you haven't forgiven Daniel?"

I clenched my hand into a fist. "He should have waited for me! If

I had known he was waiting, I would never have gotten involved with Marcus!"

The words burst out before I even formed them in my mind. I listened to what I had said, and then I slid off the bench to kneel at his feet. "Tell me what I should do, Master. Tell me, how can I get rid of this anger?"

His voice was gentle, the way it was when he spoke to children. "I know it's hard, but you must forgive him, Mary. Daniel, Daniel's father, your father, the Roman, they are the ones who set your feet upon the path to me."

I drank in his words as a person dying of thirst would drink in water.

He continued, "The ones who cannot find forgiveness in their hearts, they're the ones who have never truly loved. That's not you, Mary."

Tears began to slide down my cheeks.

"All your life you have been walking toward me. Forgive Daniel for abandoning you, Mary. It is you, not he, who has seen the light. Follow me with all your heart, and you will know eternal joy in my kingdom."

I looked at him through my tears and felt shackles loosen and fall away from my heart. He was right. All that mattered about my life was that I should be here, with him.

In the red glow of the sun he looked suddenly weary. Then we heard Martha's voice calling my name.

From my position at the Master's feet, I turned to see her coming toward us. She wasn't even wearing a cloak in the cold winter dusk.

"What is it?" I asked, getting to my feet. She was almost in tears and I felt a flash of alarm. "Has something happened?"

"Yes. The girls who were going to help me with supper had to go home. Rebecca isn't here, and Ruth has fallen asleep, and I dropped my favorite pot on the floor." She gulped like a child. "The men are hungry, and I don't see how I'm going to make supper all by myself." She looked at Jesus. "Mary must help me, Master, or the supper will never be ready in time."

He gave her the smile he reserved only for her. "Martha, Martha. The food you are cooking is good for the body, but the food Mary seeks is good for the soul. Do not be so anxious. The supper will get done."

I rose to my feet. "Of course it will, and I will help you, Martha."

"Thank you." Her voice was watery.

I grinned. "You must be desperate if you came seeking me."

She managed a chuckle.

"Come along." I put my hand on her elbow and walked her back to the house.

WE GOT THE SUPPER on the table, and after we had eaten, I retired to the chamber I shared with Martha, Rebecca, and Ruth. I curled up under my cloak and blanket and closed my eyes, bringing back the day when I had felt such perfect union with Jesus, the day I realized who he really was. The room was quiet, and I lay still, all my concentration on my inward being.

I am the light of the world. Follow me with all your heart, and you will know eternal joy.

How could I continue to be angry with the people who had put my feet on the path to Jesus? Instead of anger I should feel sorrow for them, for the blindness that kept them from knowing the perfect joy of oneness with God.

Poor Marcus. He had loved me, but he had been born into an immoral society, and there was no one to show him the true path. I certainly hadn't done so. Instead, I had taken up his ways, and then I'd rejected him when he committed what he thought of as an act of love. Even the loss of my baby . . . if my child had lived, I would have married Marcus. Tears trickled from my eyes. The greatest loss I'd ever known had brought me to the greatest joy.

Forgiving Daniel was harder. I had truly thought our love would last forever. During the time I had spent in Bethany after leaving Sepphoris, I believed he would come to me. But his ardent spirit had found a resting place with the Essenes, and that betrayal had made me angry. I had buried it deep. But when he acknowledged that he had known I was a widow, that anger surged to the surface.

Daniel had rejected me.

I thought again of the Master's words. How could I regret anything that had happened in my past? It had all led me to the greatest experience a person could have. My soul had been opened to the Infinite. I was a disciple of the Son of God.

I whispered into the darkness: *I forgive you, Lord Benjamin. I forgive you, Father. I forgive you, Marcus. And Daniel—I forgive you, and I love you. I will pray that you see the truth about Jesus and come to know him as the Messiah.*

I listened. The room was silent, but I felt a presence. I could see no one, but the presence was stronger because it was unseen. I had no doubt that God was in the room with me.

I whispered, "I will take care of Your Son."

The presence remained, and I fell asleep.

Chapter Thirty-Two

THE FOLLOWING MORNING LAZARUS and I went into Jerusalem while Jesus remained in Bethany. Lazarus was friendly with a Pharisee who, even though he was a member of the Sanhedrin, was also a secret follower of the Master. His name was Nicodemus, and he would know whether or not it was safe for Jesus to return to Jerusalem.

I accompanied Lazarus because I wanted to see Daniel again. I hoped to convince him to give up his dream of an earthly prince and see Jesus for who he truly was—the Messiah, the Son of God.

I saw Daniel as soon as we walked into the Court of the Women, and I knew he was waiting for me. Lazarus brought me over and said to him, "I'm going to the Court of the Priests to see if I can find my friend. Will my sister be all right with you?"

"She'll be safe with me," Daniel promised.

We watched as Lazarus passed through the Nicanor Gate, and then Daniel turned to me. "Did your friends tell you the reason why the priests tried to arrest Jesus yesterday? He not only said he was the Messiah, he proclaimed that he was the Son of God. The Son of God! How can you believe this nonsense, Mary? This man doesn't come from God. He's a madman."

"He speaks the truth, Daniel." I struggled to remain calm and sensible. "You don't know him, and it's necessary to spend time with him to understand. You haven't learned the truths he's brought to us."

"We already have the truth! I copy it every day in my scriptorium."

We were standing along the wall to the right of the Nicanor Gate, facing each other like adversaries. "I know our scripture is true," I told him, "but we have forgotten its most important lessons. Why else did you leave the Temple and become an Essene? You were revolted by what our religion has turned into—our lives are bound by an endless number of man-made rules, and we worship by the mindless slaughter of animals. Jesus only wants what our scriptures tell us the Lord wants—that we should love Him and love one another."

"That is what we Essenes believe. Jesus was with us once, but he left for an easier life."

I felt my temper begin to rise. *"An easier life?* He owns his sandals, his cloak, and his robe. He has nothing more, he wants nothing more—he needs nothing more. He's an example to us all of how unimportant the things of this world are."

"It's a good thing he has you then, to pay for his food and lodging," Daniel shot back.

Now I was really angry. I put up my chin. "It's my honor to help him. He turns away nobody, Daniel. Nobody. He shares himself with the destitute, the defiled, the despised, the unclean. He preaches love and forgiveness. What can be wrong with such a message?"

A man had come up behind Daniel while I was talking, and from his clothing I guessed he was also an Essene. The newcomer curled his lip in scorn. "Jesus of Nazareth is unclean. I've heard he doesn't even wash his hands before he eats." He put a hand on Daniel's shoulder and directed his next remarks to him. "He also consorts with women, my brother. Like this one." Another scornful look came my way. "She has no husband, and she follows an unmarried man around the countryside like a . . . a wanton. Look at her, here today with no man as her escort!"

Daniel flushed. "Watch your tongue, Ezra. Mary is a good woman."

I glared at this Ezra. "I am a good woman, and Jesus of Nazareth is the only man I've ever met who believes that women are just as capable of being holy as men. All other Jewish men think we are unclean and stupid."

"I never thought you were unclean or stupid!" Daniel said.

I continued to glare at Ezra. "Jesus doesn't think people are unclean because they're ill or lame or because of what they eat. They're unclean because of the filth of greed and hypocrisy and bigotry that's inside them."

Ezra glared back, but Daniel held up his hand to stop his friend from answering. In a milder voice he said, "I agree that much of what he says is true. We Essenes do not believe in animal sacrifice, and we believe that what's on the inside of a man is more important than what's on the outside. In many ways Jesus is in the tradition of our prophets, who came to remind us of our duty to the Lord. But he's not content to say he's a prophet, Mary. He says he's the Messiah. Even worse, he says he's the Son of God. That is blasphemy. A blasphemer cannot be the Messiah."

A man walking in front of us tripped over his own sandal and fell into me. Daniel put his arm around me, holding me upright, and said angrily, "Watch where you're going!"

It felt strange to be so close to him, to feel his body against mine. It felt even stranger that I had no urge to turn toward him and hold him tight. When he released me, I stepped away without a second thought.

We looked at each other, and the distance between us seemed much wider than the few inches that actually separated us. He said, "This man is not the Messiah, Mary. The Messiah will be a man like Judas Maccabeus, a man who is a leader, a soldier, a prince. This man may have some true things to say about where we have gone wrong in our duty to the Lord, but he will never lead armies. He is no David come to save us. He is a prophet, that is all."

I felt a rush of sorrow. "Oh Daniel, how I wish you could see as I do."

Ezra said, "Perhaps he's the Messiah for women."

"Be quiet," Daniel snapped. "You don't know what you're talking about."

I reached up to touch Daniel's cheek. "I love you. I will always love you. But it seems as if our lives must part again."

"Yes." His red-brown eyes reflected back my sadness. "My life has taken a path I hadn't planned, but I think it's the right path for me."

I looked over his shoulder and saw Lazarus and Nicodemus coming through the Nicanor Gate. "I must go. My brother is here." I rose up on my toes and kissed his cheek. "God bless you, Daniel."

He nodded, turned to his friend, and said, "Let's go back to Qumran. There's nothing for us here."

He walked away, and I turned to greet my brother and his friend.

ON THE WAY HOME Lazarus told me about his conversation with Nicodemus. "The Master escaped yesterday because the Temple guards refused to go after him. Nicodemus says the priests are beginning to regard Jesus as a genuine threat. His talk yesterday was provocative, to say the least. He told the people he was the Messiah and the Son of God. The priests of the Sanhedrin were livid."

"He cannot go back to Jerusalem," I said. "It's not safe."

"I agree. He would be better off in Galilee than here."

"I don't think Galilee is safe either," I said.

The truth of my statement was made clear as soon as we reached Bethany. An elegant looking litter, with uniformed litter carriers, stood in front of Lazarus' house. As we watched, a woman came out of the house and approached us. It took me a moment to recognize Joanna, the wife of Herod's steward who had been one of the women on our tour of Galilee. She was dressed in a draped Grecian-style tunic, and jewelry glinted at her throat, arms and fingers.

"Joanna!" I stared at her thin, high-nosed face. "What are you doing here?"

"I have come to warn the Master. Galilee is dangerous, Mary. Herod Antipas wants to kill him the way he killed John the Baptizer."

Sharp as an arrow, fear stabbed through my heart. "Are you certain?"

"Yes. I heard it from a reliable source in the palace." She stepped closer. "No one must know I've been here. My maid is telling everyone in Tiberias that I am ill and must keep to my room. I have to get back as quickly as I can."

"It's dangerous for him in Judea too, Joanna. Where can he go?"

"North," she said, "to Philip's territory. Once Philip hears that Antipas wants the Master, he'll do everything in his power to protect him. There is no love lost between those brothers."

The bearers had moved to the four corners of the litter, ready to pick it up. "I must go," Joanna said.

"Thank you for coming," Lazarus said.

She looked from his face to mine. "Convince him to get away."

"We will try," Lazarus said and I agreed.

Chapter Thirty-Three

Jesus and the disciples left Bethany the following day. It was a difficult parting. With Jesus in the north, my house in Capernaum was going to feel painfully empty. But I was relieved to see him go. I hoped the Master's absence from Jerusalem would allow heads to cool and the tide of danger to recede. Nothing in my life was more important than Jesus' safety.

I returned to Capernaum after the worst of the winter rains had passed and took up my old life. A letter arrived from Julia telling me there was a great deal of unease in Sepphoris over Jesus and asking if I thought he posed a threat to Roman rule. I wrote back that Jesus had less political ambition than the rest of the Jewish hierarchy, and it would be safer for Rome to protect him than to persecute him.

The flax harvest had just begun when a paid messenger arrived with a message from Martha that Lazarus was ill in his lungs. She was worried about him and begged me to come.

I called on Fulvius and asked if he would send a soldier on horseback to my sister with a letter. He agreed, and my letter to Martha went off at a gallop only two hours after I had received hers.

Lazarus had to be very ill for Martha to ask me to come. I packed and was away the following day, escorted by Fulvius Petrus. We went by horseback with an escort of a dozen mounted Roman soldiers. I had never ridden a horse in my life, but I managed somehow. It was a scary, painful experience, but it kept my mind off my brother for a while.

We were in Bethany by the end of the day. Fulvius left his men in the village and walked me out to Martha's himself. He practically had to hold me up, my legs were so unsteady from the horse. But the look on Martha's face when she saw me was worth all the pain. She threw herself into my arms and burst into tears.

Fulvius refused to come in, saying he needed to get back to his men. I thanked him profusely for his help and followed Martha into the house.

"What's wrong with him?" I asked as soon as the door closed behind us.

"Oh, Mary, I don't know! He's burning with fever, and when he breathes, he makes the most terrible noise, as if every breath is a struggle.

"Take me to him."

Lazarus was lying on his mat clad only in a thin cotton tunic. It was cold in the room, and as she went to cover him, Martha said, "I'm trying to keep him warm, but he keeps kicking off his blankets."

I went to kneel beside him and spoke his name. After a moment his eyes opened.

"Mary," he said. His voice was weak and hoarse. He looked dreadful.

I bent to kiss his forehead. His skin was on fire.

Martha tried to get him to drink some water, but after two sips he closed his eyes. "Tired," he muttered and fell silent.

Martha and I stayed for a little, listening to his labored breathing. Then we went out into the front room and sat together on a bench. Her voice trembling, she said, "He's worse today. Nothing I do seems to help. Mary . . . I think we should send for the Master."

Her eyes were filled with tears.

I shivered. I was so afraid—afraid for Jesus if he came back to Judea, and afraid for my brother who might be dying. I said, "Fulvius must still be in the village. I'll ask him to get a letter to Jesus. If it goes by horse, it will get there quickly."

"Thank you," Martha said.

Fulvius agreed to get the letter to the Master, and Martha and I settled in to do everything we could to keep Lazarus alive. If Jesus and the disciples moved as quickly as possible, without stopping to preach, he could be with us in four days.

We succeeded in keeping Lazarus alive for those four days, but on the fifth day he died.

❧

LOSING MY BABY HAD been terrible. Losing my brother was just as bad. Martha and I were sitting with him when he drew his last breath. We sat for another hour, on either side of the bed, holding his hands until they began to cool.

Then there was all the business of anointing and burying the body. I had done it once for Aaron, but this was so much worse. This was Lazarus.

In the midst of all the weeping, wailing, and moaning, my little sister was amazingly strong. She had been closer to Lazarus than anyone else. They had lived together for her entire lifetime. She had given up marriage for him. He had been everything to her. What was she going to do without him?

The entire village followed as we bore him to the cave that was to be his final resting place. Everyone had loved Lazarus. But all the wailing and crying and screaming didn't help Martha or me. Neither of us rent our garments or lifted our arms to heaven. We followed behind the bier, holding hands, keeping silent.

All during that painful walk, my mind kept repeating, *Lazarus. This is Lazarus we're entombing. My brother, Lazarus. How can this have happened? Where is Jesus? Why didn't he come?*

When the men rolled the stone over the entrance to the cave, I felt Martha flinch, as if she had been physically assaulted.

I tightened my hand on hers and put my arm around her shoulders. *This is a mistake. Jesus cured him. He shouldn't die like this. Where was he? Where was the Master?*

I had a hard time convincing Martha to turn away from the cave, but finally she did. There was nothing else to be done for Lazarus except return home for the mourning period.

The house was already filled with women when we got there. They had brought food and planned to sit with us day and night, weeping and wailing in their genuine sorrow for our brother's death.

It was exhausting. Perhaps it was supposed to be exhausting so the bereaved wouldn't feel their loss so acutely. It worked for me in that I found the women so irritating that they distracted me from other thoughts. It didn't work for Martha, however. She had been strong during the anointing and the funeral, but now she couldn't seem to stop weeping.

On the fourth day of mourning I pulled Martha aside. She needed to get away. "Why don't you go out to the road and keep watch for the Master? He must be close by now, and one of us should be there to greet him when he arrives."

A little light came into her swollen, tear-stained face. "It will be so good to see him."

It would have been even better to see him four days ago.

But I didn't say that. I knew Jesus would have come if it were possible. I knew it wasn't his fault that he was too late. And I knew that he would help Martha.

She slipped out the door, and I went back to the women.

Time passed. It was stuffy in the crowded front room, but hospitality forbade me from leaving. My eyes were glazed over, and I was half asleep sitting up when a village boy came in and whispered in my ear, "You must come quickly, my lady. The Master is just outside the town."

I jumped up and ran out of the house, leaving all the women twittering behind me. I ran through the village and up the road. As I ran, others began to run after me.

Then I saw him. He was standing on the road next to Martha, and his face looked tense and drawn. I didn't notice anyone else. I didn't think. I just threw myself at his feet and began to cry uncontrollably.

"Where have you been?" I sobbed through my tears. "If only you had been here, my brother would never have died."

I felt his hand rest on my bare head—I hadn't even stopped to put on my veil. "Don't cry, Mary," he said. "Have you lost your faith in me? Your brother will rise. Don't you remember? I am the resurrection and the life. He who believes in me will have everlasting life. Lazarus believed that—don't you?"

I raised my face to look up at him and was astonished to see tears flowing down his cheeks. My heart contracted in grief for him. He felt dreadful that he had been too late. "I do believe Master," I said.

It was the truth. I did believe, and I understood what he was telling me. I understood that he couldn't raise a man who had been dead for four days. He'd raised people to life before, but they had been the newly dead. Lazarus was alive, but only in the Kingdom of God, not here in Bethany.

Jesus reached a hand to help me to my feet. "Where have you laid him?" he asked, making no attempt to stem the tears that continued to flow down his anguished face.

Martha, who was standing on his other side, said, "It's this way, Master."

The three of us walked along the narrow path that led to the cave where my brother lay. The disciples followed behind us, and behind them came the inevitable crowd from the village. As we drew near the tomb, Jesus slowed. It was a warm day, but I could see he was shivering as if it were midwinter.

He turned to John and said, "Take away the stone."

Martha's breath caught. "He's been dead for four days, Master! There will be a stench."

I pressed my knuckles to my mouth to keep from speaking. I didn't want my memory of Lazarus tainted by the foul evidence of his death, but I trusted Jesus.

We were standing just behind him, and he turned to face us. The shivering had stopped, and he was sweating. His face had gone white, and the sweat mixed with his tears. "Didn't I tell you that if you believe, you will see the glory of God?"

I put my arm around Martha's shoulders and said, "Go ahead."

John was able to roll the stone away by himself, and once the opening was revealed, Jesus raised his eyes to the heavens. When he spoke, his voice was clear and composed. "Father, I thank you for hearing me. I know you always hear me, but I wish these people to hear me also, so that they may know who I am and believe."

I felt Martha's whole body trembling. Then Jesus walked into the tomb entrance, and she whimpered.

Jesus called into the darkness, in the same clear, composed voice, "Lazarus, come forth."

I stopped breathing, and we waited in absolute silence.

First we saw a shadow in the doorway of the tomb, and then a figure stepped out into the sunlight. He wore the winding sheet we had wrapped him in, and when he slowly reached up to remove the cloth that covered his face and stood blinking in the sunlight, we all recognized my brother. My healthy-looking, perfectly intact brother.

Lazarus had been raised from the dead.

Chapter Thirty-Four

I FELT HIM IN my arms, warm and vibrant and alive. I looked into his brown eyes, and they were the same. I laughed. I cried. I laughed and cried at once. It was impossible, but it had happened. Jesus had raised my brother from the dead.

The crowd was hysterical, and we had a difficult time trying to leave. The disciples once more turned themselves into a military guard and managed to get us home. Once we were inside the house, Peter barred the doors. We didn't dare go out into the courtyard, where we could be seen from the street. Instead we all huddled together in the front room, where only a short time ago I had been the center of a group of mourning women, and stared at my brother.

"I'm hungry," Lazarus said.

Martha leaped up and rushed into the kitchen. I just sat on the floor looking from my brother to Jesus and back again.

The Master wasn't fully recovered from the emotion that had overtaken him at the tomb; he was tired and quiet.

We all wanted to know what it was like to be dead, but Lazarus didn't have many details. For him, it had seemed but a moment in time from when he died to when he had awakened in the tomb. All he remembered was being filled with joy and enveloped in a beautiful light.

"Did you see God?" Thomas asked.

"No." Lazarus shook his head in bewilderment. "I can't believe I was dead for four days. It went by so fast. I must have been in a place of waiting." He turned to look at Jesus, who was sitting by the high window, with the sun streaming in on his head. "Your Father must have known that I would be coming back to life again."

Jesus didn't reply.

I listened to the chatter going on around me and thought with satisfaction, *This will show Daniel and all the rest of the doubters. How can anyone not believe Jesus is the long-awaited Messiah, the Son of God, after this?*

⸎

THOSE WHO HAD WITNESSED the miracle raced into Jerusalem to spread the word, and people started to come out to Bethany to see Lazarus for themselves. Passover was near, and Jews were already pouring into the city for the holy day. As soon as they heard about the miracle, they too wanted to see Lazarus.

And everyone wanted to see Jesus of Nazareth.

However, Jesus and the disciples had moved to Ephraim, a Judean town close to the eastern mountains. He told Martha and me he needed some quiet time before he returned for Passover. The raising of Lazarus had drained him, and I was glad to see him go. Bethany wasn't a quiet refuge these days.

The one sour note in all the euphoria about Lazarus came from Nicodemus, Lazarus' Pharisee friend. He came out to Bethany to warn us that the Sanhedrin had met, and Caiaphas, the high priest, had told the assembly that Jesus was too dangerous to be allowed to go free.

So now the Master, who already had influential enemies in the scribes and Pharisees, had the priests of the Sanhedrin against him as well.

When Jesus returned to Bethany two days before Passover, I told him what Caiaphas had said. He shrugged as if the Sanhedrin was of no importance. I thought he was wrong, but I knew nothing I might say would keep him from going into Jerusalem.

That evening Martha served one of her wonderful suppers. We set up the long table in the front room, as it was too chilly to eat outdoors, and the girls who helped Martha passed around platters filled with fish, lamb, and fruits. Flagons of good wine circulated as well.

The conversation was cheerful and excited. The disciples were confident that Jesus would receive a rousing reception in Jerusalem. By now everyone had heard about the raising of Lazarus, and many were hailing the Master as the Messiah.

I was nervous, but I kept one reassuring thought in my mind: *Even if the worst happens and the Sanhedrin arrests Jesus, there is little they can do to him. Herod beheaded John the Baptizer because he has the power to execute in Galilee, but only Rome can execute a prisoner in Judea.*

Rome wouldn't intervene in Jewish religious affairs. I comforted myself with this thought. Even if the Sanhedrin should act, Jesus' life would be safe.

As we sat around the table, the meal done, the conversation quieter, I slipped out of my seat and went to fetch the jar of nard I had purchased from one of the most expensive merchants in Jerusalem. I lifted the thin-necked alabaster container in my hands and carried the precious oil into the front room. I went up to Jesus and knelt before him, the alabastron in my hands. I looked up, to see if what I was going to do would be acceptable, and he gave a slight nod.

I anointed his feet. It was usual to do this service at the beginning of a meal, but I did it at the end. I poured the scented oil lavishly, and when I finished I pulled off my scarf and dried his feet with my unbound hair. When I straightened up, my hair fell around my shoulders and down my back, and the room was filled with the fragrance of the oil.

We looked at each other, and what I saw in his eyes frightened me.

Judas said, "That oil must have cost a fortune, Mary. You should have spent the money on the poor."

I opened my mouth to make a sharp reply, but Jesus spoke first. "Leave her alone. It is right for her to anoint me now. The rest of the oil must be kept for the day of my burial." He turned to Judas. "The poor you will always have with you, but you will not always have me."

His look and his words were like a sword to my heart. He knew that something dreadful was going to happen to him.

I returned the nard to its place with shaking hands. I would have given my life to protect him, but I knew he would not allow me to do that.

∾

Jesus and the Twelve went into the city early the following morning. We had decided that it would be best for Lazarus to stay away from Jerusalem. He would be mobbed if he should show himself. Martha, of course, would remain home with her brother, and I decided to stay in Bethany as well. Jesus' mother was coming to stay with us for Passover and I wanted to be at home when she arrived.

Mary came late that afternoon, having traveled from Nazareth with a group of friends, who then went on into the city. She looked smaller than I remembered, fragile, and weary. Martha fussed over her and fed her and sent her upstairs to rest.

While Mary was sleeping, Martha, Lazarus, and I sat in the courtyard, wondering what might be happening in the city. At least the crowds around our house had disappeared; everyone was in Jerusalem for Passover.

We were still sitting there when one of Lazarus' neighbors, Joachim, saw us from the road and came into the courtyard. He raised his hands dramatically and said, "Why are you here today and not in Jerusalem? You missed the most amazing sight!"

"What sight?" Lazarus demanded.

"The Master entered Jerusalem in triumph! He sat on the back of a colt, and the people strewed his path with palm leaves. Some even threw their cloaks down before him! It started at the Mount of Olives and went all the way to the city gates. Everyone was crying out *Hosannah!* They were calling him the Messiah and even King of Israel!" Joachim beamed at us. "It's all because of what happened to you, Lazarus. I don't think there's a soul in Jerusalem who hasn't heard about the miracle."

Martha's dimples flashed in her rosy cheeks. "This is wonderful news!" She put her hand over Lazarus' and smiled up at him.

"There was no trouble at all?" Lazarus asked.

The man grinned. "Only if you call the Master throwing the money changers and merchants out of the Court of the Gentiles 'trouble.'"

"What?" Surely Jesus wouldn't do such an outrageous thing now, when the priests already hated him.

"I saw it myself," Joachim said, his eyes bright with delight that he was the first with this news. "He overturned the money changers' tables—the coins were bouncing everywhere! Then he kicked over the birdcages and loosed the lambs. The whole court was in turmoil. And all the time he was doing this, Jesus was calling the priests names. He called them a den of thieves and vipers. He said the Temple was his Father's house and they were turning it into a cave of robbers!"

My hand was at my mouth. This wasn't good news. "What did the priests do, Joachim?"

He raised his thick eyebrows. "They pounced on his words. They asked him who he was that he should think he had the authority to vandalize the Temple."

Lazarus and I were silent. It was Martha who asked in her sweet, soft voice, "What did the Master answer?"

"He said something very odd. He said if the Temple was destroyed, he would raise it up again in three days' time."

We were silent, trying to make sense of this. Then Lazarus said, "They didn't try to arrest him?"

"No, there were too many people there who believed in him. They all know about you, Lazarus. The priests are afraid to touch him."

"Well, that is good news," Lazarus said.

I smiled and agreed with him, but in my heart I was worried. Why had the Master let his temper get the best of him? He was winning the war against the hypocrites. Why would he do anything to endanger his victory?

At this point, Mary came out of the house, and Joachim repeated his story. She sighed when she heard about Jesus' behavior in the Temple. "Yeshua is usually the kindest of men. He must have been furious."

I said, "I suppose we can't blame him—the Temple *is* a disgrace. But I wish he hadn't done anything else to stir up the priests."

"Yeshua is not like us, my dear," his mother said. "He does what he feels he must do, what he is called upon to do. It's not for us to judge him."

I felt rebuked. I looked into the face of Mary and for the first time saw the strength that lay behind that delicate bone structure. This was the woman God had chosen to be the mother of His Son. Everything in Jesus that was human came from her.

I said, "You're right. It's not for me to question what the Master chooses to do."

Joachim took his leave, and the four of us lingered in the courtyard until the air began to chill. We were just getting ready to move inside when Andrew arrived.

"I'm to tell you that the Master is spending the night on the Mount of Olives. He will go into Jerusalem tomorrow and celebrate Passover there. Thomas has gone to secure a room for us."

I put my hand on Mary's shoulder. "Does he know his mother has arrived?"

"He didn't say anything about his mother." Andrew shot Mary an apologetic look. "He's fixed upon spending Passover in Jerusalem."

Mary put her hand upon mine where it rested on her shoulder. "Don't be upset, Mary. You should know Yeshua by now. He has his own plans, and we must abide by them."

Martha said, "Won't you eat something before you leave, Andrew?"

"Thank you, Martha, but I must get back to the others before dark."

I accompanied Andrew to the front gate. "We have heard the Master was well received in the city today," I said.

"It was magnificent! There must have been thousands of people throwing palms. His hour is coming, Mary! Finally we will see the revelation that we have all been hoping for. The Jewish people will see the Master for who he truly is: the Messiah and the Son of God."

I watched as he walked down the street to join the others on the Mount of Olives and I prayed that he was right.

Chapter Thirty-Five

Martha woke up feeling sick. She was rarely sick, so I was concerned. Mary and I had planned to go into Jerusalem for Passover, but I couldn't leave Lazarus with sole care of his sister, so we changed our plans and remained in Bethany.

Martha had always prepared the Passover meal, but fortunately Mary knew what needed to be done. I helped her as best I could, but our thoughts were in Jerusalem. Still, we got the food together, and at sundown the three of us, without Martha, ate our Passover meal.

It was a dismal Passover. We followed the centuries-old ritual, but our hearts weren't in it.

Why did Jesus want to have his Passover meal in Jerusalem and not with us?

It was a question I could not answer, which made me uneasy. I kept insisting to myself that Jerusalem was safe, but I remained unconvinced. I couldn't forget the look he had given me when I anointed him. And I couldn't forget his words: *Save the rest for my burial.*

I looked at Lazarus and Mary, who were sitting in silence, and I knew they felt it too.

Something bad is going to happen.

It was dark when the three of us finished the meal. I had just risen to my feet when Martha came into the room. She was clutching a cloak around her shoulders, and her hair was rumpled.

I went to her. "Martha! I thought you were sleeping. You should have called for me."

"I'm feeling better, Mary, truly." She regarded the remnants of our feast. "I'm so sorry I didn't cook the Passover supper." She looked at me anxiously. "Did you manage?"

"We managed beautifully. Mary knew exactly what to do. Are you sure you should be out of bed?"

She was assuring me she felt fine when we heard a knock upon the door. My heart jumped. People didn't go visiting on the first evening of Passover.

"I'll go," Lazarus said.

He came back with a man who had a scarf pulled over his face. He pushed the scarf away as he came into the room, and I saw it was Nicodemus.

"I have bad news," he said to Lazarus. "The Sanhedrin has issued an arrest warrant for you."

I was stunned. In my concern for Jesus, I hadn't considered that my brother might be in danger as well.

"But why would they do that?" Martha's eyes swung from Lazarus to Nicodemus and back to Lazarus again.

"The Sanhedrin has seen how the people are turning away from them and embracing Jesus." Nicodemus put a hand on Lazarus' arm. "You are living proof of a tremendous miracle, my friend, and they don't want you around to verify the story."

Mary asked quietly, "And what of my son?"

"I'm afraid there is an arrest warrant out for the Master too, dear lady."

Mary went pale.

"The Master was dining somewhere in the city tonight. Does the Sanhedrin know where he is?"

"No. But they're looking for him."

"That's why he didn't dine with us tonight. He didn't want to put Lazarus in danger."

"But he *is* in danger." Nicodemus turned to Lazarus. "You must get away from Bethany tonight, while everyone is home celebrating Passover. Go to Mary's house in Capernaum. I'm sure she has friends who will hide you."

I thought immediately of my cousin Ruth. "Of course I do. Nicodemus is right, Lazarus. You must leave tonight."

"I can't do that. Suppose the Sanhedrin arrests you, Mary? You're known to be a follower of the Master."

Nicodemus disagreed. "They won't arrest Mary. There wasn't a single mention of the Master's female followers at the meeting tonight. The Sanhedrin doesn't consider them of any importance."

I sighed at the likely truth of that statement.

I urged my brother. "You must go, Lazarus. The Temple guards may come for you at any moment. Pack a few things and get away from here. Immediately!"

"I want to go with you," Martha said. She had crossed the floor and was standing beside him.

"I'm not leaving you all here." Lazarus' face was set and unusually hard.

Mary spoke. "Lazarus, Yeshua did not raise you from the dead to see you throw away your life. You must live so you can testify to the truth of who my son is."

We were silent as the two of them looked at each other. Finally Lazarus bowed his head. "If you wish me to go, my lady, I will go."

"Thank you," Mary said.

"I want to go with you," Martha said again.

I went to put my arm around her. "Listen to me, little sister. You will only hold him up. Let him go, and he'll send for you when it's safe."

"She's right, Martha," Lazarus said gruffly.

"Go and help him pack his things," Mary said.

As the two of them left the room, I turned to Nicodemus. "The Sanhedrin must be very frightened. This action will outrage all the people who only yesterday proclaimed Jesus to be the Messiah."

"It's not only because people are calling him the Messiah that the Sanhedrin has stirred into action. People have begun to call him king of Israel. And Jesus himself has said that he's the Son of God. The Sanhedrin is terrified that people will turn away from the Temple. They fear they'll lose their power to a man the high priest once dismissed as 'a peasant from Nazareth.'"

Mary said with a catch in her voice, "I keep thinking of my cousin Elizabeth's son, John. He was beheaded for saying far less than Yeshua."

I hastened to assure her, "The Sanhedrin doesn't have the right to put anyone to death here."

Some of the shadow left her face. "But what if Rome . . . ?"

"Rome won't become involved in a religious struggle." I was certain of this.

When Pilate had first been appointed procurator of Judea, he made the mistake of bringing into Jerusalem Roman standards bearing a likeness of Caesar. Jewish law forbids the making of images, and this move had provoked a huge demonstration, which forced Pilate to back down. I didn't think he'd want to repeat that situation. Marcus had told me the episode tarnished Pilate's image with the emperor.

Lazarus and Martha came back into the room and, after gently pushing her away, Lazarus left with Nicodemus, who was returning to Jerusalem. After the men had gone, Martha began to clean the table. I tried to convince her to go back to bed, but Mary told me softly to leave her alone, that this was her way of handling fear.

I wished I could find something that would help me handle mine.

❦

I DOZED ON AND off during the night, dreaming restlessly, waking, then dreaming again. I woke fully to the sound of someone pounding on the front door.

They've come for Lazarus, I thought. I blessed Nicodemus for getting him away as I grabbed my cloak and went to the door, an oil lamp in my hand.

I opened the door, and John was standing there.

"Let me in, Mary. I have something to tell you."

I opened the door wide.

"Who is there?" It was Mary, also wrapped in her cloak and carrying a lamp.

"It's John." I closed the door behind him. "Let's go into the kitchen so that no one will be able to see the lamplight."

As soon as we were away from the window, John said, "The Master has been arrested."

Mary was silent, but when I reached out to touch her shoulder I could feel her shaking.

"When?" I asked.

"A few hours ago. They came upon us as we were leaving the garden of Gethsemane to return to Jerusalem."

I knew the garden. It was a quiet place, not frequented by many people. "How did they know to look for you there?"

"It was Judas who gave him up, may he rot in the fires of Gehenna."

"Judas!"

"Yes, Judas. He brought a troop of armed Temple guards with him to arrest the Master. Peter tried to fight the guards, and James and I did too, but we were overpowered. The rest of the disciples scattered, but Peter and I followed behind to see where they were taking him. They went to the high priest's house. Peter volunteered to wait outside in the courtyard if I would come to tell you."

"Thank you for that, John," Mary said. "Do you know what they will do at the high priest's?"

He shook his head.

I knew. I don't know how I knew, but I did. "Caiaphas has probably already called the Sanhedrin together, and they will put him on trial. They'll want to do it in the middle of the night, so no one will know what's happening."

Mary said, "I must go to him."

"We'll both go," I said. "Just let me run next door and get one of the neighbors to sit with Martha. She's been ill, and she's worried enough about Lazarus."

The sun was fully up by the time we passed through the Valley Gate and into the city. Jerusalem was filling up with Passover crowds, but we avoided the worst of them by heading west toward the high priest's house instead of north toward the Temple.

It was less crowded in the Upper City, and the streets were wider, so we quickly reached the large stone mansion that housed Caiaphas. A substantial crowd was gathered in front, and as we joined it, we heard shouting from down the street. John grabbed Mary and me and pushed us back as a detachment of Roman cavalry came trotting up the street. They were shouting in marketplace Greek, the shared language of the Empire, "Clear the way! Clear the way! Horses coming through!"

Everyone moved as far off the street as possible, afraid of the huge horses that towered over us. As the soldiers formed two lines in front of the high priest's house, the front door opened—and I saw him.

They had tied his hands in front of him and surrounded him with a phalanx of Temple guards. My heart dropped into my stomach. *Why are the Romans here?*

The situation was more dangerous than I had realized.

They made Jesus walk between the horses, with the Temple guard marching in front and behind. Jesus seemed untouched and composed. As he passed a few feet in front of us, his eyes fixed straight ahead, I heard Mary whisper, "Yeshua."

The childhood name brought tears to my eyes, and I turned to her. She was standing perfectly still, her eyes on the procession as it marched away from us down the street.

John said to me, "What should we do now?"

I knew exactly what we must do. "Go to the Temple and find Nicodemus. He will have been at the Sanhedrin meeting, and he can tell us what was decided."

John bent down to Mary. "Will that be all right with you, my lady? Do you want to come to the Temple with us?"

She looked up as he towered over her and said in a firm voice, "Yes. Let us go to the Temple."

Chapter Thirty-Six

THE CLOSER WE GOT to the Temple, the thicker the crowds became. People chattering in foreign languages milled all around us, filling the air with the aroma of the different foods and spices that emanated from breath and skin. John pushed doggedly through the streets, and Mary and I followed close behind him. It took an hour to get to the Temple, through the *mikvahs*, and into the Court of the Gentiles where Mary and I met up again with John.

The Court of the Gentiles was also packed with foreigners; we may have been the only ones from Judea in the whole place. John said that local people would have been to the Temple yesterday for the sacrifice of the lambs and were probably at home with their families.

I thought Nicodemus would be in the Court of the Women, so we pushed our way up the staircase and finally spotted him standing by the Nicanor Gate. Nicodemus shepherded us to a quiet spot near the Chamber of Oils.

"Caiaphas brought forward a parade of false witnesses to testify against the Master, but they kept contradicting each other. The high priest was furious and finally turned to the Master, who had been silent during the whole proceeding. Caiaphas asked him one question: 'Are you the Messiah, the Son of the Blessed One?'"

I shut my eyes, afraid of what was coming next.

"The Master said, 'I am. And you will see the Son of Man seated at the right hand of the Power of God and coming on the clouds of heaven.'"

We were silent as those words resonated in our minds and hearts. A child came running past us holding a dove in a cage, and my eyes followed him while I tried not to think of what must have happened next.

Nicodemus continued, "The high priest said to the Sanhedrin, 'Why do we need witnesses? You have all heard this blasphemy. What is your decision?'"

Mary pressed her hand against her mouth, and I put my arm around her, as much for my comfort as for hers.

Nicodemus said, "The Sanhedrin answered that he should die."

"The Sanhedrin doesn't have the right to execute prisoners," John said quickly.

"They took him to Pilate," Nicodemus said.

I was starting to feel frantic. "Pilate won't condemn Jesus! Calling himself the Son of God isn't a crime against Rome."

Nicodemus shook his head. "Too many people are calling him king of the Jews, and that's a political, not a religious issue."

John lifted his head to stare around the crowded court. "Then we will rouse his followers to free him. Think of all the people who threw palms at him the other day! They will rise to defend him. I know they will!"

I had to force the words through my closed throat, "But those aren't the people who are in Jerusalem today. You said it yourself, John. The people here are foreigners, not followers of the Master."

Mary said, "If my son has been sent to Pilate, then that's where I must go."

"That's where we will all go," John said. We left Nicodemus and once more fought our way through the crowded streets of the city.

～

It was turning into a beautiful day, and the blue skies and bright sun seemed a mockery of what was happening in Jerusalem. Apparently word had gotten around that the Sanhedrin was asking Rome to execute a Jewish dissident, and crowds of people were flocking to see, like vultures to a wounded animal.

The fortress of the Antonia, the most visible sign of the Roman occupation in Jerusalem, was a huge building just north of the Temple. Though chiefly a military garrison, it also contained a fortified palace for the Roman procurator to use when he was in the city.

A crowd had already gathered when we arrived. Caiaphas and a group of priests from the Sanhedrin were standing in front of the palace. A contingent of Temple guards kept the crowd at a distance. There was no sign of Jesus.

Speaking in Greek, John asked the man standing next to us what was happening. The man said, "They have some fellow in with Pilate who has been going around saying he's the Son of God. The Sanhedrin wants him executed, but Pilate has been trying to get them to change their minds."

We stood waiting, sick with fear. I couldn't get the image of John the Baptizer out of my mind. Pilate wouldn't behead Jesus. His Father would never allow such a dreadful thing to happen to His Son.

We saw movement among the group of priests, and John, who was tall, told us that the procurator had come out.

We could all hear Pilate's voice as he told the Sanhedrin that he found no fault with this man.

The priests of the Sanhedrin yelled back. "He has said he is the Son of God. *Crucify him!*"

All around me the crowd took up the cry. "Crucify him! Crucify him!"

Crucifixion was for common criminals. How could these people be asking for crucifixion?

John grabbed the arm of the man we had been speaking to and shook him. "You don't even know him! How can you call for him to be crucified?"

The man tried to pull away. "Are you mad? Let go of me, or I'll have you arrested!"

"John," I said, tugging on his robe, "don't do anything stupid. We need you."

I could see the effort it took for him to contain his fury, but finally he stepped away from the angry, frightened man.

The crowd had quieted, and Pilate's raised voice came clearly. "Do you want me to crucify your king?"

A chorus of voices shouted back, "We have no king but Caesar."

I hated them. I hated every single person in that crowd of foreign Jews. How could they say such a thing? How *could* they?

Pilate's voice sounded for the last time. "Take him, then, and do with him as you please. I will put my guards at your disposal."

⸏

"Hold onto my cloak and stay behind me," John said to Mary and me, and he began to push his way forward. He must have looked like the Son of Thunder that Jesus had called him, because the crowd fell away before us.

We were almost to the front when I saw him. They had put a circle of thorns on his head and pressed them in so that blood ran down his face. Blood stained his robe as well. They must have whipped him. His face was drawn and pale and set like stone.

Mary made a whimpering sound, and I put my hand on her shoulder.

As we watched they put a great wooden crossbar on Jesus' back for him to carry from the Antonia to his place of execution, a distance of about two miles. He would have to walk first through the narrow streets southwest of the Antonia, then cross the hot Tyropoeon Valley to Golgotha.

A procession formed, with Roman soldiers in front to clear the path, then Jesus with his cross, and then another group of Romans on horseback behind him. A crowd of Jews began to fill in behind the procession, and John managed to edge us into the front, directly behind the horses.

The narrow city streets were lined with people as the death march wound along the prescribed route. Many of the watchers shouted vicious remarks at the vulnerable figure of the Master as he passed, bent under the heavy crossbar, but a number of women called out blessings and tried to follow him from the side. One woman even dashed into the street to wipe his face with her veil.

The Romans pushed her away.

We passed through the city gate and came out into the sunlight of the valley. We couldn't see over the horses, so we didn't know what had happened when the procession suddenly stopped.

"The prisoner's down!" someone shouted.

I shut my eyes. *Please let him be dead*, I prayed. *Please, dear Lord, don't make him go through the horror of crucifixion. Take him home to paradise. Please let him be dead.*

John shouted at the horsemen in front of us, "What's happening?"

One of the soldiers turned his head, "They got someone else to carry the crossbar. The prisoner can't do it anymore."

John's face was ashen. He said, "He's exhausted himself with his preaching. He's lost too much weight."

I looked at the crowd of strange Jews behind us and thought, *Where is everyone else? Peter? James? Andrew? Where are they? They should be here for him. Where are they?*

The procession started to move again, and we followed. I looked at Mary. This was worse for her than it was for John and me. But she never faltered; she kept walking steadily under the hot sun, stepping over the leavings of the horses, until the hill of Calvary appeared in the distance.

Two men were already hanging there, and between them was a single empty post.

My knees started to buckle. John grabbed my elbow and held me up. I looked at Mary. Her face was set in stone, just like her son's. She wasn't going to collapse. She was going to see this through.

I strove to pull myself together. The least I could do was see it through with her.

"I'm all right," I said to John. "I will be all right."

⤚∾⤙

A LARGE CROWD HAD assembled by the time our procession arrived, pushing us farther away from the Master. The Temple guards and some of the Roman soldiers went up the hill with him while the horsemen remained behind to keep the crowd under control. People were shrieking, and children were crying.

Children, I thought in horror. *How could anyone bring a child to a crucifixion?*

Mary said to John, "We have to get through. I have to be with him."

John made a battering ram with his elbows and pushed through the crowd. The people he shoved out of his way cursed him, but Mary and I held onto his belt and followed him through.

As we reached the front, we saw the Romans raise the middle cross.

Mary's hand closed on my arm so tightly that it would leave bruises.

John said to the horseman in front of us, "Let us through. We're friends of Jesus of Nazareth."

"No one gets through," the guard returned, swinging his horse's haunches toward us to keep us back.

I stepped forward boldly and said, in the aristocratic Latin I had learned from Julia, "You must let us through. This is Jesus of Nazareth's mother."

The guard gave me a sharp glance but repeated his refusal, this time in Latin.

I summoned up my most arrogant expression. "I don't believe you understand. I have friends in Rome—highly placed friends. They won't be pleased to learn you denied my request."

The guard looked at me suspiciously, taking in the way I was dressed. "You don't look like a Roman. You look like a Jew."

"What I am is a close friend of Marcus Novius Claudius. If you know what's good for you, you'll stop wasting my time and let us through."

"How do you know a man like that?"

I narrowed my eyes. "Stop asking me useless questions, and let us go stand by the cross. Now."

He grumbled, but he backed his horse up and let us pass.

⤫

I COULDN'T LOOK AT him.

This is unbearable.

But Mary moved forward, and John and I followed behind her.

He was so thin. He was like a skeleton covered with a thin layer of flesh as he hung there under the brilliant sun. His eyes were closed. We stopped at the foot of the cross, and Mary reached up, put her hand on his bloody foot, and said, "Yeshua, I am here."

His eyes opened. She looked up at him, her spine straight, her face concentrated, willing him to see her, to know that she was with him, to know that he was not alone.

He said nothing, but for a long moment they looked at each other. He was the Son of God, but she was his mother, and I knew he was glad for her presence.

Chapter Thirty-Seven

We remained there beneath him, Mary, John, and I, as the clouds covered the sun and the sky grew dark. When Mary could no longer keep her arm up to touch his foot, I took her place. Then, when I tired, she took mine.

It was unspeakable. Jesus was silent, acknowledging us only once, when he asked John to take Mary into his care. She was incredibly strong. She stood with him until the end, once or twice murmuring to him so he would know she was still there.

I thought, *There is more bravery in this small woman than in the entire army of Rome. Jesus didn't get his strength only from his Father.*

I felt as if it would never end, that we would stand enduring this agony until the end of time. It was late in the afternoon when Jesus whispered in a cracked voice, "I thirst."

"Get him something to drink," I snapped in Latin to the soldiers around us.

They dipped a sponge in the bucket and held it to his lips. After he had tasted the drink, he looked up to heaven. This time when he spoke his voice was clear.

"It is finished."

His head dropped forward, and all his muscles, which had been concentrated on bearing him up against the tearing of the nails, relaxed.

"He's done for," one of the soldiers said.

I looked at his chest, to see if it was moving. It wasn't. He was dead.

Thank God.

They lowered him from the cross, and we ran to kneel next to him. There was blood on his face, but he looked peaceful, as if asleep.

"He is with his Father," Mary said, brushing his hair away from his forehead with a steady hand.

"Yes, he is." I took off my cloak and settled it over him gently, as if afraid that, even in death, he might feel it on his poor wounded body.

The Temple guards who had been watching with the crowd came up to us, and one of them said to John, "The Sabbath begins at sundown. You must take him away before then."

John and I looked at each other, the same thought in both our minds. Where could we take him?

The crowd had grown bored with the spectacle and dispersed. The two other men were still hanging in their agony, watched over by the soldiers. The sky was gray, and it was growing cold.

"We have no place to put him," John said.

The Temple guard shrugged in supreme indifference. "We cannot have a dead body lying here on the Sabbath. Take him away."

Then, as I looked wildly around for some kind of help, I saw Nicodemus and another man toiling up the hill.

Neither the Roman nor the Temple guards attempted to stop them. Nicodemus fell to his knees next to Jesus, and tears ran down his cheeks. "They are evil men," he said. "Evil men."

I didn't think he was speaking of the Romans.

Mary was still kneeling beside her son, and Nicodemus said to her, "Don't worry, dear woman. I have with me one of the Master's followers, Joseph by name. He's recently purchased some land over there." He gestured toward the area north of Golgotha. "There's an empty tomb on the property, and Joseph wants you to have it for the Master."

Mary held out her hand, stained by her son's blood. "Thank you, sir. With all my heart, I thank you."

I tried to think practically. "He'll have to be washed and anointed."

"I have servants coming after me with burial cloths and oils." Nicodemus looked toward the city and then pointed. "There, do you see?"

I looked and saw two men approaching the base of the hill.

John said, "We will carry him to the tomb, and your men can follow us. We must get him away from here as soon as possible."

Nicodemus agreed. "The three of us can surely carry him. It isn't that far."

"No," said John, his voice adamant. "I will carry him myself."

He bent and lifted Jesus into his arms as if he weighed no more than a child, and we started off. A Roman soldier and a Temple guard followed behind.

It was a long walk, but John never faltered. Joseph's property turned out to be a small garden dotted with almond trees at the end of their bloom. The delicate pink flowers lay scattered all over the ground, dying. A rocky hillside formed one of the property lines, and carved into the hillside was a cave. It was there that we carried him.

Nicodemus' servants caught up to us, and as John laid Jesus on a rocky shelf inside the cave, I said to Mary, "Do you want to help me with the anointing? Are you able to face this?"

"I think so," she whispered.

I put my arms around her. She was shivering. "Go with John. You've borne enough. I will see to this for you."

As we were speaking, the Temple guard came into the cave. "You must clear out now," he said. "The Sabbath will begin within the hour and you must be away from here before then."

"I am not leaving until I've prepared his body!" My voice shook, I was so angry. If I had been a man, I would have punched him in his broad flat face.

"You can come back when the Sabbath is over," and he gestured impatiently for us to leave the tomb.

The Roman guard said, in Latin so the Temple guard couldn't understand, "I will roll a smaller stone in front of the entrance, one you can remove easily when you return. Don't give your friend's enemies a reason to take his body someplace where you can't get to it."

I stared at him, uncertain.

"Be smart," he said softly. "You can come back and perform your rites tomorrow."

The Temple guard was scowling. "What did you just say to her?" he demanded.

The Roman shrugged. "I told her she had better do as you asked, or she would be arrested."

"He's right," the Temple guard said to me. "You don't want to end up under guard at the Antonia, do you?"

My fingers twitched. I wanted so much to slap his ugly face. But I said to the others, "We must leave. We're no good to the Master if we are arrested."

Nicodemus instructed his servants to leave the oils and burial cloths, and the Temple guard herded us out of the cave, telling us to get to our homes before the Sabbath began. As John, Mary, and I looked at each other in bewilderment—where should we go?—Nicodemus said, "I'll take you to the others."

John nodded and beckoned to us to follow, leading us back into the now-empty streets of Jerusalem.

⁓

NICODEMUS TOLD US THE disciples were gathered in the room where they had celebrated Passover the night before. It was located in the Upper City, near the house of the high priest. Like Nicodemus, the owner was a secret follower of the Master.

We walked quickly through the silent streets until we reached the house. Nicodemus led us through a side door and up a flight of stairs. As we ascended, I heard the sound of men talking, but once we knocked at the door the voices stopped.

"Who is there?" I recognized Peter's voice.

"It's Nicodemus. I'm here with John, Mary of Magdala, and the Master's mother."

Peter opened the door and closed it quickly behind us. I looked at all the pale faces staring at us. They were all there except Judas.

Peter spoke first, his booming voice no more than a husky whisper. "Is he dead?"

Nicodemus answered. "Yes. We brought him to a nearby tomb, but the guards forced us to leave because of the Sabbath. It was too late for the women to return to Bethany."

Peter began to sob. I saw tears in the eyes of most of the others, and suddenly I was furious. "Where were you while the Master was being crucified?" I shouted. "John, Mary, and I were there. Where were you?"

No one would look at me.

Mary said, "I would like to sit down."

The long, low table at which they must have celebrated their Passover supper last evening took up half the room. Andrew hurried to push one of the couches against the wall, and Mary and I sat.

Nicodemus said, "Let me find the owner and see if he has a room the women can use."

After the door closed behind the Pharisee, John said, his face grim, "Who is going to answer Mary's question? Where were you?" His gaze fixed on Peter. "You were supposed to be in the high priest's courtyard, but when we arrived, you were gone."

Peter began to cry again and tears continued to rain down his cheeks as he told us his story. At last night's supper, here in this very room, Jesus had told him that, before the cock crowed twice this morning, Peter would deny him thrice. And that's what happened. The servants in the high priest's courtyard kept asking him if he was a follower of the Master, and Peter kept saying he didn't know the man. The last time Peter denied knowing him, he heard the cock crow for the second time.

"I betrayed him," Peter sobbed. "I loved him, and I betrayed him."

"Well, no one else even made it to Caiaphas' house," I snapped and looked around again.

Every man looked miserable. "It's true," Thomas said. "We failed him."

I looked at their grieving, humiliated faces, and my anger died as suddenly as if a bucket of water had been thrown on it. For the first time I understood why Jesus had chosen these ill-educated, hardworking men to be his disciples. They loved him with all their hearts. Unlike Daniel, they were open to what he expected of them—not what they expected of him. They were human, and they had their flaws, but arrogance was not one of them. They had let fear drive them, and they grieved for their failure to stand by their beloved Master. They knew they were wrong and that Jesus was right. Even now, faced with his death, a death they never expected, they believed in him.

Judas had been like Daniel. He wanted the Messiah to fit into the mold he had envisioned. John said, "Have you seen or heard from Judas? He knows about this house. We may not be safe here."

Matthew rubbed his eyes. "We have nowhere else to go."

I said, "I don't think Judas will give us away."

Heads turned my way.

I had thought about why Judas had done this heinous thing. "I don't think he ever meant this to happen. He wanted the Master to be a warrior messiah, and he thought that being arrested would make him more radical. I don't think he ever thought Jesus would be executed."

"I don't care what he thought," Peter growled. "I'd like to get my hands around his throat!"

Rumbles of agreement came from every male in the room.

The door opened, and Nicodemus came back in. "I spoke to the owner, and he has offered a downstairs room to the women."

I helped Mary to her feet, and we followed Nicodemus downstairs, into a room that, miraculously, had two Roman beds with cushions. Mary and I washed in the water that was waiting on a marble-topped table and crawled under the wool blankets. Within minutes I was asleep.

Chapter Thirty-Eight

T̲HE NEXT DAY WAS̲ the Sabbath, so I couldn't go to the tomb to wash and anoint Jesus. Mary and I sat in the upper room with the disciples, and I counted the minutes until sundown. I told myself that the weather was cool, and it would be even colder inside the stone tomb.

I couldn't bear the thought of finding him with decay.

I wouldn't think about it. I would think of something else.

I sat on the couch against the wall and tried to understand what had happened and what it could mean. How could the Son of God die? Why should he die? And in such a horrible way?

Was it possible he wasn't who he said he was?

But then I thought of that transcendent moment in my garden. I had looked into his eyes, and I had known.

He was the Son of God. He was the Messiah we had been praying for. He had raised my brother from the dead. And now he was dead himself.

It had to mean something. It must mean something.

It hurt to look at Mary, who sat beside me. She had aged twenty years overnight.

At one point John came over to us. He squatted in front of her and said, "The Master gave you into my care. I will do anything in the world that you ask of me."

She had just looked at him helplessly.

I took her hand into mine and said, "I'm sure your son James will want you to come home."

"James. Yes." She closed her eyes. The skin under them was deeply shadowed. "I will have to tell him about Yeshua."

I said, "I'll go to the tomb tomorrow morning and anoint him. Then I'll come back here, and we'll decide what to do."

"You can't anoint him alone."

It would be difficult, but there was no other woman to help me, and she was too fragile. She had spent all her resources yesterday.

"Of course I can. I'm used to being on my own, remember?"

"You will do it properly, Mary. I have every confidence in you." John's voice was deferential, a note I had never heard from him before.

"Thank you, John. And thank you for being there for him. And for us."

He just shook his head, unable to answer, and moved away.

☙

MARY AND I WENT to bed as soon as it was dark and I lay awake all night, willing the sun to show itself. As soon as I saw the first faint light in the high window, I was up and moving.

The streets were still dark and empty as I approached the Dung Gate. In an hour's time the farm carts would be rolling into the city with produce to sell, but for now I was alone.

The gate was not yet open, and I called to the guardroom above. A guard stuck his head out and told me it was too early.

I debated what I should do to convince him to change his mind.

Latin? No, not with these fellows. I slipped my veil from my head to my shoulders and shook out my loose hair. I produced my most dazzling smile and said, "Please? My brother is ill, and I must go to him."

He looked at me. I kept on smiling. "Oh, all right, I suppose I can open a little early."

I passed through the heavy doors, giving him another smile and saying, "Thank you. I'll remember your kindness."

The sky grew brighter as I walked. Jesus' tomb was near the intersection of the roads to Joppa and Caesarea. As I walked along, I tried not to think. I looked at the Grecian magnificence of Herod's palace rising above the city walls to my right. I stopped to pick a stone out of my sandal. I thought of Lazarus, who I prayed was safe in Capernaum. I worried about Martha, who must be frantic with fear for all of us.

Then I saw the hill of Calvary, with three empty crosses stark against the morning sky.

I turned away from the sight and proceeded to Joseph's garden.

THE SUN WAS FULLY up by the time I arrived. I found my way through the almond trees to the tomb, half expecting to find a guard posted outside. No one was there.

I narrowed my eyes against the sun, abruptly realizing there was no stone at the cave entrance. My heart began to pound. The Roman guard had put one there. I had seen him do it.

I heard the Roman's words again: "Don't give your friend's enemies a reason to take the body someplace you can't get to."

I ran, tripping and almost falling over a branch in my way.

The mouth of the cave yawned wide and empty. Slowly, fearfully, almost on tiptoe, I went inside. After my eyes adjusted to the dark, I looked toward the rock shelf where we had left him. Folded neatly upon it was the cloak I had covered him with. The oils and burial garments were untouched where we had left them.

Jesus was gone.

Blind rage possessed me. *They've taken him! The Sanhedrin has taken him so we cannot give him a proper burial!*

I backed out of the cave, my fists clenched, my body vibrating with fury.

I have to tell the others. I have to tell them what has happened.

I ran all the way to the city, through the Dung Gate, where the guards yelled after me, and back to the upper room where they were all waiting for me. By the time I arrived, I was so out of breath I could barely speak.

The disciples listened to my story, a mixture of horror and confusion on their faces.

"I'll go and see for myself," Peter said.

"I'll go with you and show you the way," John said.

"I'm coming too," I said.

We went quietly down the stairs, not wishing to disturb Mary, who was still asleep. Then the three of us retraced the journey I had already made twice. The guards at the Dung Gate made jocular comments as we went through.

We were almost at the garden when John ran on ahead of us. By the time Peter and I reached the tomb he was coming out of it. "Mary's right. He's not there."

Peter went in and I followed. I saw once again the empty shelf. Peter buried his face in his hands. "What can have happened?"

"The Sanhedrin has taken him." I wasn't angry anymore. All I felt was a bleak chill emptiness.

We were silent, staring at the shelf and the robe. Peter's shoulders shook, and I knew he was crying.

John said slowly, "Surely it's in the Sanhedrin's interest to keep the Master's body visible?"

I didn't know what to say.

Peter turned his tearstained face to me. "We must tell the others."

"You and John go. I'm too tired; I'll come after I have rested."

They left, and I sat for a while on the stone that had held his body. I lay down on it, pressing myself into it, hoping to feel something of him in the cold hardness. Finally I stood up and went outside.

The daylight was so bright after the darkness of the cave that it dazzled my eyes. It was a moment before I saw the outline of a white-robed figure standing a few feet away from me. I blinked, thinking the man must be a gardener. Perhaps he had been here earlier and had seen what happened.

"Sir," I said, approaching him and squinting in the sunlight, "I beg you, if you know where they have taken him, tell me. I promise I won't tell anyone who gave me the information."

The man replied with one word, spoken in a familiar, beloved voice.

"Mary."

I blinked again, my vision cleared, and I saw him.

"Master!" I dropped to my knees at his feet and bent to embrace them.

"Do not touch me, Mary," he said quietly. "I have been with my Father, and my body is not as yours."

I pulled away and jumped to my feet. Tears began to pour down my face. "I thought the Sanhedrin had stolen you away," I sobbed.

Through my tears I could see that he was unmarked—he didn't even have the scar above his eyebrow.

He said, "Did you not understand? Did I not raise your brother from the dead? I thought that you, of all of them, would know I would rise. How else was I to show the world that I have conquered death? That all who follow me will conquer death?"

I tried to wipe away my tears. "I'm sorry, Master," I said. "I didn't understand."

He smiled at me, the rare smile that went straight to my heart. "You must go to my brothers and tell them. I shall appear to them soon, but they must know what has happened. They must know so they can preach the word to all the world."

I didn't want to let him out of my sight. "Will I see you again?"

"Yes. You are the first to see me, and you will see me again. Go now, and bring the news to your fellow disciples. Go back to Bethany, you and my mother, and I will see you there."

"I will, Master. I will."

I returned to Jerusalem, as free and light as a bird gliding through the air.

❧

AT FIRST PETER DIDN'T believe me. "You say he was outside the tomb, but we were outside the tomb, and he wasn't there." He looked at the amazed faces that were gathered around me. "He wasn't there," he repeated.

John said, with a gentleness that was new to him, "He wanted to see Mary first, Peter."

That was the problem, of course. Peter was jealous that he hadn't been first.

I said, "He told me he would appear to all of you. And, remember, Peter, he named you as our leader. You are our rock. He depends upon you to spread the word of his resurrection to the world."

Peter's chin lifted. "I will never fail him. Never."

None of us mentioned that Peter had already failed Jesus by denying him three times.

"I know you won't," I said.

❧

MARY AND I LEFT for Bethany early in the afternoon. We met Martha on the way; she was coming into the city to find us. I told her what had happened, and she turned and accompanied us back to Bethany.

We received word from Lazarus the following day. He was safe in Capernaum and begged us to let him know what was happening in Jerusalem. Clearly he had not yet heard of Jesus' crucifixion.

Mary, Martha, and I were sitting silently in the courtyard sun when I saw him come through the gate. He was dressed in the same white robe, yet he looked different. The scar was back on his face, and I saw the wounds in his hands and his feet.

"Yeshua!" Mary leaped up and ran into his open arms.

"Be at peace, Mother," he said. "Be at peace."

"I didn't know. I didn't know you would rise! I'm so glad to see you!"

She stepped away from his arms and looked up into his face. Her voice shook. "It was so awful, Yeshua. So awful."

His voice was tender. "I know, but it is over."

She touched his cheek and nodded.

He looked from his mother to where Martha and I were standing beside the table. He said to me, "Now the real work must begin. Do you understand, Mary? The good news of my teachings and my resurrection must be brought to all the nations of the world. That will be the mission of my disciples, to be apostles of my Word."

The way he was looking at me, I knew he was including me in his mission. Our eyes held, and I felt the union of my spirit with his. I was filled with such love, such joy, such hope. I could do anything he asked of me. Anything.

He said, "You have always understood more than the others. Can you take my Word out into the world and bring it to the souls who hunger and thirst for the truth?"

I fell to my knees in front of him. "Yes, Lord, I can do that."

"Always remember this—I will be with you, even unto the end of time."

"I know that, Lord."

He reached out a hand and drew me to my feet.

Martha had been standing by the table as if transfixed. Now she said, "Are you hungry, Master? Can I get you something to eat and drink?"

He gave her his "Martha" smile.

"I would like that very much," he said.

Martha's face lighted to radiance. "I'll go and prepare something," she said and ran off in the direction of the house.

Epilogue

We had him with us for forty days. During that time he appeared to all the apostles and to many of his faithful disciples as well, including Lazarus. He also came again to me, to his mother, to Ruth, and to Peter's wife, Rebecca.

I cannot begin to express the infinite joy it was to be with him. I knew his time on earth would end, but when it finally did, when we saw him return to his Father, instead of feeling deserted, I was filled with anticipation and hope. Before he left, he told us that the Holy Spirit would give us the strength to witness to his Word in Jerusalem, throughout Judea and Samaria, and all the way to the ends of the earth. I believed him. We all did.

During his stay among us, the apostles had remained in the upper room while a smaller group of us stayed in Bethany. Word of Jesus' resurrection had spread among his disciples, but no one had dared yet to preach it in the Temple. The Sanhedrin left us alone because they thought the death of our leader had crushed us, but we were waiting for the promised strength of the Holy Spirit to give us the courage to go forth as Jesus wanted.

Lazarus had returned to Bethany after Jesus appeared to him, and we also had the company of Jesus' brother James. When he saw his mother sitting in the courtyard, he fell to his knees before her, buried his face in her lap, and began to sob like a child.

"I failed him, Mother. I didn't understand. I thought he was deserting us, and I couldn't forgive him. But I never stopped loving him!" His broad shoulders shook with grief. "Yeshua!" It was a cry of anguish. "I should have known. Why didn't he tell me?"

Mary gently stroked his hair. "He had to work out for himself who he was and what he was supposed to do. But he always understood your feelings, James. He always knew you loved him."

"I know. I saw him." He lifted his head. "I saw him. It was the greatest moment of my life."

He rose to his feet and turned to look at Lazarus, Martha, and me. "Yeshua asked me to come to Jerusalem to be a leader of his church. I told him I wasn't worthy, that such an honor should go to those who had followed him, but he said he wanted me. So I promised I would do it. I will devote the rest of my life to telling other people about my brother, the Son of God."

"So will we all," said Lazarus. "So will we all."

❧

TWO DAYS AFTER JESUS' return to his Father, Peter sent a message to Bethany to let us know he was calling a meeting. On the appointed day we made the familiar journey to the house in the Upper City.

The upper room was filled with disciples from Jerusalem and the surrounding area. I noticed in particular the women. They had been devoted to the Lord, many of them following him on the terrible journey to Calvary. I saw the woman who had defied the Romans by wiping his face as he went by. We were too far apart to speak, but we shared a knowing, tearful smile.

John came over to Mary immediately and brought all of us to a space by the window. Then he went back to join the ten remaining apostles standing in the front of the room.

Peter opened the meeting by leading us all in prayer. When we finished he looked up at us and said, "I have called you here today to choose a replacement for Judas. We have always been the Twelve, and it is important that we become the Twelve again. I believe this is what the Lord would have wished. It is crucial that we choose someone who has been a longtime disciple, who has often listened to the Lord preach, and who has the ability to spread his message to others."

I hadn't thought about replacing Judas, who had hanged himself when he realized what his betrayal had caused. The apostles hated him, but I couldn't help feeling pity for the young man who had misjudged his actions so fatally. I considered Peter's idea now and thought it was a good one. To leave Judas' place empty would always be a reminder of his betrayal. Better for them to fill it and become the Twelve again.

A man standing near the front of the room called out the name of Barsabbas, saying, "He has been a disciple of the Lord since his earliest days in Galilee. He would be a good addition to the Twelve."

I searched for Barsabbas in the group and found him. Behind his black beard and thick black eyebrows, he was looking very grave. He was a good man, I thought. He would do very well.

Nicodemus spoke next. "I would like to suggest Matthias. He's been one of the most faithful of disciples, also following the Lord throughout Galilee and Judea."

Matthias, who was standing next to Nicodemus, lowered his eyes.

Matthias was younger than Barsabbas and more of a leader. I thought I might prefer him.

Peter waited, offering other people a chance to put a name before the group. There was a long pause, and Peter was lifting his hand to close the suggestions when Andrew spoke up. "I think our twelfth apostle should be Mary of Magdala."

James, who was standing next to me, stiffened. Most of the male faces in the room looked stunned. Andrew moved his eyes from face to face as he spoke. "Mary is the only one among us who never failed him. She always understood what he meant. And—if you remember—she was the one who stayed with him during the whole of his crucifixion, while the rest of us hid in this room, afraid."

The men who had been looking so stunned dropped their eyes. The women were smiling at me.

The apostle James said truculently, "My brother John didn't desert him. Mary wasn't the only one who stood under his cross!"

John shook his head slowly. "That may be true, James, but I often disappointed him. We all did." He looked along the line of the apostles standing next to him. "We all failed him at one time or another. We quarreled over foolish things. We worried about our rank in his kingdom. We didn't understand."

He moved his eyes to me.

"Mary always understood. The Master loved her more than any of us because she was the one who saw him most clearly. She was the one he appeared to first."

Our eyes held. There would always be a special bond between John and me. Then he smiled. "That's why I don't think we should name Mary to be one of the Twelve."

Martha put her hand on my arm, as if to comfort me.

I patted her fingers. John continued to look at me. "You stand alone, Mary of Magdala. You were beloved of the Lord, and your honor is your own, not to be shared with anyone else."

My heart swelled as we looked at each other. *Oh, John. You will be a great witness for the Lord. And thank you for being there for us on that terrible day.*

He nodded slightly, as if he had understood my thoughts.

I was so deeply moved that I had to struggle to hold back my tears.

Lazarus put an arm around my shoulders and said, "Thank you, John."

John nodded. Then he turned back to Peter and said gruffly, "So we have Barsabbas and Matthias. Are there any other names?"

There were none. Peter raised his arms in prayer and we all followed his lead. *"Lord, who knows the hearts of all, show us which one of these two you have chosen to take the place in this ministry from which Judas has turned away."*

The apostles handed two small pieces of marked parchment to everyone in the room. The X was for Barsabbas and the O for Matthias. Thomas went around with a basket, and each of us put one piece into it, signifying our choice. When the lots were counted, Matthias had been chosen.

The Twelve were complete once more.

THE HOLY SPIRIT DESCENDED in wind and fire upon the apostles. I heard about it from Nicodemus, who was there when it happened. Perhaps the most amazing thing was the way the apostles' preaching had been heard by many foreign Jews who were in Jerusalem on pilgrimage. They had understood the apostles as if they were speaking in the visitors' own languages.

The Holy Spirit came to me in a different way. Ever since Jesus left I had been thinking about what he wanted from me. He hadn't given any specific instructions; he simply wanted me to go out and "teach all nations." Those words had set me on fire when he spoke them, but once the radiance of his presence was gone, I was faced with reality. How would I accomplish this mission?

My enlightenment was not as remarkable as the tongues of fire that descended on the apostles. It came one afternoon as I was in the village, and a troop of Roman soldiers came riding in. They were heading for Jerusalem and had stopped to water their horses.

Now Jerusalem lay only two miles to the south of Bethany, and normally soldiers would have waited to water their horses at the cavalry headquarters there. But these didn't; they stopped in Bethany. And their leader, a lieutenant who had been stationed in Sepphoris, recognized me.

We began to talk in Latin, and he asked me if I knew anything about the so-called prophet recently executed by Pontius Pilate. I told him I was one of the man's followers.

He was intrigued, and all the rest of the troop listened intently as we spoke. It occurred to me that few of the Romans I had known in Sepphoris believed in their gods anymore. They paid lip service to the deities they had modeled after the Greek gods, but they didn't believe in their reality. The emperor had become their god, but the recent emperors had failed catastrophically as moral examples to the people. Tiberius had turned into a degenerate and had moved to the island of Capri, leaving his hated general, Sejanus, as acting emperor in Rome.

Romans, particularly the lesser folk, might be eager to learn about a God who cared about the poor, the outcast, the women and children. I thought of Fulvius Petrus in Capernaum, who had become a follower of Jesus. And then I thought of Julia. How much I longed to have my second mother become a believer in the Lord.

And why shouldn't she? Jesus didn't care what she ate or what she wore. He didn't care about her past life. What he cared about was her present, and I knew from Julia's letters that she was finding her present life increasingly empty.

My rejection of Marcus had made a deep impression on her, and I felt she was searching for more to believe in than a successful social life. In her letters she had often inquired about Jesus and what I saw in him.

After the soldiers left, I walked back to the house. Lazarus had just come in from a day with the apostles, who had begun to preach about Jesus in the very courtyard of the Temple. We sat down to talk.

"There have been many baptisms in Jerusalem, Mary. I don't know how long the Sanhedrin will tolerate our open presence in the Temple, but many of the people who heard the apostles have been asking for someone to go to their country and tell about the Lord. Soon we will have to decide who is to go where. James, the brother of the Lord, has sworn to remain in Jerusalem no matter how difficult the Sanhedrin might make it for him."

It was starting.

"I think I might have a different mission," I said, and then I told Lazarus everything I had been thinking about since speaking to the Roman lieutenant.

"There are certainly many Jews in Sepphoris," he said. "Perhaps Martha and I could spread the word to them while you work with the Romans."

"And there are so many villages around Sepphoris, Lazarus. These people are hard-working farmers and workmen. They need to hear the Word of the Lord; they need to know how important they are to him."

He reached out and took both my hands into his. "We may not be going to the ends of the earth, Mary, but I think we can make a good start in Sepphoris. There will be plenty for us to do there, I think."

And so that's what we did. Lazarus, Martha, and I went to stay with Julia and commenced the conversion of western Galilee, both Jews and Romans, to the religion preached by Jesus, the Christ. He was with us all the while, as he had promised, and our successes came because of the faith he had in us and the faith we had in him.

Glory be to God the Father, God the Son, and God the Holy Spirit.
Amen.

About the Author

Joan Wolf was born in the Bronx, only a few miles from Yankee Stadium. She has spent most of her adult life in Connecticut, where she and her husband raised two children and a wide assortment of animals. She started out writing books by hand at a table in the Milford Public Library more years ago than she cares to remember. She's the author of *A Reluctant Queen* and *The Road to Avalon*, lauded as "historical fiction at its finest," by *Publisher's Weekly*.

WORTHY

PUBLISHING

IF YOU ENJOYED THIS BOOK, WILL YOU CONSIDER SHARING THE MESSAGE WITH OTHERS?

- Mention the book in a Facebook post, Twitter update, Pinterest pin, or blog post.

- Recommend this book to those in your small group, book club, workplace, and classes.

- Head over to facebook.com/authorjoanwolf, "LIKE" the page, and post a comment as to what you enjoyed the most.

- Tweet "I recommend reading #DaughterofJerusalem by @joanwolf // @worthypub"

- Pick up a copy for someone you know who would be challenged and encouraged by this message.

- Write a review on amazon.com, bn.com, or cbd.com.

You can subscribe to Worthy Publishing's newsletter at worthypublishing.com.

**WORTHY PUBLISHING
FACEBOOK PAGE**

**WORTHY PUBLISHING
WEBSITE**